MIDNIGHT'S CURSE

Midnight's Curse

A Cinderella Retelling
Beyond the Tales Book Two

Tricia Mingerink

Sword & Cross
Publishing

The Seven Kingdoms of Tallahatchia
Castle Fonthaven
Pohatomie
Pohatomie River
Buckhannock
Buckhannock River
Castle Firlin
Monongadotte
Monongadotte River
Rand Clan Home
Kanawhee
Chattakee
Gaulee River
Nanooga
Neskahana
Cheyandooh Trace
Onohio River
Castle Eyota
Clearwater Creek
Castle Deeling
Neskahana River
Kanawhee River
Kikataw
Grassy Lick Creek
Fishrock Cove
Fort Last Chance
Tuckawassee
Aunt Frennie's Cabin
Guyangahela
Nanahootchie Creek
Guyangahela River
Castle Greenbrier
Tuckawassee River

Chapter 1

Daemyn

Daemyn Rand sliced his paddle into the swift-flowing Onohio River as it pressed against the canoe's birchbark sides, wild and alive and thrumming deep in his bones as if begging him to remember what it was like to embrace life instead of a numb existence. Life awaited ahead, where Rosanna, his curse-breaking princess, said she'd meet him.

In the canoe's prow, Zeke, Daemyn's great-great-grand-nephew, wielded his own paddle, the fringes on his buck-skin shirt swinging with each movement. He set a steady rhythm, one well-practiced from the miles they'd canoed across the Seven Kingdoms of Tallahatchia, searching for the princess who would wake the high prince from his cursed sleep.

In the center, wedged between the packs of their personal items, the awakened and crowned High King Alexander of Tallahatchia clung to the sides of the canoe as if unnerved by the river's swift current. If this scared him, then the rapids ahead would be downright terrifying.

Though it could simply be Alex's disorientation. He'd slept through decades of war and woken to splintered kingdoms far different from the ones he'd known a hundred years ago.

This would be Alex's first attempt at a diplomatic mission to unite the kingdoms under his rule and hopefully prevent another war from further tearing the kingdoms apart. Alex had chosen to start with Neskahana, probably to honor Rosanna and her family for their loyalty that led to breaking the cursed sleep. And, perhaps, due to Daemyn's hinting it was a good idea.

Four canoes with Alex's eight guards swooped swift and sure ahead and behind. Everything in Daemyn longed to push the canoe harder, faster, outrace the river and the guards to reach that next bend.

They swept into the curve, and Daemyn fought the press of the river, centering the canoe in the current. When he glanced up, there on a rock promontory stood two women, one with her long black hair in a braid and the other with her black curls tied back from her face. They wore beaded buckskin shirts and leggings.

Princess Rosanna and her maid and bodyguard Isi Degotaga waved. Then Rosanna, with a running leap, dove from the promontory in a perfect, fearless arc before plunging into the river.

On the rock, Isi shook her head, turned, and raced down from the rocks with the surefootedness of a deer.

With a gasp, Rosanna surfaced a few yards from Daemyn's canoe, her black hair glistening, and her bronze skin glowing with the river water. Daemyn leaned into the paddle, turning the canoe toward her. He itched to jump into the river himself and swim toward her, but he couldn't without tipping the canoe and spilling both Zeke and Alex into the river with him.

As they neared, Daemyn let his paddle fall flat against the river instead of dipping it in edge-first, showering Rosanna with a light spray of water. "That was a mighty fine leap, Princess."

She grinned and flicked her hand, sending a spray of water in his direction. "It isn't that high. Besides, is that any way to greet a princess?"

"Princess?" Zeke splashed water in her direction. "I reckoned you for an otter. Maybe a fish."

"A fish?" Rosanna swiped her hand through the water. The wave washed over the side of the canoe, drenching Zeke's sleeve.

A few drops spattered Alex, and Alex grimaced, scrubbing at his face with the back of his hand.

"Your Majesty! I'm so sorry." Rosanna clapped a hand to her mouth, but Daemyn couldn't tell if it was from horror that she splashed the high king or to hide her laughter. "It seems I'm always getting you wet."

Daemyn wasn't sure if he wanted to grin at that or shudder. Three months ago, Rosanna awakened Alex by pouring a canteen of water over his head. The moment she'd done that, Daemyn had rapidly died of old age. The ninth of the many times he hadn't stayed dead.

"I will dry." Alex straightened his shirt and his expression into his official, cordially blank mask. "It is a pleasure to meet you again, Princess Rosanna."

Rosanna bobbed her head, still treading water next to their canoe. "I'm glad you could come, Your Majesty." Her gaze flicked to Daemyn.

The river had to be cold, even this late in the summer. Daemyn dipped his paddle in. "Reckon we'd best get a move on and finish the welcomes on the bank before your teeth set to chattering."

Rosanna flashed a grin before she stroked toward the rocks. Daemyn curved the canoe in behind her, though he was able to cut the corner across the current sharper than she did as they swept around the promontory into the still water sheltered by the rocks.

As they reached the shallows, Zeke hopped from their canoe first, and Daemyn was only a moment behind him. The water squished through his moccasins, cold yet not bitter. Refreshing after the warmth of the sun beating on him.

Daemyn glanced between the shore and Alex, his body tensed. A hundred years ago, when he'd been Alex's manservant, he would've been expected to hold the canoe while Alex hiked to the bank.

But all he wanted to do was leave Alex to fend for himself and dash to where Rosanna squished her way from the river farther downstream.

Alex shifted his legs over the side and fumbled his way out of the canoe. At least he'd gotten better than the first time when he'd tipped the canoe over. Grabbing the canoe, Alex glanced up. His smile was a mite hesitant, but it was there. "Go on. I have the canoe."

Daemyn shifted, every muscle tensed to dash to Rosanna, but duty to Alex tied him in place. It wouldn't hardly be right at all, leaving his high king standing knee-deep in the muddy river while he ran off.

Zeke had already made it to the bank, where he swung Isi off her feet, both of them laughing.

Captain Taum, the captain of Alex's guards, splashed toward them. He'd be there in a moment. Daemyn wouldn't have to leave Alex unattended for long.

Alex huffed out a breath and waved toward Rosanna with one hand while gripping their canoe with the other. "Go. Do I have to make it an order?"

"Reckon not." Daemyn forced himself to release the canoe. He spun, only to find Rosanna already racing toward him, stepping high through the shallows. He managed only two strides before she leapt at him, clasping her arms around his neck. He had to wrap his arms around her waist and swing her from the water to keep them both from toppling from her momentum.

Her face pressed against his shoulder as he held her, her braid still dripping and her buckskins seeping cold water. When she glanced up at him, she grinned. "This is how you greet a princess."

"Is it?" With her face only inches from his, it was tempting to lean in and kiss her. But he hesitated. They were surrounded by her guards, Alex's guards, Zeke, and Isi.

It wasn't only that. He wasn't sure he could put his hesitation into words.

With something like a laugh, Rosanna stretched, planted a kiss on his jaw, then leaned back to set her feet on the semi-solid ground of the river's mucky bottom. But she didn't step out of his hold, nor fully release him. "I missed you. That was far too long."

"Yes." Daemyn held her close, savoring the feel of her in his arms. A reminder that she was real. His future. Not just another person he would watch outgrow and out-age him while he remained stuck at twenty-one.

What would their relationship be like now that it wasn't defined by the quest to wake Alex? Where did they go now that they weren't bonded by the adventure of it? It was her courage that had drawn him to her. She'd left without looking back. Kept going when things fell apart. Held him together when he fell apart.

In some ways, he was still falling apart and trying to put the pieces together. When he was with her, he thought he knew who he was. He was the Daemyn Rand he saw in her eyes, and that month she'd spent at Castle Eyota before she'd returned to Neskahana with her father and his army had been one of the best of his life.

Then he'd been alone at Castle Eyota again.

Not totally alone. Zeke had refused to leave, and there had been Alex.

That was part of the problem. Alex was the past Daemyn had left behind decades ago. Whenever Daemyn was with Alex, he felt more like the quiet, unassuming manservant he'd trained to be back when he'd been Jadon Rand.

And yet Zeke was still there, reminding Daemyn of who he was now. Or, at least, who he was supposed to be.

Was he Jadon? Bland. Obedient. Unnoticed.

Or Daemyn? Confident. A leader. Someone an entire family looked up to.

He cleared his throat and stepped back, growing aware of the cold water squishing between his toes inside his moccasins. "I brought you something."

"You did?" Rosanna clasped his hand, her fingers cold after her swim in the river.

Glancing around, he spotted his canoe drawn up on the bank. After they tromped from the river, he fished in his pack and drew out a leather-wrapped bundle. "For our canoe."

Rosanna unwrapped the bundle to reveal a coil of spruce roots, all stripped and pulled apart into the strings that were used to stitch pieces of birch bark together when making a canoe. "These are perfect. I have a whole stack of birch bark in the shed I've set aside. We can start working on it while you're here."

Their canoe. It was an old Tallahatchian tradition, going farther back even than the past Daemyn had lived as Jadon, that a couple who intended to get married would build a canoe together. It wasn't something often done anymore, but he liked that Rosanna valued old traditions.

"Look what Zeke brought me." Isi dashed toward them, a similar leather-wrapped bundle grasped in both hands. She shoved it at Rosanna. "Look. Fabric. From Guyangahela. Feel it. Have you ever felt fabric that soft before?"

Rosanna reached out and ran her fingers over the silk Zeke had traded a whole stack of furs for. Her eyes widened. "We've had some silk here before, but never that fine."

"What did Daemyn bring you?" Isi peered down at the package. "Spruce roots? You've been separated for two months and the most romantic thing he brought you was spruce roots?"

Should he have gotten her silk like Zeke had for Isi? His chest tightened. What if Rosanna wanted something more than a few roots he'd dug from the ground?

"They're just what I wanted." Rosanna smiled and reached for his hand again.

When she squeezed his fingers, his heart beat harder, though less in the panic from a few moments ago and more at her nearness. How he'd missed her. Her smiles and understanding. The way she strolled through the forest seeing each tree and fold of the land with wonder.

"If you want silk, His Majesty brought some silk and linen along as part of a trade gesture from the king of

Guyangahela to your father." Daemyn glanced from Rosanna to where Captain Degotaga, Isi's father, welcomed Alex to Neskahana.

Rosanna hugged the package of spruce roots with her free hand. "This is the best gift you could have brought me."

Something in him relaxed. He'd thought so, but for a moment he'd been worried he didn't know her as well as he thought he did.

She glanced past him, her nose wrinkling. "I probably should officially welcome the high king but we're going to do all that stuff all over again at the castle. Unless..." Rosanna's frown quirked upward. "Captain Degotaga, can you see to getting the high king and his guards safely through the rapids? Daemyn and I might as well set off now."

Captain Degotaga turned in their direction, eyes sharp.

Daemyn didn't flinch away from that gaze. A few months ago, he'd earned Captain Degotaga's respect enough to be entrusted with Rosanna's safety when a Tuckawassee war party caught up to them. But since then, he'd broken a guard's unwritten code by falling in love with the princess he'd been charged to protect.

After one last piercing look, Captain Degotaga nodded as if satisfied and motioned to Rosanna's knot of guards. "Chogan, Ilma, Nikan, and Otho. Scout ahead of the princess."

"Yes, sir." The guards hurried to their canoes with Chogan and his wife Ilma setting off in the first canoe, Nikan and Otho shortly after them. If it weren't for the presence of Alex and his guards, it would've been all too like the familiar pattern they'd set during their weeks of travel together.

And yet everything was different. Then Daemyn had been stuck under the weight of a hundred years of not-aging, burdened by the task he'd been given to lead the promised princess to wake Alex. Now he was courting Rosanna. That journey had been a task. This one was personal.

Leaving his side, Rosanna took his paddle from his canoe and held it out to him. "Think you can steer through the rapids?"

Daemyn accepted the paddle, the wood worn to a smooth shine. Her words were light. A challenge. But there was something buried underneath, like a test he didn't dare answer wrong.

On the way to Castle Eyota a few months ago, they'd fallen into a rhythm with him in the canoe's stern and her in the prow. It was, perhaps, expected.

He might be the expert when it came to most of Tallahatchia, but this was her river. No one knew these waters better than Rosanna and her guards after shooting these rapids several mornings a week for years. In this case, the wise decision meant stepping aside so she could do what she knew best.

"This is your river." Daemyn found himself smiling. "You steer."

"Really?" Rosanna's face lit up, and the tightness in his chest eased. He'd made the right choice. She headed for a canoe with a line of blue paint and beadwork around the top edge.

Together, they lifted it from the bank and carried it into the shallows. Daemyn settled into the prow, then kept the canoe steady by shifting his weight as Rosanna slid in and grabbed her paddle.

When she met his gaze, her grin was mountain-wild.

Strands of her black hair fell from her braid to frame her face while her river-deep brown eyes glinted. "Ready?"

She was a girl to ride the river with, and it reminded him that, right now, he didn't have to be the invisible manservant silently killing the mountain side of himself.

That twinkle in her eye set the daring in his own blood surging. A grin tugged at the corner of his mouth. "Always, Princess."

CHAPTER 2

ALEXANDER

High King Alexander stood on the bank of the Onohio River in annoyingly wet moccasins and watched while he was abandoned to the hands of near strangers.

First Jadon and Princess Rosanna, then Jadon's nephew Zeke and the princess's maid Isi, hopped into canoes and flew off downriver. As if they were excited to face the harrowing stretch of rapids for which this river was known.

He shouldn't care. He was fine. He had plenty of guards around him, and it wasn't Jadon's job anymore to be at his every beck and call.

Daemyn. Not Jadon. Friend. Not manservant. Even after three months, Alex struggled to use Jadon's new name. In some ways, it shouldn't be that difficult. While Alex had known Jadon, he didn't know Daemyn. The hundred years Daemyn had lived and the many names he'd worn while Alex slept had changed him.

It had changed Alex too. He hoped. At least, he felt different.

For three months, they'd said they were friends. And they were. Maybe. Alex didn't know a whole lot about how to be a friend.

But he supposed, as a friend, he should allow Daemyn to go off with Rosanna. They'd been parted for two months after all. And Alex was trying to be better. More observant of the needs of those below him.

Something twisted deep in Alex's chest. An ache growing by the day. He was alone. Yes, he had his mother and Daemyn. But Daemyn had Princess Rosanna. Zeke had Isi.

And Alex had no one.

As superficial as their relationship had been, he missed Mirabelle, a baron's daughter he'd been courting before he fell into the cursed sleep. He longed for the feel of a woman in his arms. Kissing. Being a part of two instead of one alone. And, he ached for what they could have had if he'd been different as he was now.

He didn't want to be alone. People who were alone did things like stand awkwardly on the bank of a river, as if he was some leftover baggage waiting to be claimed instead of a high king in command of everyone around him.

Alex lifted his chin and straightened his shoulders. What had Princess Rosanna called the captain of her guard? He wasn't sure why she'd presumed to place her guard captain in charge, even if this was her kingdom. "Captain Degotaga, please arrange our departure."

Captain Degotaga swept a glance over Alex's guards, making them stand straighter. "Listen up. If you don't, then you will likely capsize, wreck your canoe, and probably die."

Alex didn't bother listening. He wasn't going to do anything besides hang on. He'd taken a few turns paddling on the way here, but he was novice enough that no one would trust him with their lives on the rapids, much less with his own.

He needed to build his muscles and skills, now that large, pole-pushed keelboats no longer plied the rivers shuttling passengers between the towns. Not that people traveled for pleasure anymore, as they had a hundred years ago. Between war parties from Tuckawassee and Pohatomie and the river pirates from all the kingdoms, the rivers weren't safe the way they once were.

Would he ever get used to looking around Tallahatchia, expecting to see the kingdoms he remembered, and instead find this? No more bridges connecting the kingdoms. The town of Eyota a crumbled, rotted shadow of what had once been the bustling, trade-filled heart of Tallahatchia.

And he was its high king, a high king only a part of the seven kingdoms wanted.

Would he even be able to visit Pohatomie or Tuckawassee without being killed? Those two kingdoms had fought against the other five for the past hundred years to keep Alex from waking and regaining the throne. What would they do now that he had done just that?

How was Alex supposed to fix Tallahatchia when it was so broken? How could he rebuild the bridges and re-establish trade when the kingdoms were currently one wrong word away from breaking into war once again? Had Alex's waking solved anything? Or had it just temporarily halted a war that would continue even with a high king on the throne?

Things had been tense a hundred years ago. Back then the other kings had been restless. Somewhat power hungry.

But compared to now, Tallahatchia had been united and peaceful. They had been connected by the Cheyandoah Trace, the rivers, and the bridges.

Now the bridges were severed and with them the links between the kingdoms. Alex wasn't even sure where to start. With the bridges? With Eyota? Trade between the kingdoms?

He needed to do all of it, yet he could do nothing if the kings under him didn't cooperate.

"Your Majesty?" Captain Taum, his guard captain, pointed to a canoe waiting in the river shallows. "We're ready to leave."

"Of course." Alex climbed into the canoe's center with Captain Taum in the prow and the princess's hard-eyed Captain Degotaga in the stern.

As they joined the current, Alex clung to the sides of the canoe so hard the blisters on his hands hurt. He drew in a deep breath of the river-cooled air rushing past his face, trying to steady his pounding heart. It didn't work.

The banks turned into cliffs of earth and trees on either side. Boulders reared from the water, the river foaming and angry at their base.

Perhaps this would be less terrifying if he closed his eyes, but his heart was beating too fast, his muscles frozen.

"Lean left." Captain Degotaga dug in his paddle and shoved the canoe hard over.

Alex leaned and clamped his mouth shut against a shout. Spray washed against his face and his buckskin shirt.

The river's rush tumbled faster, wilder. The breeze clawed at his eyes until tears ran down his cheeks.

He couldn't have moved even if he wanted to, except for Captain Degotaga's shouted commands that had more control over him than his own brain.

Ahead, Zeke and Isi's canoe sliced through the raging river, and even farther downriver, Daemyn and Princess Rosanna flew between a pair of boulders.

The river dropped away, and Daemyn and Rosanna vanished. Zeke and Isi followed a few seconds later.

Then the river ended in front of Alex's canoe.

"Lean back!" Captain Degotaga shouted.

Their canoe shot off the small waterfall into open air. A shout burst from Alex, and for a heartbeat, they hung suspended. Then they crashed into the river. Sheets of water washed over the canoe, cold and far too wet.

Alex couldn't force his fingers to release the sides of the canoe, not even to swipe the water from his face as it streamed from the ends of his hair.

Princess Rosanna was laughing as Daemyn shook water from his hair, the whole front of his fringed shirt damp.

Isi wrung water from her curls. "Ugh. I hate getting wet."

"And yet you never say no to shooting the rapids." Princess Rosanna glanced at Alex. "And what about you, High King? What did you think about shooting the Falls of the Onohio?"

Alex swallowed and cleared his throat. Even then, his voice still had a strained squeak. "It was...exhilarating."

Not the word he wanted to use, but he didn't want to say *terrifying*. Not when he was apparently the only one.

Behind Alex, Captain Degotaga dug his paddle into the river. "We should continue on, otherwise the high king will be late to his own welcome banquet."

After a brief stop at Castle Deeling's side docks for Princess Rosanna and her maid to disembark and slip up the back stairs into the castle, Captain Degotaga led Alex and his guards to the main docks downriver, just before the roiling Onohio River converged with the Neskahana. Here, the cliffs on either side of the river eased their heights into a gentle slope. The town of Deeling huddled by the bank, protected inside a stockade wall.

A wall. Did Alex need another reminder of how things had changed? He remembered the sprawling towns that filled the valleys along the rivers. Bustling towns where all the Seven Kingdoms—from the red-haired, fur-wearing Monongadotte to the dark-skinned warriors of Guyangahela dressed in finest, colorful fabrics—blended into one on the streets.

And now there were walls. Marching soldiers parading on the parapets.

He was responsible for all of it. He had fallen into his curse and left Tallahatchia without a high king for a hundred years. He hadn't been there to halt the tensions and war. Because of his own mistake, Tallahatchia had fallen apart.

And now it was his responsibility to put it back together.

The canoes pulled alongside the docks, and Alex crawled out, flopping onto the boards before he pushed himself to his feet. Not the most dignified of exits from his canoe, but at least he hadn't gotten wet.

More wet, anyway. Alex frowned down at his buckskin leggings and sturdy linen shirt. After two weeks of travel, his clothes were stained. Thanks to the wild ride down the Onohio, his shirt clung to his chest, dripping water in rivulets onto the dock. His leggings were dark with water from the knees down while river muck coated his moccasins.

Such a terrible condition to be in for his first official visit to Castle Deeling. Was it too much to ask to duck inside to change into clothing befitting a high king before he made his grand entrance?

Daemyn swung onto the dock from his canoe, landing on his feet before straightening. He was just as wet, from the fringes of his buckskin shirt shedding water to the moccasins leaving damp footprints on the boards. But he looked a lot more comfortable in the buckskins and dirt than Alex felt.

Alex tugged on his shirt and tried to brush a lump of mud from where it had somehow spattered the front. Instead he only managed to smear it.

"From what I know of King Faron, he's more likely to respect you in this than he would in fancy clothes." Daemyn retrieved his hardwood staff from the canoe, then he set to work untying their packs from where they had been stowed on either side of where Alex spent most of their trip up the Gaulee and down the Onohio.

"You're only saying that because you don't want all the hard work it's going to take to remove the wrinkles from my silk shirts after they've spent the past weeks crammed in a pack." Alex shuddered. His poor silk shirts wouldn't be presentable even if he had time to change into them at this point.

Daemyn stilled, and when he glanced up, he had the bland, perfect manservant mask he'd worn so often when Alex had known him as Jadon. "Of course, Your Highness."

"That was a joke, you know." It was, mostly. Had there been a hint of the old Alex still in those words? The one that, deep inside, still expected Jadon to go out of his way to deal with the wrinkled silk and travel stains even though Jadon was now Daemyn. A friend. An advisor. Someone more than a lackey to order according to his every whim.

"Of course, Your Highness." As Daemyn said it, there was a hint of a spark in his eyes, a quirk to his mouth, and Alex couldn't be sure Daemyn wasn't the one pulling a joke over on him with the bland manservant thing. How many times had Jadon been secretly amused behind that impassive mask? Laughing behind Alex's back.

No. Alex brushed aside that thought before it simmered hot inside his chest. No, with the way Alex had been, Jadon had probably needed his secret amusement to keep him from wanting to pummel the smug look from Alex's face.

Daemyn stood and held something out to Alex. "You'll want this."

Alex glanced down at the circle of gold in Daemyn's hand. Alex's crown.

Not the fancy, seven-spiked and bejeweled crown he'd worn for the coronation ceremony. No, this was a gold circle barely larger than a circlet. Yet, there was symbolism too, in the etchings ringing the sides. Corn for Pohatomie, antlers for Monongadotte, a miner's pickax for Buckhannock, jewels for Tuckawassee, pottery for Neskahana, a loom for Guyangahela, and, in the center of the crown, a canoe for Kanawhee, all held together with a twining pattern of maple, oak, and rhododendron leaves.

Alex took the crown and settled it on his head. He stood straighter, held his head higher. There was something about a crown that made a man feel braver. Stronger. More worthy.

Zeke joined them, his own pack already slung on his

back next to his unstrung bow and quiver filled with arrows. He flung a pack at Alex.

Alex barely managed to lower his hands in time to catch the pack, though it still thumped against his stomach.

Zeke grinned, though his dark brown eyes were hard as he glanced at Alex. "I think we've given Isi and Rosanna enough time to change and assemble in the great hall."

Alex forced his smile to remain in place. He wasn't entirely sure what he'd done to make Zeke dislike him. Zeke had fought for Alex. He'd even been wounded in the battle. When had that loyalty changed?

Had it changed? Or had Zeke always been more loyal to Daemyn than Alex?

With Captain Degotaga leading the way, they marched up the steep hillside toward Castle Deeling. It perched on the cliffs with the Onohio River on one side and the Neskahana River on the other.

Castle Deeling wasn't the grandest castle in Tallahatchia, especially not when compared to the sweeping turrets and soaring towers of Castle Eyota. Rather than round turrets with sloped roofs, Castle Deeling was formed of rectangular buildings with peaked roofs forming triangles at the ends of the buildings. A curtain wall surrounded the castle.

It might not be the most beautiful, but it was formidable. Imposing.

Alex tipped his chin higher. He was the high king. He would not be intimidated. He marched through the castle gates and tried to ignore all the soldiers and their glinting spears and knives.

In the courtyard, King Faron stepped forward. His black hair showed only the hints of gray at his temples beneath the silver crown he wore. While his mouth remained flat in a somber expression, his dark brown eyes held a gleam as if a part of him, like his daughter, still yearned for adventure.

At his side, Queen Erina's curly black hair flowed down her back. Her posture was flawlessly regal, but her smile held warmth. Her beauty reminded Alex of what Mirabelle might have looked like when she reached Queen Erina's age.

He shook that thought away. It was too strange thinking that Mirabelle grew old and died decades ago when to him it still felt like she was the young woman he'd left behind.

King Faron bowed fully from the waist while Queen Erina curtsied. When King Faron spoke, his voice was deep, his tone polite but not harsh. "Welcome to Neskahana, Your Majesty."

"A pleasure to be here." Alex bowed in return, though not as deeply since he was the high king.

A young man, a few years older than Alex and wearing a circlet over his black hair, joined King Faron and Queen Erina and bowed. "Your Majesty."

Since Alex had already met Princess Rosanna's younger brother Prince Berend, this must be her older brother, Crown Prince Willem. He was cursed to be unable to leave the borders of Neskahana. His gift of charismatic writing helped make up for it, at least partially. Alex gave another half-bow in greeting.

The main doors flew open, and Princess Rosanna rushed through, dressed in a dark green cotton dress and straightening a tiara that looked to be woven of silver strands and glass beads. She bobbed something between a bow and a curtsy. "Welcome, Your Majesty. I apologize, but my younger brother Berend will be unable to greet you this morning."

Behind Rosanna, Queen Erina's shoulders heaved with something that might have been a sigh.

Alex probably should be offended that the youngest Neskahana prince couldn't manage to drag himself out of bed to greet his high king. Staying up all night romping around the forest as a bear due to his curse wasn't much of an excuse.

But Alex needed to be better than that. He would never unite the kingdoms if he took every little thing as a slight.

"I understand. A bear needs his rest." Alex glanced behind him until he spotted Daemyn lingering in the background. "Thank you for hosting me. This is the captain of my guard, Captain Taum. And you're already acquainted with Daemyn Rand."

The gaze King Faron turned to Daemyn glinted both hard and speculative. As if he wasn't sure what he thought of Daemyn yet. "Yes. It seems I've known him for far longer than I thought."

Daemyn stiffened and bowed.

Queen Erina patted King Faron's arm and gave him a glare before turning to Alex. "We have refreshments set out in the hall, Your Majesty, if you'd care to come this way."

He fell into step with them and climbed the stairs into the castle. And yet, as he entered the main hall surrounded by his guards, Zeke, Daemyn, and the royal family of Neskahana, he still was very much alone.

Chapter 3

Daemyn

Daemyn kept his breathing steady and his body relaxed. What had awakened him?

He lay on a pallet in the outer room of the suite given to Alex for the night. He'd been offered his own room, but he'd thought it best to sleep here. Even in Castle Deeling surrounded by friends, there could be a Tuckawassee spy who wouldn't hesitate to kill Alex if given a chance.

A few feet away, just within reach, Zeke slept on his pallet.

A creaking sound. A shaft of light fell across Daemyn's closed eyelids.

The door to the hall was being pushed open. A spy? An assassin? Had the guards outside in the hall been injured or killed? Whatever had happened, the fight had been swift and silent if it had failed to wake him.

Daemyn eased his hand to the long knife next to him on the pallet and mentally rehearsed the moves he'd make the moment the intruder was fully in the room.

The door creaked again. More light fell across his face, more sensed than seen with his eyes closed.

Then there was a shuffling and a...clicking sound? Like a wolf's claws clacking on stone.

He cracked his eyes into slits and peered at the intruder shambling toward his pallet.

No, not a wolf. Not a spy or an assassin either.

A bear.

Was this Rosanna's brother Berend? He was cursed to turn into a black bear at night. And this bear resembled him. A medium-sized bear, lanky and skinny like a yearling bear rather than full grown, with patches of brown around the face and paws while the rest of the fur remained glossy black.

Daemyn slowly sat up, keeping his gaze focused on the bear lumbering toward him. "Prince Berend? Is that you? Is something wrong?"

The bear bared its teeth. In the flickering torchlight from the hall outside the door, his teeth gleamed white and sharp, the bear's eyes glittering black against his even blacker fur.

Why would Prince Berend be angry with him? It wasn't like he had just broken his Rosanna's heart or anything like that.

"Zeke." Without taking his eyes off the bear that might or might not be Berend, Daemyn leaned back and shoved Zeke. "Wake up."

Zeke's breathing hitched, then whooshed out. "What in the—" His pallet rustled and creaked.

Daemyn risked looking away from the bear long enough to glance over his shoulder. Zeke was scrambling for his bow and reaching for an arrow. "Don't. This might be Rosanna's brother."

Zeke halted, one hand on his bow, the other gripping an arrow. "Are you sure?"

Daemyn eyed the bear where it had halted only a few feet away from him. "Not really. But I don't want to risk accidentally killing him."

The bear made a wheezing, growling sound in its throat, and its lips parted to reveal even more teeth.

"I've never heard a bear make a sound like that. Maybe it's a rabid bear that stumbled its way into the castle?" Zeke remained where he was, as if he wasn't ready to put away his bow and arrow just yet.

The bear took another step closer, still making that snarling noise.

"And slipped past all the guards to climb to the third floor and just happened into our room?" No, this had to be Rosanna's brother. Daemyn looked the bear straight in its beady black eyes. "Prince Berend, you of all people should know black bears don't actually growl. They huff and sometimes grunt, but they never growl or roar."

Something flashed in the bear's eyes, and for a moment, the bear's mouth curved almost in a grin before he went back to growling.

What had he done to make Rosanna's brother so angry at him? Was it merely because he was courting her? Was this some kind of test?

Of course it was. Daemyn had lived a hundred and twenty-one years, worn numerous names, been born to the mountain folk, and spent much of his early life as a lowly manservant. Now he had the nerve to court Berend's only sister. Of course Berend wouldn't think he was worthy of her.

And he happened to agree.

"Zeke, set down your bow." Daemyn spread his hands

to show they were empty, though he left his long knife within reach. "I don't know what you're looking for me to say, Prince Berend. If this is about Rosanna, please know I would never do anything to hurt her. I care for her too much for that."

Prince Berend didn't stop snarling. Instead, he stalked closer, until his nose was only inches from Daemyn's. Hot breath washed over Daemyn's face, but he forced himself not to flinch.

He might not think himself worthy of Rosanna, but he wouldn't be if he flinched now.

Prince Berend lunged. Before Daemyn could react with more than a startled lurch, Prince Berend planted both forepaws on Daemyn's chest and shoved him backwards.

Daemyn landed flat on his back on his pallet, his breath whooshing out of him as Prince Berend's weight landed on him. All he could see was a furry bear face, then sharp teeth, pink gums, and a dark throat as Prince Berend roared.

Daemyn's heart pounded into his throat in time with the ringing in his ears. His palms were sweaty, his hands shaky, his stomach churning. This was an emotion he hadn't felt in decades.

Fear.

For the past hundred years, once he'd figured out he wouldn't stay dead, he'd become numb to this emotion. As much as it would hurt, he'd known he wouldn't remain dead long, nor had the small glimpses of Beyond while he knelt at the threshold been anything other than something to long for.

Yet now he was...afraid. Irrational as it was. Even though he knew this was Prince Berend. He'd been in a worse scrape face-to-face with a real, wild bear, after all.

Zeke scrambled to his feet, reaching for his bow again, but Daemyn shook his head and waved for him to stand down.

The connecting door flew open, and Alex stumbled through, his linen shirt askew and his feet bare. "What is going on—what the..."

"Stay there, Your Majesty." Zeke stepped between Alex and the bear. Good. Just what Daemyn would've done had he not been pinned to his pallet by a bear that was far heavier than he looked. Zeke glanced down at his bow, as if he still itched to pick it up. "We think it's Prince Berend."

"What's wrong with him?" Alex took a step back as Prince Berend snarled next to Daemyn's ear.

Zeke grimaced and shook his head. "What has his dander up like this, we don't know."

Prince Berend's claws dug into Daemyn's shoulders, hard enough to hurt, but not hard enough to draw blood. Hot, bear breath washed over his face with each growl. Wet, warm drool landed on his neck. Another line of drool was working its way from Prince Berend's mouth as he roared in Daemyn's face again.

Daemyn had played along so far, but enough was enough. He was mountain born and bred, and the mountain folk didn't scare easy. Even if his heart was pulsing fast and hard inside his chest. He'd faced worse at the paws of a real, wild bear years ago, back when he'd been Jubal Rand, a wild hunter of the mountains. Berend wasn't nothing to be scared of.

Closing his fingers over his long knife, Daemyn dredged up a snarl of his own. This wasn't the first time he'd growled back to a bear. "You may be a bear, but you ain't invincible. Those stories about me ain't just tall tales." Daemyn raised the knife enough to press the flat against

Berend's ribs. With all his fur, he wouldn't feel it much. But it did make him jump and quit growling, his mouth hanging a touch slack. Daemyn didn't try to hold back the growl to his voice. "I love her, and you ain't going to scare me off with that roaring."

"Have you told her that?" A new voice spoke from the doorway.

Daemyn peered past Berend's drooling, teeth-filled muzzle to see Prince Willem, leaning against the door jamb, his face impassive.

Had Daemyn ever told Rosanna he loved her? Maybe not that plainly. He was working his way there, though. And she knew his heart, perhaps better than he did.

Prince Willem looked past Daemyn to where Zeke and Alex stood. He gave a small nod. "I apologize, Your Majesty, for disturbing your sleep like this. When we'd planned this, we expected him to sleep in his own room as he'd been offered. Feel free to return to your rest. We'll be done shortly."

Alex's gaze flicked from Prince Willem down to Daemyn. "Please don't let your brother eat my advisor. He's the only advisor I have at the moment."

"Berend won't eat him. Gnaw on him a little, maybe. But not eat him. Besides, he's the one holding my brother at knife point." Prince Willem's face remained blank, much like the blank expression Daemyn wore when around Alex. "We'll keep the noise down."

Did that mean the torture part of the evening was over or that Prince Willem expected Daemyn to remain silent during torture?

"Very well." Alex turned to Zeke. "I believe it would be best if we retreated to the other room."

"Uncle Daemyn?" Zeke crossed his arms, not budging.

"I'll be fine." Hopefully. Maybe. Hard to know when Prince Berend still loomed over him with teeth bared.

Finally, Zeke followed Alex and closed the door after him.

Prince Willem stepped into the room and took a seat on the floor. "Well, Bere-Bear, I think you've scared him enough for one night."

Instantly, the growling stopped. When Daemyn looked up, Prince Berend's lips were drawn back in what could only be called a huge grin that showed plenty of teeth. Meeting Daemyn's gaze, Prince Berend stuck out his big, slobbery tongue. A blob of sticky drool landed on Daemyn's cheek.

Still wearing his bear grin, Prince Berend released Daemyn.

Wiping the bear drool from his face with a sleeve, Daemyn drew in his first decent breath in several minutes and rolled upright, swinging into a cross-legged position on his pallet. His shoulders ached from Prince Berend's weight, but he wasn't hurt. Not any more than he would've expected from a confrontation with Rosanna's brothers.

Prince Berend plopped onto the foot of the pallet, causing the whole straw mattress to whoosh and crinkle as his weight settled onto it. He sat upright, his back straight, as if trying to appear dignified. Rather hard to do when his hind legs stuck straight out and his fur poofed around him.

Both brothers remained silent, staring at Daemyn.

Apparently he was supposed to make the first move. "I meant what I said. I wasn't just saying that because I was pinned under a growling bear. I care for Rosanna."

Prince Willem stiffened, his gaze hardening. "You said care that time. It was love earlier."

Trust Prince Willem to pick up on that. Prince Willem

had been given the gift of charismatic writing by the Fae when he was born. Apparently that gift with words wasn't only confined to the page.

"We spent several weeks traveling to Castle Eyota. Then we spent only another months together before she returned here. So, yes. I care for her. I'm falling for her."

"And yet you're building a canoe together. You're talking about marrying her." Willem's gaze didn't waver. Prince Berend let out a grunting huff that sounded much more like the threatening noises black bears normally made than the growls he'd been making earlier.

Daemyn wasn't explaining this like he meant to. He'd watched his siblings, his nieces and nephews, his grand nieces and nephews, fall in love, get married, and stay loving each other until death parted them. If anyone could learn what love looked like through observation, then he had a better chance than most.

But putting something like love into words...he hesitated. He hadn't even revealed the depth of what was in his heart to Rosanna yet. Surely she deserved to be the first to hear it, rather than her brothers.

Still, he was going to have to be honest, painfully so, if he wanted them to believe he was worthy to court Rosanna.

That was the problem, wasn't it? The hesitation. The reason he still held back. Something in him was waiting to lose Rosanna too. As he'd lost his family as the years had gone by, when they aged, and he didn't. As he'd lost his strong father to the mines, only to have a crippled father return, leaving Daemyn responsible for earning enough to support his family. And he had, by leaving home at the age of ten to become Alex's manservant.

There was the heart of it. Yes, Rosanna loved the

mountains and adventure. Yet she was still a princess, and he, for all of the years he'd lived and the position Alex was trying to give him now, was still a humble manservant born in a small cabin in the mountains.

While they'd traveled from Neskahana to Kanawhee to wake Alex from his cursed sleep, they'd been on the rivers, deep in the mountains, where status and titles hadn't mattered.

But in Rosanna's world, titles mattered. And not just the title, but everything that went with it. How long would it take Rosanna to realize that while she fit into his world, he would never fit into hers?

"Well?" Prince Willem's voice broke into the silence.

Right. Rosanna's brothers were still waiting on an answer.

Daemyn drew in a deep breath and faced them. "I love her, and that love is only going to deepen with time. I know I don't have any more experience with love than anyone else my age, but I've also lived long enough to know I don't say that lightly or for something that's a passing feeling. But I'm also not going to trap her. If she doesn't feel the same way, I'll let her go."

Prince Berend grunted and jabbed Daemyn in the chest with one of his claws. He waved his other paw in the air as he made a series of growling noises as if he was talking, just he couldn't form the words with his bear's mouth and tongue.

"Exactly." Prince Willem nodded, as if he understood what Prince Berend said, though Daemyn doubted it. Rosanna hadn't understood Berend when he'd tried to warn them about a Tuckawassee ambush while in bear form.

Prince Willem turned to Daemyn, and his gaze was

hard. "That might sound all noble, saying you'd let her go, but it just means you don't understand how much Rosanna already loves you. She's made her choice, and it's you. So you're either going to have to choose her in return or you're going to break her heart. Because doubting her isn't love."

"It's not her I'm doubting." Daemyn stared down at the floor, unable to hold Prince Willem's gaze any longer. How could he doubt Rosanna? She'd seen through his attempts to push her away after Alex was awakened. She'd stuck with him even as he'd been sorting out where he went after being gifted another lifetime.

"She's not the one we're doubting either." Prince Willem leaned forward. "From what we heard, she's the one who had to chase after you. She's the one who asked to court you. She's the one who said she loves you. I haven't heard you doing or saying any of that in return. You need to figure out why that is and either fix it or leave our sister alone. Understand?"

"Perfectly, Your Highness." Of course he understood. He even agreed. Rosanna deserved to be loved whole heartedly, unreservedly.

And that was the problem. She deserved someone much better than him.

"Good." For the first time, a smile crossed Prince Willem's face. "In that case, no more calling me Your Highness. If we're going to be brothers-in-law eventually, then you'd better call me Willem."

Prince Berend patted his furry chest with a paw and pronounced something unintelligible in bear grunts and growls.

"And he's Berend." Willem climbed to his feet, his expression sobering. "For what it's worth, I think you'll be good for her. You're the first one who hasn't screamed in terror and run away as soon as Berend threatened him."

"I didn't think Rosanna had ever courted anyone else before." Daemyn had always had that impression.

"She's never courted anyone, but that doesn't mean there weren't a few boys who have been interested." Willem's mouth turned into something that would've been called a smirk if it had been less controlled. "They were all decidedly less interested after we got done with them. They couldn't make it past the drool."

Berend was definitely smirking. As much as a bear could smirk, anyway.

"I see." Daemyn held out his hands, palm up. "I can assure you. I will be on my very best behavior."

"Your *beary* best." Willem's smirk turned into a full-on grin.

"What?" Daemyn stared up at Willem. Was he supposed to laugh at that?

"I know. It can *bear*ly be considered humor. But it's our thing, so if you intend to join this family, then you'd better get good at bear puns."

He'd forgotten about Willem and Berend's bear pun habit. The one time he'd overheard one of their pun conversations, he'd been more focused on observing Rosanna and wondering how she'd take the news that she was the princess who was supposed to wake Alex. "I will *bear* that in mind."

Berend gave a huff, and Willem glanced toward his brother. "Not bad for a first attempt. It wasn't a complete em*bear*assment of a pun. You'll get better."

"What did I do wrong?" Daemyn was still missing something.

"Willem turned to him, straight-faced, even if his eyes

twinkled. "You'll figure out the rules eventually. Good job on not smiling, even if Berend tends to say them with *bear-faced smirking*."

There were rules for bear puns? Daemyn shook his head, then met Willem's gaze. "I don't see why my ability to pun should have any *bear*ing on my relationship with your sister. She *bear*ly tolerates the puns."

Berend snorted, then made a choking, coughing sound. He thumped Daemyn's shoulder with a paw.

Willem let out a bark of laughter and slapped his knee. "Now that's un*bear*able. I'd declare you the pun victor, but I already used *bearly*. You can't use the same pun someone else has already used. That would be bar*bear*ic."

Another punning rule.

The door at the other side of the room opened, and Zeke stalked in. "This is nuttier than a henhouse full of squirrels. You're keeping me and the High King of all Tallahatchia awake because you're having a bear pun war."

Daemyn shifted. It was a tad foolish when put that way.

Willem smirked. "We'd better go, Bere-Bear. I'm not sure how much longer the high king's fore*bear*ance will last."

With one last thump with a paw on Daemyn's shoulder, Berend rolled to his feet and shuffled out the door after Willem.

Zeke shut the door and leaned against it. "We ain't going to get any sleep unless we barricade this door."

Daemyn eyed Zeke. How long would it take him to realize what he'd just said?

Zeke glanced at him, then closed his eyes and groaned. "Ain't that just a hollering coon's tail. They've got me doing it too."

Daemyn flopped back onto his pallet. "Frennie would sure as maple sap get a hoot out of them."

"Ain't that the truth." In the near darkness now that the door blocked the light from the corridor, Zeke crossed the room, his bare feet scuffing on the stone floor, and settled back onto his pallet. After a moment, his pallet rustled. "Uncle Daemyn, you ain't going to let them rattle you none? You love Princess Rosanna, and she loves you. It's that simple."

Was it? Daemyn wasn't so sure. He was mountain folk. She was a princess.

Yes, it had happened before. He'd been there when it had. But that wasn't the usual way of things.

Zeke was waiting for an answer. Daemyn forced confidence into his voice. "Don't worry. I ain't scaring off that easy."

Chapter 4

Elara

Elara Ashen trailed behind the baroness and her two daughters, keeping the proper distance behind them, as they wound their way through the streets of Fonthaven, the capital of Pohatomie, on their way to Castle Fonthaven rising on the hill above the town.

Summons from King Cassius himself had been delivered this morning to Baroness Hackett, asking for her and her daughters, Monica and Beatrice, to come to the castle. And of course they dragged along Elara, as their maid. What a tragedy it would be if the baroness or one of her beautiful daughters had to appear before the king with the hems of their dresses dusty or their golden curls out of place.

Elara glared at the two sets of perfect curls dancing in front of her. She had spent so much time on their hair that she'd only had time to messily tie her own hair back from her face. It wasn't fair. Her hair was just as blonde and beautiful. Was it too much to ask to have five minutes to spend putting her own hair into curls?

It hadn't always been like this. Growing up as the daughter of the captain of the late Baron Hackett's guards, Elara had felt almost like another sister to Monica and Beatrice. Certainly a friend. But the moment her father died, she'd become just a servant.

Ahead, a crowd filled the entire street, pressing around a couple of the market stalls. What was going on? Elara stood on her tiptoes, trying to see over the crowd.

Monica, the oldest of the two daughters, halted and pointed. "It's fabric!"

Baroness Hackett peered toward the market stall. "I heard there was a cargo of cloth from Guyangahela coming, but I wasn't sure I believed it. We haven't had trade with Guyangahela, except for a few smugglers, for decades."

Elara hung back as the baroness and her daughters worked their way into the crowd to take their turn touching the silk and admiring the fine linen, in colors so vibrant and beautiful it was hard to believe they were real. Certainly no dyes like that existed in Pohatomie. Guyangahela guarded the secrets of its dyes, fabrics, and weaving techniques closely.

Perhaps the presence of fabric from Guyangahela signaled a return to those long past golden days that Elara had heard about only in rumors. Days when the high king had ruled and goods from each of the seven kingdoms flowed to the others through the great market at Eyota.

Not that it would make a difference to Elara, at least any time soon. The baroness and her daughters would probably soon wear dresses made from the fine fabrics arrayed in that market stall, once regular trade made the price of such fabrics affordable to the likes of them.

But not for Elara. She'd be stuck in homespun. If she

was lucky, maybe some lesser fabric coming from Guyangahela. But never silk. Never those bright colors.

Wasn't she just as good as any of them? Didn't she deserve to wear silk just like they did?

After a few minutes, Baroness Hackett extricated herself from the crowd, motioning for her daughters to follow. "We mustn't keep the king waiting."

Monica and Beatrice followed their mother while Elara sighed and trailed behind them. Did she get a chance to look at the fabric? No. She was just the servant.

At the far end of the main street, the ground rose steeply. Elara's calves ached as they approached Castle Fonthaven.

The palace perched at the top of a sheer mountain overlooking the Pohatomie River, inaccessible except for a paved causeway. The castle itself was a grand thing, rising in three towers clustered together. The lower floors of the towers were built in stone while they were topped with wooden upper floors with turrets spiraling from them.

At the base of the causeway, a guardhouse and two squat towers guarded the cobblestone bridge that connected the castle with the town. Off to one side, a log barn stood next to a corral blocking off the end of a steep-sided gorge along one of the side creeks flowing into the river.

Baroness Hackett halted and patted her hair.

Elara sighed and stepped forward. This was the life of a maidservant. She knelt and brushed at first the baroness's skirts, then her daughters'. Elara pulled a few more hair pins from her apron pocket and pinned Monica's curls back in place.

Monica smiled at her. "Thanks, Elara. What would we do without you?"

Not much at all. Elara gritted her teeth and pasted on a smile. "I'm here to help."

Baroness Hackett swept a glance over her and her daughters' appearances before she nodded. "I believe we look presentable now. Elara, please wait for us here."

"Of course, ma'am." Elara bobbed her head. As she'd expected. She was just a lowly servant. Not even worthy of entering the castle.

Baroness Hackett swept to the gatehouse, her homespun, dark green dress elegant and her head held high as she announced to the guards, "Baroness Hackett and her daughters Monica and Beatrice to see the king, on the order of His Majesty King Cassius."

The guards eyed the baroness for a moment before they pulled the gate open.

Elara turned away and headed for the barn down the slope. Here, the rushing river gurgled louder.

In the corral ahead, a matched pair of elk grazed on the grass while a buffalo with sandy colored, nearly white fur rubbed against one of the posts.

On the other side of the fence stood a young man with hair almost the same sandy yellow-brown as the buffalo leaned against a post. He was tall and muscled. Solid. Elara smiled. Terrence had been her friend since they were children when their parents had been friends.

He reached beneath the top rail, which was level with his head, and scratched the buffalo's head behind its ear.

The buffalo leaned harder against the fence. The wood creaked.

Elara halted next to Terrence, reached through the fence, and buried her fingers in the soft, thick fur around the buffalo's ruff. "You shouldn't encourage him. Toho is going to stumble his way through the fence again."

"He could knock this fence down whenever he wanted." Terrence shook his head. "There isn't a fence built that can hold a buffalo for long."

One of the elk raised its head and trotted toward the fence. The points of its antlers were filed smooth, like Toho's were, for safety. The elk stuck its face as far as it could through the rails, sticking its tongue out to lap Elara's hand. She rubbed the elk's forehead. "At least Kal and Kio are well behaved. Aren't you, boy?"

"Well, mostly." Terrence huffed out a breath.

Elara held her palm out and let Kio slobber across her fingers, looking for a treat. "Did you see the new fabrics they brought in from Guyangahela? There was a display in the market."

Terrence scratched Toho's ruff. "Yes. Right pretty, aren't they?"

"The baroness and her daughters are probably going to have new, fancy dresses before the week is out." Elara leaned against the fence. "They will probably be all generous and give me their old clothes. As if I'm worth nothing more than cast-offs."

"That *is* generous, Elara." Terrence stopped scratching Toho and turned to her. "Most barons and baronesses aren't that generous with their servants."

"That's not the point." Elara bit her bottom lip to stop her sigh, which might have come out as more a scream. Couldn't he see the point? She was just as good as Monica or Beatrice. Why couldn't she have a nice, new dress for once? Something made of fancy silk?

What would silk feel like against her skin? Soft and swishing. Smooth, without the itchiness of wool homespun.

"You have delusions of grandeur." Terrence laughed

and faced the buffalo and elk once again. "You know life isn't like that. Some are given much, and from them is demanded much. That's why the nobles, like the baroness and her daughters, have curses."

"They have gifts too." Elara rolled her eyes. As if they had needed more than natural beauty, status, and wealth. They are given Fae gifts on top of all that. And, really, how bad were the curses? Especially for the lesser nobles. It was the princes and princesses that received the terrible curses. Beatrice was cursed with sensitive skin, and Monica was cursed with fast growing hair. And their gifts of a head for numbers and the ability to paint beautifully more than made up for it.

"Yes, they do. But the Highest King distributes gifts as he wishes. Sometimes those gifts are obvious, like the Fae gifts. Others not so much. Doesn't mean they are worth less. Or any position in life is worth any less." Terrence smiled as Toho bumped his arm with a nose. "And some of those curses, I wouldn't want them. I'd much rather be the king's buffalo boy than take a king's curse."

Elara suppressed a growl. Terrence's gifts speech. How many times had she heard it? Why did he have to be so infuriatingly content with his lot in life? Couldn't he see how unfair it was? "Life shouldn't work like this."

"Maybe it shouldn't. When they unleashed the true curse, the first kings brought curses and unfairness and a life that's hard." Terrence pushed off the fence and headed for the barn. "I reckon I see Baroness Hackett on her way back over the causeway. Looks like you'll be heading home soon."

Already?

Elara scanned the causeway. Baroness Hackett's dull green skirt swished as she led the way across the cobblestones. Monica and Beatrice trailed in her footsteps, as they always did. Living in their mother's shadow. Elara fell into step with Terrence. "That was hardly worth the hassle of the trip. The king believes he is entitled to order everyone around as he sees fit."

"He is the king." Terrence halted by the barn. "Feel free to stop by next time you're in Fonthaven."

"Of course I will." Elara patted his arm. He was her only friend after all. She didn't know what she would do without him.

When Elara reached Baroness Hackett, Monica, and Beatrice, she bobbed a curtsy. "Did you have a profitable meeting with His Majesty?"

Baroness Hackett glanced over her shoulder at Monica. Monica's head hung, her shoulders stiff. Baroness Hackett was frowning, deep grooves cutting around her mouth and her eyes.

Something wasn't right. What had the king said to them? What had he wanted?

They wouldn't speak about it here, whatever it was. Elara took her place a few steps behind Baroness Hackett and her daughters, leaving the imposing Castle Fonthaven behind.

ELARA RAN the brush through Monica's thick, golden hair, then reached for the shears. Monica's hair had already reached the floor even though Elara had cut it above her shoulders that morning.

Monica stared at her reflection in a pitted, wavy mirror, though her eyes were unfocused.

"Are you all right, milady?" As a servant, Elara was

expected to ask such questions, listen intently to whatever Monica had to say, and keep it all to herself.

She sliced into the hair above Monica's shoulders, the shears making a soft, crisp sound as they parted the hair. She didn't have to be neat or straight. This trim was just to keep Monica from tangling herself in her hair as she slept. Elara would have to trim the hair again in the morning to keep it manageable during the day.

Monica hugged her arms around herself. "King Cassius intends to invite High King Alexander and the princess from Neskahana to the Harvest Festival Balls."

Elara froze, a chunk of Monica's hair gripped in her hand. Invite the high king here? She wasn't sure how she felt about that. He was the legendary sleeping high prince. Somewhat of a romantic figure, even here in Pohatomie. Why would King Cassius invite the high king here? King Cassius had fought against him.

Monica turned in her seat to look at Elara, still hugging herself, while the untrimmed half of her hair wrapped around her. "But it's a trick. King Cassius wants me to lure the high king into some kind of trap."

"What?" Elara gaped. Sweet, innocent Monica? She wouldn't know how to even begin such a task. Not unless the high king was attracted to someone with an abundance of long, golden, hair.

Monica rocked back and forth on her chair and toyed with the end of her hair. "He wants me to make the high king fall in love with me, then publicly reject and embarrass him."

"Why?" Elara shook her head. What did King Cassius plan to gain?

"He wants to cause a scandal. I don't know more than that. Not even Mother dared ask King Cassius what his plans are. What else could we do? We nodded and said yes." Monica blinked up at Elara. "But what if I don't want to do this? What if I'm not sure hurting the high king is the right thing to do? We fought, but we lost. Maybe it's time the kingdoms united again. It might be what is best for Pohatomie."

Maybe. Elara didn't know. In some ways, she didn't care.

Her mind filled with images of swirling, silk dresses and a handsome high king. What would it be like to attend the Harvest Festival Balls, the three nights of dancing ending on the night of the harvest full moon? To wear a beautiful dress fit for a princess worthy of the high king himself?

"What should I do?" Monica's quiet voice shook Elara from her glimmering daydreams.

"I don't know. You can't exactly refuse the king." Elara reached for the shears again. "Besides, the high king may not even come. He will surely expect a trap. He would be foolish to come here."

CHAPTER 5

DAEMYN

Daemyn dug his knife into the bark, scraping it away from the sapling in one, smooth stroke. He ran his fingers over the exposed wood, using his knife to peel away any rough edges. Once bent into a curve and dried, this sapling would become one of the canoe's ribs.

This early in the process, their canoe was nothing but piles of birch bark, spruce roots, and fresh-cut saplings all stacked neatly inside a stone shed tucked along one side of Castle Deeling's outer wall across a small courtyard from the castle's keep. He and Rosanna worked just outside the shed, forming the beginnings of the canoe's framework.

"What is..." Rosanna tightened a wooden clamp to hold one of the green saplings in a curve while it dried. "What is your scariest memory, not counting the times you died?"

It was a game they'd started during that month at Castle Eyota, asking each other the most interesting questions they could. Daemyn slid his hand over the sapling.

What was his scariest memory? There were a number to choose from, even ignoring the memories of dying nine times.

He let the curl of bark fall into the pile of wood shavings at his feet. The other night with her brothers brought to mind a story he'd yet to tell her.

"Well, there was this time I was sneaking through a tangle up in Monongadotte, trying to elude a war party from Pohatomie when I brushed aside some brambles and came face-to-face with a bear." Daemyn dropped his voice into the low, bated tone he used when telling stories to his nieces and nephews. "And not a nice bear like Berend, but a big, ornery bear that took one look at me and decided I looked mighty tasty."

Rosanna halted and gaped at him. "What did you do then?"

Daemyn leaned closer, as if he was going to impart a great secret. "I wrassled him, of course."

"That story is true?" Rosanna lightly swatted his chest with the back of her hand. "There is no way you took on a bear with just your knife."

"It was all I had." Daemyn shrugged. He wasn't about to mention that gut-wrenching, desperate moment when he'd thought he might add getting eaten by a bear to what was at that time a short list of deaths.

"That was when you were Jubal Rand, wasn't it?" Rosanna leaned on the sapling to bend it into shape. "Surely not all of those stories about Jubal are true. There are some awful wild ones about him. Well, you."

"Most are yarns stretched about as tall as oak trees." Daemyn worked at a particularly stubborn patch of bark around a knot in the sapling. The sun warmed his back, seeping through his buckskin shirt. He had his sleeves rolled up to his elbows, the better to feel the wisp of a breeze. "But they ain't all tall tales. They got some truth to them."

"Then what happened? With you and the bear?" Rosanna reached for the next sapling.

It felt too good to fall back into his mountain speech to stop now. Instead, he exaggerated the mountain even more. "He got one taste of me and reckoned I weren't worth the hassle of fighting no more, on account of me being a stringy, tough mountain boy. So he up and runned off."

Rosanna huffed out a laugh. "No wonder the tales got all stretched when you tell them like that."

"It ain't a proper mountain yarn 'til it's growed some in the telling." Daemyn held his smile for another moment before he shook his head and dropped the exaggerated story-telling voice. "Truth is, that Pohatomie war party made such a ruckus looking for me they scared the bear off before it had a chance to do more than gnaw on me some."

If she looked too closely at his left forearm, she'd see the scars left by the bear's teeth. Though, the bear came out worse in that scrape, knifed as it had been.

"When I was little, I thought all bears were nice and friendly and cuddly like Berend. He would turn into the cutest, fluffiest cub you've ever seen back when he was a baby and toddler. I about gave my father a heart attack when we came across a wild bear on a family hike and I wanted to pet it." Ducking her head, Rosanna laughed softly. "If you see any bite marks on the chair or table legs, that was Berend when he was little. He went through a phase where he chewed everything he could get his paws on during the night. He ate my favorite pair of moccasins."

If he'd ever wondered why she managed to take all his

non-aging weirdness so well, it would be this. She'd grown up with a brother who turned into a bear at night.

Daemyn picked up another sapling, and the two of them worked in silence. It was the same sort of silence they had when paddling a canoe together. A steady rhythm that needed no words.

"Is your father still watching and pretending he isn't?" Daemyn sliced another long curl of bark from a sapling.

Rosanna glanced up long enough to peek past his shoulder before she tightened another clamp. "Yes. He and High King Alexander are still watching our soldiers drill, though Father is glaring in this direction every chance he gets."

"It's an odd situation for him to be in. I get the feeling none of your family knows what to think." Daemyn resisted the urge to glance over his shoulder. He could feel the sharp itch of eyes watching him.

"They'll come around." Rosanna reached for the sapling he'd peeled and handed him a new one. "High King Alexander also seems to be glancing this way a lot."

Why? Was Alex angry he was taking time away from working? Should he be over there, standing a few steps behind Alex in case Alex wished to summon him?

No, that was how he would've thought as Jadon, Alex's manservant. Was he still Jadon? He'd left that part of himself back a hundred years ago.

Yet who was Daemyn Rand? He wasn't sure. He'd worn so many false names over the years. Changed his personality to become different people. Was Daemyn another one of those false names? Was the person he was now real or false?

Did he even know how to be himself anymore?

"Daemyn?"

He started at Rosanna's touch on his arm. This was his here and now. After a hundred years, he was free to join life again. If he could figure out how.

He managed a small smile. "I'm fine."

"No, you're not." Rosanna leaned closer and slid her hand into his. "But I understand. Or, at least, I'm trying to understand."

He wasn't sure how to explain this disorientation from feeling the weight of aging and the churn of emotions in a way he hadn't in a hundred years.

He opened his mouth, but her fingers tightened on his.

She was staring past him, her smile dropping into something taut. "A messenger has arrived. It looks serious."

When Daemyn turned, it wasn't Rosanna's father gripping a note as he'd expected. Instead the messenger stood in front of Alex, and Alex stared at something in his hands.

His time alone with Rosanna was over, at least for now. With her at his side, Daemyn strode toward Alex and King Faron.

As Daemyn approached, Alex's frown deepened as he stared at the message, written on real paper. A hard commodity to come by. This had to be something important, probably from one of the kings. Alex glanced at Daemyn before turning to King Faron. "Is there somewhere we can talk privately?"

"Yes. The Great Hall will suffice." King Faron motioned over his shoulder at the square keep behind him. "I will station my guards at the door so we aren't disturbed."

"Very well." Alex turned. "Jadon—uh, Daemyn—and Princess Rosanna, I'd like you both present as well. This concerns you, too."

Daemyn's chest tightened. The past few days had been too good to last.

Queen Erina joined them in the Great Hall along with Prince Berend, Prince Willem, and their guard captains. Zeke and Isi, too, stood off to one side.

Except for Alex and Zeke, it was almost an exact replica of the moment Daemyn told Rosanna and her family that she was the promised princess.

Had it only been a few months? It felt like he'd known Rosanna much longer, as if she'd been the person he'd been missing for a hundred years.

Alex frowned, as if annoyed with the extra people who had invited themselves to his meeting without his permission.

But as Daemyn had learned, this was Rosanna's family. What concerned one of them affected them all.

As they claimed seats around the table on the dais, Daemyn found himself part way down the table with Rosanna on one side and Berend on the other. Willem took the seat on the other side of Rosanna while Zeke and Isi sat across from them.

"High King Alexander is being un*bear*ably grim about that message." Willem had his arms crossed, his face blank.

"Whatever it is, we shall have to grin and *bear* it." Berend leaned forward and grinned, showing off his square, human teeth. Yet Daemyn couldn't help but remember Berend's sharp fangs.

"Ugh, please. Don't get started on the bear puns." Rosanna slouched in her chair.

"Aww, come on, Ro-row. Now is the *beary* best time

for puns." Berend nudged Daemyn with an elbow. "We even taught Daemyn. Show her, Daemyn. Lay your best pun on us."

"Bere-bear. Please tell me you didn't." Rosanna gave Daemyn a don't-you-dare look.

What was he supposed to do? If he said a pun, he'd annoy Rosanna. If he didn't, he might lose the progress he'd gained with her brothers.

Then he noticed the gleam in Rosanna's eyes, the hint of a smile at one corner of her mouth.

She was pretending to be more annoyed than she really was, giving him a chance to earn goodwill with her brothers.

Now he just needed a pun, and fast. He nearly said *bear with me*, but Berend had already used something too similar.

"If we could get this meeting started?" King Faron's voice was hard, and even though it had been the princes doing the talking, his glare was locked on Daemyn.

This was why Daemyn preferred to be invisible. To be the overlooked servant.

"Thank you, Your Majesty." Alex tipped a small nod in King Faron's direction before he smoothed the message on the table in front of him. "This is an invitation from the king of Pohatomie."

Silence hushed the room. Daemyn's back tightened. Pohatomie was the last place Alex should go. Well, second to last. Tuckawassee would be worse. But only barely. A hundred years ago, the Pohatomie had sabotaged the bridges and escalated the tensions between kingdoms.

"What do they want?" King Faron leaned forward.

Alex shook his head and stared down at the message. "This is an invitation for their Harvest Balls for me and for..." Alex glanced at Rosanna. "And for Princess Rosanna."

"What?" Berend bolted upright.

"Me?" Rosanna's grip on Daemyn's hand tightened, and her eyes widened, as if she couldn't imagine why the Pohatomie would specifically ask for her in the invitation.

Alex grimaced and cleared his throat. "It appears they want us to be their honored guests at this ball—me as the newly awakened and crowned high king and you as the princess who woke me. By the wording, it seems they are under the impression there is something...romantic between us."

The legend of true love's kiss waking the high prince. Daemyn suppressed a grimace. It wasn't too surprising the Pohatomie would think that. It was what all the old stories rumored. Rosanna and Daemyn hadn't been all that demonstrative together when at Castle Eyota while the king of Pohatomie had been present. Rosanna had stayed at her father's side while Daemyn lurked in the background.

"The message also indicates that royalty from Buckhannock and Monongadotte have been invited, as well. It seems King Cassius of Pohatomie wishes this to be a gesture to symbolize the renewed unity of Tallahatchia."

"If that is the case, then why wouldn't he invite all of the kingdoms? He's excluded Tuckawassee, his ally, and Guyangahela, the first kingdom to reopen trade." Prince Willem sat back in his chair, tapping his chin as if he was contemplating the answer to his own question.

"I suspect because of the time it would take them to travel to Pohatomie." Alex stared at the paper in front of him with narrowed eyes. "It will be difficult for us to arrive in Pohatomie in time. It would be impossible for a messenger to carry the invitation all the way to either Guyangahela or Tuckawassee and have time for their representatives to travel north to Pohatomie."

Willem's frown deepened. "King Cassius has had three months to send out this invitation if celebrating the high king's awakening was his true intention. Why wait until now?"

Daemyn's mind raced as he tried to put the pieces together. Perhaps Guyangahela's re-establishment of trade had sparked the king of Pohatomie into action. This had to be a trap of some sort. Maybe he was hoping the short notice would make it hard for Alex to prepare countermeasures? What was King Cassius planning?

"It has to be a trick." Alex tapped the paper. "That much is obvious. But I'm not sure I, at least, can refuse."

King Faron scowled. "Why walk into King Cassius's trap?"

"He's already maneuvered me into a corner." Alex shook his head. "By sending these invitations across the country, he's made a public gesture. If I refuse, he can claim I'm not as committed toward peace and rebuilding Tallahatchia as I claim. He will use it to undermine everything I've managed to do in the past few months. Besides, I planned to visit Pohatomie eventually. Sooner rather than later won't make a difference."

But it could, if they went to Pohatomie on King Cassius's terms. No telling what he had simmering in the stewpot.

"Daemyn?" Rosanna squeezed his hand. "What's your opinion?"

His opinion? Daemyn raised his head. He hadn't realized his thoughts would matter. Not in a discussion between kings.

Alex glanced at him. "Right. Daemyn. You're my advisor. What is your advice for this situation?"

Daemyn let out a long breath. This whole advising thing took some getting used to. "I suspect it's a trap no matter if you go or stay. King Cassius is wily. There's a reason he immediately surrendered as soon as the battle turned against the Pohatomie and the Tuckawassee."

He didn't want to give his next advice. He'd rather Alex stayed far away from Pohatomie and the danger there.

But Alex was right. He planned to go there eventually. And no matter when they went, they would be walking into a trap. Better to face it head on while surrounded by allies.

"I think you should go." Daemyn glanced at Alex but couldn't hold his gaze. It still felt odd having a room filled with royalty listening to what he had to say. A manservant. A boy from the mountain folk. A miner's son. "With members of the royal family of Monongadotte and Buckhannock there, you will have allies and witnesses who will prevent King Cassius from striking at you in an obvious way. If we can discover what he's planning, we can reveal his treachery in front of nearly all the kingdoms."

"Turn his trap into a trap of our own." Alex's mouth twitched in something of a smile. "I would prefer facing his trap than running from it."

Rosanna lifted her chin. "In that case, I'll have to accept the invitation as well."

Daemyn's heart stuttered. It was one thing to risk Alex, but another to have Rosanna there, facing danger. It had been bad enough, guarding her on the journey to Kanawhee, knowing the Tuckawassee would try to kill her. This time, he wasn't indestructible. She could be hurt, and he might not be able to prevent it.

"No." King Faron's face twisted. "I sent you into danger once. It was necessary then. But I cannot give my approval when it isn't necessary."

"But it is, Father." Rosanna's face was composed, her back straight. "If High King Alexander intends to walk into this trap, then he will need his allies at his side. That's the only way he's going to survive whatever King Cassius has planned. That means a representative of the royal family of Neskahana must be there. Willem can't go because his curse prevents him from leaving Neskahana. Berend can't go because he is liable to be shot and killed by one of Pohatomie's hunters while he's a bear at night. Besides, the invitation names me specifically. King Cassius could see it as an affront if you send someone else in my place."

"If he needs a member of our family, then I'll go personally." King Faron crossed his arms, steel in his eyes. "I'll not risk one of my children again."

"It's a risk we inherit because we are royal. You can't protect us from it forever." Willem met and held his father's gaze, though something in Willem's expression was tight and almost pained. "Until my curse is broken, I cannot rule Neskahana the way you do. You can't risk that King Cassius will take the opportunity to kill you off, knowing that Neskahana will struggle to retaliate without a king to lead them into battle the way a king should."

"That's why it has to be me." Rosanna's voice was firm. "King Cassius will have no reason to hurt or kill me. I'm not a crown princess where he would disrupt the line of succession. And, if I were to be hurt in a way that could be linked to Pohatomie, King Cassius knows he will have Neskahana's armies to face. With royalty from Kanawhee, Monongadotte, and Buckhannock also there, Pohatomie wouldn't dare risk an outright attack against any of us, not when the resulting war would be four kingdoms against one. No, whatever he has planned, it must be more subtle than that, and I doubt it involves bodily injury to any of us."

"Still, you won't be safe." King Faron's hands tightened into fists in his crossed arms.

Queen Erina rested her hand on King Faron's forearm. "It was only a few months ago that we watched you leave into terrible danger. It isn't easy to think about you walking into danger like that again. You're our daughter."

"I know it isn't easy. But you've also raised me to know my duty. And this is what a princess does."

Daemyn drew in a deep breath. He had to speak up. "I'll protect her."

King Faron's gaze shot to him, searching. It had to be strange for him, knowing Daemyn was the same Arlen Rand he'd known years ago.

Daemyn looked away. This was one reason he usually kept his secret confined to his family. Because it was too strange to come face-to-face with people he'd known as friends in one name, only to know them again as mentors or father figures in another name.

By this point, he was used to the way relationships changed—had to change—while he had stayed un-aging, unchanging. Nephews and nieces he'd held as babies grew into little brothers and sisters, then friends, and eventually out-grew him to become almost parental figures. Daemyn had a grandnephew who was like a grandfather to him. It was strange, yes. But it was his reality.

King Faron let out a long breath. "The Arlen Rand I knew was a good man. I mourned when I heard of his death."

Daemyn traced the length of the scar running beneath his chin across his windpipe. "The part of me that was Arlen did die. I just didn't stay dead."

King Faron scrubbed his jaw, as if he still couldn't wrap his mind around it fully.

"Daemyn is a good man." Rosanna swayed closer to him. "And he won't be the only one protecting me. His family will help." She turned to him. "How many relatives do you have in Pohatomie?"

Daemyn hesitated. He never spoke about his many great-great grandnephews and nieces, often not even to each other. It was safer if no one knew exactly who was related to him. "A few. I have one relative at Castle Fonthaven, and I'm sure a few of the delegation from Buckhannock will be family."

Including Buckhannock's prince or princess, whoever ended up going. Probably not Keziah. Her curse made it impossible for her to represent Buckhannock as its princess in diplomatic situations like this. And probably not Zephaniah, the crown prince either.

He would have to send a message out tonight, using the flashing light relay system he had established, and let the family in Buckhannock know what the plan was and to confirm which of the princes were going. He would be better prepared when he arrived in Pohatomie if he knew which allies he could plan on being there.

He glanced over his shoulder to where Zeke stood guard along one of the walls with Isi near him. It would also help to make sure Zeke was prepared as well.

"Can I go? I can help protect Ro." Berend grinned, and Daemyn saw again the reflection of the bear's toothy grin in the expression.

"No, Rosanna is right. The Pohatomie hunters don't

know not to hunt bear at night, and it would give King Cassius too easy of an excuse to pass your death off as an accident."

Daemyn breathed a sigh under his breath. He had enough to worry about with having to protect both Rosanna and Alex.

Rosanna's hand was warm in his where they still clasped hands beneath the table, and his pulse thumped in his throat. Would she be in danger again because of this? Could he protect her this time?

And if he did, would it cost him his life yet again?

As if sensing his worries through their clasped fingers, Rosanna glanced over her shoulder at him. "I'll be fine."

"I know." He tried to muster up a smile.

"This is your life, Daemyn. And it's the life I want, paddling beside you into adventures in the far distant parts of Tallahatchia." Rosanna turned in her seat so she could face him more fully. "I know there will be dangers. But we'll face them together. That's how this works, you know."

It was, yet how could he ask Rosanna to share in the kind of life he led? Not that he knew what his life would be like now that Alex was awake. Surely it would be less dangerous than the last hundred years.

His heart ached with something he didn't even dare name to himself. He couldn't watch her die as he'd watched so many others. It would break him in a way all the other losses hadn't.

She smiled, and he couldn't help a small smile in return.

A part of him was glad she was coming. He didn't like the danger, but she was the woman he wanted at his side. The wonder on her face when she saw the Pohatomie fields rolling away into the distance would be a sight to see.

He cupped her chin with his hand. "The adventure might be more than you can *bear*."

Next to him, Berend howled a laugh and thumped his back, and behind Rosanna, Willem smirked.

But it was Rosanna's huff and grin that held Daemyn's attention. Yes, she was exactly the girl he wanted to ride the river with on this adventure.

CHAPTER 6

ALEXANDER

Alex tried to stay out of the way as the guardsmen and women set up their camp along the banks of the upper Onohio River.

The soldiers had their own rhythm as they pitched tents, started fires, and stowed the canoes. Laughter filled the campsite, and even Daemyn had an almost smile as he and Zeke carried the last of the gear from the river.

Princess Rosanna halted by a fire where one of her guards was putting a pot on. "Otho, do you think you could show me how you make your stew?"

"You'd like to learn, princess?" Otho's brow wrinkled.

"If I'm going to keep traveling like this, I think I should learn how to cook and wash my own clothes and stuff like that." Rosanna flicked a glance toward Daemyn before focusing back on the guard. "I may not always have people around to do the work for me."

Interesting. Alex scrubbed a hand along his jaw as he perched on a fallen log. The princess was thinking she wasn't going to be a princess forever.

That seemed a poor reward, after everything she'd done to wake him from his curse. He had offered Daemyn a barony. But Daemyn hadn't wanted it. He wasn't quite sure what Daemyn's new position was going to look like yet.

Alex swept a glance around the camp. He'd failed a hundred years ago because, while he'd been intelligent, he hadn't truly seen what was around him.

This time he needed to observe. To do better than he did back then.

If only he could figure out what it meant to be more than an arrogant high prince.

Princess Rosanna greeted several of her guards—and his—by name as they passed by on their various tasks and chopped vegetables. Otho skinned the muskrat Zeke had shot as they'd canoed up river.

Muskrat. A large, rat-like creature with a ropy tail and mud-brown fur. Alex swallowed. He was going to try hard not to think about what he was eating when the stew was done.

Alex tried to remember his guards' names. It wasn't like he conversed with them.

But, no. That was the sort of thinking that had gotten him into trouble before. He shook his head. Was he ever going to learn how to be different than he'd been? It was so easy to fall back into his old ways. Seeing those beneath him as less than him. Ordering Daemyn around as a manservant instead of an advisor. Standing by and letting others do the work for him.

His pride was ingrained. How did he go about changing something so fundamentally a part of himself?

He'd knelt before the Highest Prince with his pride and

darkness inside laid bare and rotten before him. He had to change.

"The stew is ready!" Rosanna called. She helped Otho dish the stew into bowls as the guards went through a line.

Daemyn strode to Alex and held out a bowl of stew. "Your supper, Your Highness."

Alex took the bowl and blew on it to delay having to take a bite. Muskrat couldn't be any worse than eating raccoon or whatever other mystery meat Jadon's family had fed him back a hundred years ago.

Daemyn perched on the log a few feet away, blew on a bite, and popped it in his mouth as if he had no hesitation about eating the nasty looking creature. After a few bites, Daemyn glanced over at him. "Is the stew not to your liking, Your Highness?"

Not really. But Rosanna had helped make it. Alex couldn't admit his squeamishness. "No, I was just waiting for it to cool down."

He dipped in his spoon and stuffed a bite into his mouth before he thought about it any more. It honestly wasn't bad. Maybe on the gamey, tangy side. But the broth was thick with the right balance of spices and vegetables.

Daemyn raised his eyebrows and kept eating, the slightest twitch to the corners of his mouth as if he knew exactly what Alex thought of the stew.

Alex forced himself to smile and take another bite. If he told himself this was just normal buffalo, then he'd be fine. "It's good."

"Thank you." Rosanna took a seat between Daemyn and Alex.

Daemyn's nephew Zeke and Rosanna's maid, Isi, sank cross-legged, facing them. Isi grinned. "Just like old times."

Zeke shot a glance toward Alex. "Mostly."

Alex tried not to shift on the log. He was the high king. He should not feel out of place. Yet, among these people who had traveled from Neskahana to Kanawhee by way of Tuckawassee to wake him from his sleep, he was the outsider. They had friendships and a history that didn't include him.

He glanced past Rosanna to Daemyn. Alex had traveled with Daemyn before. Sort of. Alex knew Jadon. But he didn't know Daemyn. Not really. Daemyn had lived a hundred years. Done more. Seen things Jadon hadn't.

Daemyn set aside his bowl, all the stew scraped clean. "I think, once we reach Pohatomie, I should go back to the role of your manservant."

"What do you mean?" Rosanna rested her hand on Daemyn's arm. Alex had to look away, a pang in his chest. How he missed the coy way Mirabelle used to look at him.

Zeke crossed his arms. "Why?"

Alex met Daemyn's gaze. "I am willing to announce you as my advisor. I'm not ashamed of that." He wouldn't be. Not with what Daemyn did for him.

"Because a servant is invisible." Daemyn shifted as if he was uncomfortable with even that much attention. "I will have a better chance of figuring out what King Cassius is planning if I can move about unnoticed."

And Daemyn—or, at least, Jadon—was good at being invisible.

Alex studied Daemyn, the way he stared at the trees across the camp instead of looking at them. Did Daemyn even want a position at Alex's side, being introduced to the kings of Tallahatchia? Or did he actually prefer a role like this, one that kept him in the shadows?

Rosanna straightened her spine. "Then Isi and I can

switch places. She can pretend to be me, and I can help you as a maidservant."

But Daemyn was already shaking his head. "No. It's too much of a risk that someone in Pohatomie might recognize you from Castle Eyota. You were at your father's side after the battle. You weren't trying to hide who you were."

"Besides." Isi shook her head. "I can pass for you from a distance, but I haven't been raised to be a princess. Yes, I know a lot of the etiquette from being around you, but there's a lot I don't know."

Rosanna reached over and twined her fingers through Daemyn's. "But I'm not going to pretend I'm in love with High King Alexander no matter what everyone else in the kingdoms thinks."

Daemyn's shoulders hunched, as if a weight settled on him. He stared at the ground.

"Daemyn?" Rosanna shook their clasped hands.

Alex's stomach clenched. What was going through Daemyn's head?

"I think we need to fit what they are expecting as much as possible. And a manservant courting a princess is noticeable."

As much as Alex had been jealous of Daemyn—even a little hurt the promised princess hadn't fallen for him—he didn't want to fake a romance with Rosanna. Not that she wasn't nice, but he wasn't horrible enough to take Daemyn's girl, not even in pretend.

He cleared his throat. "Perhaps we don't have to feign romance. We don't avoid each other either. I escort you to the balls, but I don't dance with you any more than normal. Let everyone speculate. We'll incite more gossip with a friendly relationship that isn't obviously romantic.

And if everyone is gossiping and focused on us, they are less likely to pay attention to our real purpose for being there."

Rosanna tugged on Daemyn's hand. "See? We'll work something out. It might even be fun, a forbidden romance."

Daemyn smiled back, but the expression didn't reach his eyes.

Zeke set aside his finished bowl of stew. "Where do you want me?"

"Outside the castle." The hard edge of command was back in Daemyn's voice. "If the worst should happen, I want someone outside the castle the king of Pohatomie doesn't know about. If I go a day without contacting you..."

"I'll rally the relatives." Zeke smirked and patted the end of his bow. "I know."

Alex swirled the remnants of his stew in the bowl. Was he being foolish, walking into a trap like this?

ELARA

Elara swept her rag over the surfaces in the manor's entry hall, dusting. Then she had dresses to wash and mend and the girls' rooms to clean. While they were lounging in the parlor doing nothing besides a bit of painting and paperwork, checking the numbers from the harvest. Hardly strenuous.

A knock sounded on the front door.

Elara groaned and tossed her rag onto an end table. The last thing she wanted to do was deal with visitors. It meant she'd spend her day serving refreshments and staying on hand near the parlor instead of getting her other duties done.

She pasted on a smile and opened the door. "Welcome to…"

A royal guard stood on the doorstep, his homespun shirt dyed a deep blue and a long knife belted at his waist. He carried a burlap-covered bundle.

Behind them, Terrence gripped Toho's lead rope. The yellow-brown buffalo was burdened with a pack. Terrence gave Elara a small wave before he looped the lead rope over the hitching post and began to unstrap the bundle.

The guard cleared his throat. "We have been sent by His Majesty King Cassius to see to dresses for the Harvest Balls."

Of course. Not only were Monica and Beatrice going to the Harvest Balls as the personal guests of the king, they were being provided dresses by him too. Well, fabric for the dresses anyway. Probably that fancy new fabric from down south.

It wasn't fair. Elara wouldn't even get a new dress of her own this year, unless Monica or Beatrice "generously" gave her one of their cast offs.

As if that's all she was good for. Used clothes. Things no one else wanted.

Didn't she deserve a dress of that new fabric? She was just as good as Monica or Beatrice. They had so much, but she had to work so hard for what she earned.

She kept her fake smile in place and stepped aside, motioning for the guard to enter. "I will fetch the baroness and her daughters, if you would like to wait in the parlor?"

After showing the guard to the parlor just off the entry hall, Elara hurried upstairs. Baroness Hackett was in the family sitting room, sitting at her desk looking over the manor's accounts. Monica perched near the window painting a landscape.

Beatrice had her back to the other window as she double-checked the numbers in a second accounts book. Like her mother, Beatrice had been given the gift of numbers.

"Milady." Elara bobbed a curtsy.

"Yes, Elara?" Baroness Hackett glanced up, her quill poised over the book.

"A guard is here from the king. Says he has been sent to see about dresses for Lady Monica and Lady Beatrice. He has fabric with him."

Beatrice's face paled. Monica quickly set aside her paint brush and hurried to her sister's side.

Baroness Hackett drew in a deep breath, carefully set her quill aside, and rose to her feet, smoothing her skirts. Her porcelain smooth face was nearly expressionless, except for a tightening around her eyes. "Then we must not keep the king's messenger waiting."

"But, Mother. This is all part of the trap." Monica gave a shiver. "He's giving me a new dress to help me lure the high king."

"Yes. But right now, we have no way to refuse the king's orders. So we might as well take advantage of his generosity while we have it." Baroness Hackett's eyes narrowed further as she swept from the room.

After a moment, Monica stepped forward, nudging Beatrice to walk with her.

Elara headed for the kitchen, set a kettle on, and gathered the supplies for tea. She turned to the cook, the only other servant. "We have guests. Do you have anything I can serve with the tea?"

There probably weren't any cookies or cake. Sugar from the southern kingdoms was too hard to get. But maybe the cook had something else.

The cook gave Elara a nod. "I baked some fresh bread this morning. You can serve that."

Elara found the bread on the side board and sliced half of it as thin as she dared without appearing rude to their guests.

After she returned to the parlor and served, Elara took a tray outside. Terrence had Toho tied to a tree with a long lead rope, letting the buffalo munch on the thick, green grass by the river's bank. Not that tying the buffalo to the tree would do much good if the animal took it in his head to bolt. He would either snap the tree or the lead rope. But at least Terrence wouldn't get dragged as well.

Terrence grinned and took the glass. "Thanks. It's a long trip from Fonthaven."

"You must have been up before dawn. It's a good eight-hour walk, at least. The guard could've been here hours ago by canoe." Elara held the tray steady as Terrence claimed some of the bread. Inconsiderate nobles. What had King Cassius been thinking?

"Actually, we left yesterday morning. The king decided his buffalo boy was easier to spare than his last canoe." Terrence shrugged and chomped half the slice of bread in one bite. It took him a few long seconds to chew and swallow. "This wasn't our first stop. We made deliveries of fabric to several nobles between here and Fonthaven. From what I overheard, the king needed his canoes to make several other deliveries farther up and down the river."

Perhaps Monica wasn't the only girl King Cassius had tasked with making High King Alexander fall in love with her. King Cassius was too sly to put all his corn in one buffalo cart. Not only had King Cassius drawn multiple families into his plot, but his generosity would make it harder for the nobles to turn on him. They owed him.

Life was truly unfair. Elara flexed her fingers on the tray of food. Terrence worked too hard. She worked too hard. And all the while the fancy nobles played their games and intrigue without caring what happened to the peasant folk.

Chapter 8

Alexander

Castle Fonthaven loomed on the horizon overlooking the Pohatomie River. The hills surrounding it were lower than anything in Kanawhee or Neskahana, yet the castle still managed an impressive location on a craggy cliff over the river, surrounded by rolling hills on all sides but one.

While not as beautiful as Castle Eyota's graceful spires, Castle Fonthaven stood taller than any other castle in Tallahatchia. The tallest of its three towers was said to be eight stories tall in one place. A causeway ran up the side of the mountain, spanning a steep ravine that cut off the castle from the land around it.

Alex settled his crown on his head once again, lifted his chin, and waited for his entourage to fall into place behind him. He strode to the gate, then motioned behind him. One of his guards stepped forward. "His Royal Majesty, High King Alexander demands entrance."

After a moment, the gates creaked open. A sentry

dressed in dark blue homespun stood in the center of the gateway. "If you would please follow me."

The guard led them up the causeway and through a second set of arched gates into the small courtyard in the castle. To their right, a few smaller buildings and a section of wall hemmed in the courtyard while to the left and in front of them, the three towers loomed far, far above. The lower floors of the tower were built in dark gray stone while the upper floors were painted wood with peaked roofs and spired towers. A large clock was set in the face of the nearest tower.

When Alex had visited Castle Fonthaven with his parents when he'd been nine, he'd felt so small with the towers so far above. The sensation was little changed as he glanced upward at the three rising towers with the narrow valley of the courtyard slicing between them and the outer wall.

A man of average height with light blond hair exited the large doors set into the first tower. His crown, a golden thing with spikes and an elaborate design of corn and squash etched into it, rested against his forehead, shining against his pale skin. This must be King Cassius. He bore a slight resemblance to his great-grandfather.

A few steps behind him, another blond-haired man strode, this one bulkier instead of slim the way King Cassius was. Was this King Cassius's seneschal? Or the captain of his guards?

King Cassius halted in front of Alex. His blue eyes were hard as he met Alex's gaze.

Alex stared back. Was King Cassius going to refuse to bow before him? As the high king, Alex had to demand that sort of respect. Not because of his own dignity, but because he couldn't appear weak with Tallahatchia as divided as it was. If the other kings saw Alex as weak, civil war would break out once again within days.

King Cassius's mouth twitched, though Alex didn't think it was with a smile. Then, he dipped his head and bowed at the waist. Not as low as Alex would have liked, but at least he bowed. "Welcome to Pohatomie, Your Majesty. It is our pleasure to host you after your hundred-year slumber."

"I am pleased to be in Pohatomie, surrounded by your bounty at harvest time." The smooth, diplomatic words came easily to Alex, as did the haughty look. He turned and held out a hand. Princess Rosanna swept forward a step. "This is Princess Rosanna, the one who woke me."

Princess Rosanna bobbed a curtsy. It was a decent curtsy, but not a particularly graceful or practiced one. "Excited to be here."

King Cassius nodded. "We will have an official dinner reception planned for you in the gold dining room."

The gold dining room. Both the smallest and the most lavish of the three dining rooms in Castle Fonthaven. Alex had been awed by it when he'd been nine. "I would appreciate being shown to my room to wash up after my travels."

King Cassius waved to the man behind him. "This is my seneschal, Major Stefan Vinzen. He will show you and Princess Rosanna to your rooms."

Major Vinzen. As the castle seneschal in charge of running the castle, he would be an important person to remember. Alex followed Major Vinzen while his guards and Daemyn fell into step behind him. Princess Rosanna followed with Isi and her guards.

They entered the main doors of the farthest of the three towers. Inside, a grand staircase wound into the second story. From there, they had to walk down a hallway before they reached another set of stairs to take them to the third story. There they walked back down the hallway to the other end.

Major Vinzen halted and pointed at a door. "Your Majesty, you have this suite while Princess Rosanna is across the hall. The ballroom where the Harvest Balls will be held is on the first floor of this tower."

"Thank you." Alex pushed into the room. It was decorated in deep burgundy and gold with a sitting room filled with a settee and padded chairs while a door on the right side of the room probably led to the bedroom.

Daemyn carried their packs inside and slipped into the bedroom. Doing what he always used to do as Alex's manservant. Unpack their travel packs. See to Alex's clothes. Lay out a matching silk shirt and linen pants.

As Alex turned, Major Vinzen stepped inside the room and shut the door behind him.

Alex tensed. Why would Major Vinzen linger? As King Cassius's seneschal, he had other tasks to attend to, and Alex no longer needed him.

But Major Vinzen's gaze swept past Alex as if he was no one important and focused on something behind Alex. "Daemyn?"

Alex jumped and half-turned to see Daemyn behind him. He hadn't even realized Daemyn had returned to the sitting room. He was just so easy to overlook.

Daemyn stepped forward and shook Major Vinzen's hand. "It has been a while. I'm amazed you even remembered I'm Daemyn and no longer Arlen."

Major Vinzen's mouth cracked into something like a smile. "I *am* King Cassius's seneschal. I'm supposed to remember details like that, especially when it comes to the family."

Family? Was Major Vinzen one of Daemyn's relatives?

Daemyn nodded and waved to Alex. "Where does that leave us? Having the high king here must put you in a difficult position."

Yes. Because Alex was the high king, and Major Vinzen served the disloyal king of Pohatomie.

Major Vinzen let out a sigh, his gaze focused on the wall somewhere behind Alex and Daemyn. "I am loyal to the family. But I'm also loyal to my king. It has been a hundred years since we've had a high king, and Pohatomie has done just fine by itself." He flicked a glance at Alex before focusing back on the wall. "I am not sure the return of a high king to Tallahatchia is the best thing for Pohatomie."

Alex swallowed. It wasn't easy to stand there and listen to others doubt him. "I know I am untested. But I remember what Tallahatchia was like before I fell asleep. There were problems, yes. But the kingdoms were better off. I know you might not believe me since you only have my word and Daemyn's for what things were like back then. But I intend to not only restore Tallahatchia to what it was before, but make the kingdoms better than they were."

Major Vinzen shook his head. "Empty promises, in the end."

"Maybe. Maybe not." Alex forced himself to let his arms hang loose at his sides instead of folding them defensively.

What would his father have done in this situation? Alex wished he had paid more attention to how his father ruled. How he'd kept the kingdoms together for as long as he had, despite their contentions.

Because it was only after his father was murdered that the kingdoms dared split apart. If his father had lived...

But would he still have fallen into his curse, trapping his father in sleep as well? In that case, they would have still woken to a fractured kingdom.

Yet his father would have been the high king. Putting the kingdoms back together would have rested on his father's shoulders.

Daemyn stepped forward, and the steel in him was something Alex hadn't seen before. "I will not force you to go against your convictions or your king, not even for the family bond. You never knew your great-grandmother, my sister. I can't expect you to keep a promise she made decades ago." Daemyn paused and only continued when Major Vinzen met his gaze. "We are not here to overthrow your king, only to stop him from further rebellion. All I ask is that you decide what help you can give me without compromising your loyalties or duties to your king."

"Not going to be easy." Major Vinzen shook his head. "King Cassius is planning something. Even I don't have all the details. But I do know it will happen at the Harvest Balls. That's all I can or will tell you."

Alex suppressed a scowl. They'd already guessed that much already, even without Major Vinzen's confirmation. He gritted his teeth. He wanted to protest. To declare that he was the high king and thus Major Vinzen owed his allegiance first of all to Alex.

But Alex was striving to be better. And going around shouting about his status wasn't going to win him any allies. As he was learning, respect had to be earned.

That had him glancing over at Daemyn. For all his bluster, Major Vinzen was looking at Daemyn with hands at his sides, head bent. Not defiant, but respectful. Almost like he would like Daemyn's approval, for all he pretended he didn't.

Much like Alex. What was it about this new Daemyn —quiet and invisible as he still was—that made others want to follow his lead? Want to earn his respect?

Somehow, Daemyn had earned the respect of generations of his nieces and nephews, holding them together in a web across Tallahatchia. How had the Jadon Alex had known managed to do that? Jadon hadn't been a leader back then.

Even now, Daemyn wasn't a leader in the usual way. He wasn't visible at the head of an army. Instead, he worked in and from the shadows, meeting with his relatives only a few at a time. He was an organizer more than a leader.

Major Vinzen tipped his head toward Daemyn. "I will pass along more information as I can."

He turned and left the room without so much as a nod in Alex's direction.

Alex suppressed another sigh. That's the way things stood, apparently. Major Vinzen would help them somewhat because of Daemyn, but he had no loyalty to Alex.

CHAPTER 9

DAEMYN

As the gray light of dawn eased the darkness, Daemyn rolled out of the bedroll he'd spread beside the door to serve as the last line of defense for Alex. Thankfully the night before had been quiet. He wasn't going to sleep soundly until both Alex and Rosanna were safely out of Pohatomie.

Alex still slept, breathing out in deep, whuffling breaths. After days on the trail, Alex probably wouldn't wake for another couple of hours, considering the feather bed he slept on.

Daemyn slipped on his moccasins and laced them up his calves, hiding a small knife in his right moccasin. It was the only weapon he could carry. Anything else would raise suspicions that he was more than Alex's manservant.

But, if he needed weapons, then he'd already failed.

Daemyn eased the door open and stepped into the sitting room of Alex's suite. There, four of Alex's guards slept, positioned on the floor to make it difficult for an attacker to get to Alex during the night. A few stirred as Daemyn stepped around them, but he waved for them to remain where they were. They had a few minutes yet until their shift.

At the outer door, Daemyn knocked on the door three times before he unlocked it and stepped outside. The rest of Alex's guards stood outside, alert and armed.

Not that eight guards and Daemyn were going to do much to stop King Cassius if that's what he decided to do. King Cassius had an army at his beck and call. This was his castle.

Daemyn tapped Captain Taum, the captain of Alex's guards, on the shoulder. "Don't let anyone in while I'm gone. Not even a maid with a tray of breakfast."

"Understood." Captain Taum nodded and swept a glance down the hallway again. After the weeks of traveling, first from Kanawhee to Neskahana, and from there to Pohatomie, Captain Taum didn't question taking orders from him. Maybe Alex had told the captain to obey his orders, or perhaps Captain Taum had heard the legends about his past lives.

Or maybe it was because Rosanna's guards, including Captain Degotaga, listened to his orders and advice.

Across the hall, Captain Degotaga guarded the door to Rosanna's room with three of her men. He gave Daemyn a nod.

Daemyn resisted the urge to clear his throat. Giving orders about Alex's security was one thing. Almost second nature. But asking to see Rosanna? That was still new and uncertain. "Is Rosanna awake?"

Captain Degotaga knocked on the door. The lock clicked, and the door swung open. Not to Isi, as Daemyn had expected but to Rosanna herself.

Captain Degotaga sighed. "It isn't safe for you to open the door yourself."

Rosanna's gaze and smile were directed at Daemyn. "I heard you talking and knew it was safe." She held the door open wider. "Do you want to step inside?"

"Actually..." Daemyn held out his hand to her. Could she see the tremble coursing through him? The way his stomach was tight, his breath catching in his throat?

Nervous. In a way he'd never experienced before. Not nervous for his life or for his family or because of an unfamiliar place without family or friends.

No, these nerves were something new altogether. As if every fiber of him ached to impress her. To have her like him. All of him. Jadon. Daemyn. Every person he'd had to become in the past hundred years.

Rosanna smiled and took his hand. "Actually, what?"

Oh, right. He had been trying to say something. His brother Luke would've sighed and shook his head at him. Zeke would've been laughing. "I have something to show you. The sunrise from Castle Fonthaven's highest tower is amazing."

Rosanna swung their clasped hands. "Sounds like my kind of adventure."

Captain Degotaga tightened his hand on his sword. "Wait a moment, and I'll send Chogan and Ilma with you."

Showing Rosanna the sunrise with two guards along wasn't what he'd had in mind. But that was the cost of courting a princess.

Rosanna huffed. "I'm safe with Daemyn. And it's rather hard to sneak off with guards following me."

Captain Degotaga swept a hard glance over Daemyn. "That's the point."

Daemyn struggled not to shift under that gaze. Captain

Degotaga probably had orders from Rosanna's father to keep a watchful eye on him.

Rosanna's grip tightened on Daemyn's hand. "If it's just the two of us, anyone who sees us will probably assume I'm Isi, not the princess. They won't look closely, not the way they would if they thought the princess of Neskahana, the one who is supposedly part of a romantic love story with the high king, was sneaking off with the high king's manservant."

That made it almost sound like something her father wouldn't approve of. Not the innocent, show-Rosanna-the-sunrise like he'd meant.

Daemyn met Captain Degotaga's gaze. "We'll be back in an hour."

Captain Degotaga remained impassive for another moment before he gave one, sharp nod. "I'll send guards after you if you aren't back by then."

That was the best Daemyn would get. He glanced to Rosanna. "Ready?"

"For an adventure? Always." Rosanna pulled him down the hallway toward the main staircase.

Something that almost felt like it could've been a laugh caught in his throat. A laugh of all things. He waved the other direction. "This way."

Rosanna turned and trotted a few steps to fall into place beside him. "Doesn't this hall dead end?"

"It does." The lightness in his chest, the feel of her hand in his, sent his head spinning. It was just so easy smiling with her. Relaxing. Not thinking about who he had to pretend to be and only be who he was, even if he wasn't certain who that exactly was at the moment. "But we'll cut through a set of rooms to get to a corridor on the other side."

"This is the oddest way to build a castle." Rosanna shook her head, grimacing at the small table and chair sitting below a window, as if waiting for someone to curl up and enjoy the view. The whole castle was decorated like that. Comfort first, before defense. The complete opposite of Castle Deeling.

Daemyn pushed open the door to their right. "The first tower is the oldest and original part of the castle and the other two towers were added as the castle expanded. Several hundred years ago, three princes couldn't get along, and their father solved the fighting by giving them each one of the towers of the castle as their own. Or so he thought, until the brothers began building on to the towers, trying to out-do each other. What they got was a rambling, scrambling mess of a castle filled with lavish rooms."

Rosanna glanced around the abandoned sitting room and bedchamber as they cut through them. What little furniture remained was mostly stacked out of the way in the corners. "That explains why this castle has so many dining rooms and ballrooms and guest rooms."

It also had several kitchens and a different kitchen staff for each wing of the castle. He'd explored them and introduced himself to the servants while she'd attended the formal welcome reception the night before.

It was a reminder of how different their stations in life truly were. Yes, Rosanna dressed in buckskin and loved the mountains. But she was also a princess. He might know castles and castle life better than some among the mountain folk, but he knew a different side of castle life than she did.

Hence they were sneaking through Castle Fonthaven in the early morning hours.

He couldn't let himself dwell on that now. Instead, he

cleared his throat. "Later kings tried their best to integrate the towers, but there was only so much they could do. The towers only connect in certain places. Sometimes stairs within a tower only go to certain floors." Daemyn opened the sitting room's door, and they stepped into corridor on the far side. It looked much like the corridor they'd just left, except that they faced a staircase instead of another room. "We have a hike to the tallest tower."

"I don't mind." Rosanna followed him into the corridor, and they started up the stairs.

Footsteps padded on the stairs coming down toward them. Daemyn pressed himself to the wall to make room as a maidservant rounded the corner. Rosanna started and stepped out of the way only a fraction after Daemyn did.

The servant, her long blonde hair tied back with a ribbon, glanced over the two of them, her eyes widening before she ducked her head and hurried past.

Daemyn grimaced. Pohatomie wasn't his favorite kingdom to infiltrate. In most of the others, his brown-black hair and bronze skin was nondescript, letting him move about unnoticed. But here in Pohatomie where most people were blond-haired, blue-eyed, and light skinned, Daemyn's hair and skin stood out.

At the top of the stairs, they reached a corridor that connected the third tower, where they were staying in the guest rooms, with the second tower that had the highest turret. In the second tower, they had to go down two flights of stairs, through a few twisting corridors, until they finally reached the stairs that would take them all the way to the top of the first tower.

"This sunrise had better be worth it." Rosanna grimaced at the curving stairs and kept pace with him.

He wanted to come up with light and teasing words

but couldn't think of anything. If only he was more like his brother Luke or Zeke or one of the many nephews who found it so easy to tease him.

Today, all he managed was a hint of a smile. "You'll see."

By the time Daemyn eased open the trap door to the upper room in the tower, both he and Rosanna were panting from all the stairs they'd climbed.

A light layer of dust coated the floor, along with bird droppings. Above, a bird chittered and swooped among the rafters of the cone-shaped, peaked roof before darting out a window missing one of its panes of glass. As this room had been built solely out of ego to make the second tower the tallest, it was often neglected now, since few of the servants wanted to make the trek up all the stairs for a room no one used.

Rosanna let go of Daemyn's hand to scramble through the trap door.

How was it possible he could miss the feel of her hand in his when it was all so new? Her hand fit so well in his. So comfortable. Right.

Daemyn rolled out of the door and to his feet, shutting the trap door after him.

Rosanna was waiting in the center of the room, shifting as if eager to dash to one of the windows. Yet she waited for him.

He took her hand again and led her to one of the windows on the east. The windows were so begrimed they were nothing but brown with dark gray beyond. He lifted the latch and pushed the windows open.

In the gray dawn, the Pohatomie River rippled far below. On the far side, the mountains rose higher and higher until they disappeared in the gray line where land blurred into the sky only faintly streaked with pink.

Rosanna leaned back against him as they watched the sky turn pink, then orange before the sun burst above the horizon in a blaze of gold.

Daemyn watched the light warm her bronze skin and shimmer across her black hair. And something in him ached.

She was the lady he would've wanted to bring home to his family a hundred years ago. Ma would've been all a-fluster, hosting a princess in the small cabin. Nancy and MarySue would've been starry-eyed. Hasil and Silas wouldn't have cared all that much. And Luke. He would've given Rosanna the side-eye until she proved herself. But he would have approved. Eventually.

If only he could go back. Tell his family he had, finally, found what they'd wanted for him all those years ago.

But that was impossible. His family wouldn't meet Rosanna, and she would never meet them, not until the life Beyond.

"You're lost in thought this morning." Rosanna pulled away to face him, and her eyes searched his face.

Could she read the churning and tugging of his past and present and everything between? "Sorry, I'm..." How much did he want to admit to her? Was it too soon to mention her meeting his parents, even hypothetically? Then again, he'd met her parents and hers were the king and queen of Neskahana. Nothing if not intimidating. "I was just wishing I could've introduced you to my parents. They would've liked you."

"Would they have worried because I'm not one of the mountain folk?"

Daemyn tried to picture it, walking into his family's

small cabin with Rosanna's hand in his. "It would've been a shock to everybody, but you did just fine at Frennie's, and they're a much wilder bunch of mountain folk than the Buckhannock ones. Someday I'll take you to see the cabin where I grew up. It's still standing, and Zeke's parents live there."

"I think I would've liked your family very much. And I look forward to visiting Buckhannock and your family there." Rosanna grimaced. "Much more than I'm looking forward to the Harvest Balls. I've heard the dances they have here are more formal and elaborate than those we have in Neskahana. We dance to the rhythm of the drums."

"Similar to the Kanawhee dances." Daemyn felt the smile return to his face. "And of course, we mountain folk have our jigs. You ain't never seen a barn-stomping dance 'til you've seen a mountain boy jig to a fiddle."

"Show me." Rosanna grinned and stepped back as if to give him more room. Her dark brown eyes twinkled with a dare.

He almost wanted to take her up on it. But he'd fail horribly if he tried. When he breathed out, the hitch in his chest almost sounded like a laugh. "I can't jig here. You can't cut a jig without a fiddle."

"You didn't jig at Aunt Frennie's."

He hadn't been able to. He could barely manage a smile then, not with what he thought would be his death looming over him and the weight of the past hundred years resting heavy on his shoulders. "No, I didn't. You got to be so full up with music and happiness that the jig just takes a hold of your knees and comes a-pounding from your toes. But I promise. Next time there's a decent fiddle, I'm going to cut you a jig like you ain't never seen."

"I love it when the mountain comes through in your

voice." Rosanna wrapped her arms around his waist. "You don't have to hide it with me, you know."

"I know." That settled into his chest. He didn't have to hide with her. Not the mountain part of him. Not the past hundred years, the names he'd worn, the things he'd seen and done.

As much as he wanted to savor this, he was pressed for time. "You need to see the view from the west windows."

After crossing the room and lifting the latch, he pushed the windows open.

Rosanna stepped in front of him to get a better view, then gasped. "The mountains end!"

To the west, the mountains gave way to rolling hills only sparsely forested with large swathes of fields cleared between the trees. Cornstalks created their own forest with climbing beans clinging to their stalks while squashes spread large, green leaves beneath.

Other places in Tallahatchia had small fields carved out of rocky highlands and the valleys by the rivers, but none were as vast or fertile as the fields of Pohatomie.

Something that might have been another laugh caught in his chest. "The mountains don't go on forever."

"I know but..." Rosanna shot a glance over her shoulder at him before she turned back to the window. Her eyes were wide, her mouth gaping as she leaned against the windowsill to catch more of the view.

Maybe he should've started with this rather than the sunrise. This was Rosanna, after all. She appreciated a beautiful sunrise over the mountains, but a new horizon...that had her eyes sparkling.

After a few minutes where they stood together, looking over the rolling fields and stands of trees, Rosanna heaved a sigh. "We probably have to head back, don't we?"

"Probably." Actually, they were already late and would be even later by the time they wound their way through the castle. Besides glaring at Daemyn and possibly barring him from taking Rosanna on a tour of the castle again, there wasn't much Captain Degotaga could do. He probably couldn't even find this tower, even if he wanted to send guards after them due to Daemyn's tardiness.

No matter. Alex was probably awake and brimming with orders by now.

Daemyn forced out a breath to keep himself from tensing. No need to ruin this moment thinking about his servant's duties waiting for him.

Rosanna started for the trap door, then halted. "Which trap door is our way out?"

"This one." Daemyn knelt and pulled open the trap door on the right. "The other one is the entrance to a secret passageway to the dungeons nine stories down."

"Really? That brother built a secret passageway to his darkest dungeon from his tallest tower? That's a lot of stairs." Rosanna dropped through the trap door to the landing below.

"As far as I can figure out, since the brother who built this tower was the only one of the three who added dungeons to his part of Castle Fonthaven, he was extra paranoid." Daemyn joined Rosanna on the landing and closed the trap door. "He built a secret passageway into the dungeons so he could escape if he needed to, but if anyone else found the passage in the dungeons and escaped, they would end up in the tallest tower where they would be easy to apprehend."

Rosanna laughed as they started down the stairs. "Very true. Someone could escape the dungeon but end up wandering this messed up castle for years trying to find the way out."

It took them nearly twenty minutes to arrive in the hallway where their rooms were located. As they neared, Daemyn caught movement by the door next to Alex's.

Daemyn put his hand on Rosanna's lower back and steered her past her door with a nod to Captain Degotaga. "Looks like I'll have a chance to introduce you to a few more of the nephews."

Asa, the man at the door, turned and a smile broke across his face. He was only a few years older than Daemyn with dark hair and eyes. "Uncle Daemyn."

"Uncle Daemyn?" Another young man, Josiah, stuck his head from the room. His black hair was long enough to tie back in more of a Kanawhee style than Buckhannock. At eighteen, Josiah was trying hard for that roguish look. He grinned and hurried into the hallway. He held his hand out to Rosanna. "You probably don't remember me. We met briefly right before..."

Rosanna flicked a gaze at Daemyn before she shook Josiah's hand. "Right before I broke the curse. You're the prince of Buckhannock."

"*A* prince. My older brother Zephaniah is *the* prince." Josiah grinned. "But I don't mind. I get to have all the adventures."

Daemyn shook his head. "Rosanna, this is Prince Josiah and his bodyguard Asa Rand."

"We're distant cousins." Josiah shrugged.

Asa stepped forward. "You met me briefly that same day. Zeke is my younger brother."

"Nice to meet you. You'll have to tell me about all the trouble Zeke got into growing up." Rosanna shook his hand.

"How are your families?" Daemyn ached to visit them all again. Even a hundred years later, his family in Buckhannock still felt the most like home.

"Pa and Ma are doing well, though the youngsters are doing their best to run them ragged." Asa glanced at Josiah. "Kezzie is still staying with them."

"Still talking to her geese and smiling, so that's a blessing." Josiah's voice had an aching tone to it.

An ache Daemyn understood. If there was anything he could do to help his great-great-grandniece Keziah break her curse, he'd do it in a heartbeat.

Before Daemyn could ask for more family updates, footsteps came down the hallway, and a large group of people headed their way, led by a pair of Pohatomie servants with their blond hair and homespun dresses a distinct contrast to the three tall, large men behind them. The men wore buffalo hide capes over shirts made of various animal hides. One of the men carried a pair of elk antlers attached to a metal crown, trying to keep from poking the servants with the branching antlers.

Daemyn drew in a deep breath and took a step back, forcing his face to smooth. He couldn't be family in front of strangers. Instead, he was just the servant.

Asa also stiffened and rested his hand on the long knife on his belt as Josiah stepped forward and greeted Prince Tyrell from Monongadotte.

Rosanna glanced over her shoulder. Daemyn gave a small shake of his head. The smile slipped from Rosanna's face. She straightened her shoulders, and a perfect princess smile took its place.

The ache in Daemyn's chest worsened as he turned around and strode toward Alex's suite of rooms. They each had their role to play here. The masks they had to wear.

Passing the guards at Alex's door, Daemyn entered and closed the door behind him. All he wanted to do was climb out the nearest window, sneak from the castle, and disappear in the forest.

"Daemyn?" Alex stepped out of the bedchamber. "Good. You're back. With the first ball tonight, I need you to make sure my shirt and trousers are pressed. And make sure the ones I chose are appropriate for this new Tallahatchia."

Daemyn gritted his teeth and forced his muscles to relax. *Before honor is humility.*

His father's words. Daemyn repeated them to himself, as he had from the time he was ten and first adjusting to servant life in a castle, so far from the little cabin in the mountains.

Pa lived by those words. He'd left every morning for the mines, a dangerous job making a living by carving through the depths of the mountains. He'd told his children that there was honor even in the humblest of jobs.

And there was honor in this. Daemyn pushed away from the door. "Of course, Your Highness. Also, the princes of Buckhannock and Monongadotte have arrived. Now would be a good time to greet them before the Harvest Balls begin."

"Of course." Alex strolled for the door, then he halted and glanced over his shoulder. "I didn't come off as arrogant back there, did I?"

"Maybe a little, but I'm your manservant at the moment. You still have to give orders, and I still have to take them." Daemyn forced himself to meet Alex's gaze. It was easier to fall back into old habits instead of forging ahead on whatever friendship sort of thing they had started.

"Still, with you, I probably should have said please." Alex stared up at the ceiling for a moment before he glanced back at Daemyn. "Don't hesitate to call me out when I'm arrogant. I won't always catch myself right away, and I need you to be my advisor."

Something that was far easier said than done.

CHAPTER 10

ELARA

Elara's knees ached as she knelt to help Monica slip into her fancy, leather slippers made by a cobbler. Real leather shoes. Brand new. What an extravagance. Elara had heard even the princess of Neskahana would be wearing moccasins.

At least they'd been offered rooms here in the second tower of Castle Fonthaven for the duration of the festival. Elara would have a chance to explore the castle and peek at the ball, even if she wasn't going herself.

As she straightened, she sighed. Monica had her fingers fisted in the shimmering pink fabric of her skirt, her knuckles nearly as white as her pale face.

Elara reached for one of Monica's hands. "You're going to wrinkle your skirt if you keep that up."

Monica let go of the skirt but twined her fingers in her recently-trimmed hair instead. That didn't still their shaking.

Elara gritted her teeth. Monica was getting everything Elara ever dreamed of—a beautiful dress, a night to dance with the high king himself—and all she had to do was flirt, yet she wanted nothing more than to walk away. It really wasn't fair.

"What am I supposed to do, Elara? I don't think I can do this." Monica wrapped her arms around herself. "I can't..."

Ugh. This girl needed to grow a spine. Elara forced a smile on her face. "You're going to go out there and smile and charm the high king like he's never been charmed. All you have to do is be your sweet self and have fun. Don't worry about doing any more. You're a nice girl. How could High King Alexander be anything but charmed?"

"But...but I have to steal him away. From a princess. How I can manage that? What if...I can't make a princess angry...I just..." Monica shook worse, her whole body quaking as if wracked by an inner storm.

What had King Cassius been thinking to task a girl like this with turning High King Alexander's head? She was a mouse.

Elara gripped Monica's shoulders, wincing at the way she was crushing the silk. Oh, well. If Monica showed up rumpled, King Cassius had only himself to blame for picking the wrong girl for whatever he was plotting. "Do your best, and if you don't manage to make the high king fall head over heels with you to cause a scandal, then King Cassius will see you aren't the right girl for the task and will pick someone else, all right?"

Monica flung her arms around Elara and hugged her tightly. "You're right. Thank you so much. I don't know what I'd do without you."

Fall apart into a weepy mess, probably. Elara patted her back and pushed her away. "You're crushing your dress.

Now let's see to a few touches of make up while you calm down. You'll be fine tonight."

Elara dabbed a hint of red onto Monica's lips, brushed pink over her cheeks, darkened her eyelashes. By the time Elara was finished, Monica's natural, sweet beauty had been transformed into something alluring.

But not seductively alluring as King Cassius probably wanted her to be. No, innocent lamb that Monica was, the pink gown and touches of make-up brought out her luminescent blue eyes framed by wisps of blonde hair in a way that made her appear like a fragile, sweet Fae.

As Elara straightened Monica's dress one last time, Baroness Hackett swept into the room. Her smile wobbled as she hugged Monica. "You look beautiful. Whatever happens tonight, I love you. You don't have to do this."

"But the king ordered me to. If I don't, it could be considered treason." Monica started shaking again.

Elara suppressed another sigh. After she just managed to calm Monica down...

"There's only so much the king can do to us if you refuse. He isn't going to want everyone to know he tried to force a young girl to throw herself at the high king for who knows what purpose." Baroness Hackett gripped her daughter's shoulders. "If we have to, we can run. The princess of Neskahana or the prince of Buckhannock would probably help us, considering their countries were enemies of Pohatomie not that long ago."

"But we'd have to give up everything. Leave our home." Monica straightened her spine and faced her mother. "I have to at least try. As Elara pointed out, if I fail tonight, King Cassius can hardly blame me, and then he'll pick someone else and that will be the end of it. We will just have to keep quiet so nothing will happen to us."

"I wish Papa was here." Beatrice's voice came from the doorway. As everyone turned toward her, Beatrice hurried across the room, her green skirts swishing softly in a way no homespun ever could, and she joined Baroness Hackett and Monica for a teary-eyed hug. Even years after his passing, the baron was missed by his family.

Elara stared at the ceiling, fighting her own ache over her long-dead family. Not that anyone would notice if she broke down in tears. She was an invisible servant that the baroness and her daughters didn't remember was in the room as they talked about personal matters.

Baroness Hackett pulled away first. "We must be on our way. We can get there early, introduce you to the high king right away, and see his reaction. After that, we'll just enjoy the rest of our time without the added pressure."

Monica gave her mother a shaky smile and straightened her back. She swished from the room with Beatrice on her heels.

Before closing the door behind her, the baroness turned to Elara. "Please wait up for us, though feel free to nap. I expect we will be back shortly after midnight."

"Yes, ma'am." Elara bobbed her head and her knees. Oh, yes. More orders. As if even her sleeping schedule was controlled by the baroness.

As soon as the door closed, Elara flopped onto the settee. All of her thrummed too much to think about resting.

She could sneak out and visit Terrence. It was something to do and someone to talk to. Maybe she would get a few glimpses of the fancy dresses along the way.

Elara slipped from the room and down one of the many staircases winding through Castle Fonthaven. The hallways and back staircases bustled with servants. On a night like this while the nobles danced, the servants had to be hard at work. No rest for them.

Elara exited a side door of the second tower and skirted the far edge of the courtyard. The towers loomed far above her, bathed with orange from the setting sun. At the other side of the courtyard by the entrance to the towers, a group of people gathered by the door, dressed in shimmering, vibrant colors.

Elara worked her way through the pack of people arriving via the causeway. None of the noble folk stepped out of her way. No, she had to dodge around them. Because the noble folk couldn't be bothered to move for a lowly servant.

There had been a time, as the daughter of a renowned soldier, she'd almost been nobility. Almost been one of them. But the moment he'd been killed, she'd been reduced to this.

On the crowded causeway, she bumped into a baroness's arm.

The baron glared and yanked his wife away from her as if she was afflicted with some dreadful plague. "Move for your betters, girl."

Betters. As if. Elara gritted her teeth, ducked her head, and kept going.

After pressing herself against the low wall of the causeway near the guardhouse as a family, dressed in their finest, strolled toward the castle, Elara finally hurried through the archway and into the night.

She entered the forest by the river and let the twilight wash around her. Not that she wandered too far. She was a castle girl after all, and she wouldn't wander in the forest by herself. She probably should've gone the other way and headed straight to talk to Terrence, but she couldn't face him like this. Not when she was a seething, roiling mess.

She stalked down to the bank of the Pohatomie River. The fading sunlight was gone except for a hint on the western horizon, but the castle far above glowed, lit from within by thousands of candles and hundreds of torches. Its glimmering reflection rippled across the river's surface.

Elara halted at the edge where the grassy section descended into mud. She wasn't about to get her shoes or dress muddy. That would only add more work on top of everything else she had to do.

It wasn't fair. None of it. Just because of the station in life she'd been born into, she couldn't go to the balls tonight. She couldn't pay for a fancy dress. She suffered humiliation and had to bow and scrape to just about everyone she met.

"Is it so wrong that I wish I could be noble for one night?" Elara grabbed a pebble and chucked it as hard as she could into the river. It landed with a faint plop, casting a few ripples that were quickly swept away by the current.

A woman's voice came from the woods behind her. "Of course it isn't wrong."

Elara whirled around but couldn't see anyone behind her. "Who's there?"

This really hadn't been a smart idea. She shouldn't be out here alone. She glanced about, searching for a handy stick or a rock she could use to defend herself. If she screamed loud enough, would the guards at the end of the causeway hear her over the din of people clamoring to enter the castle for the ball tonight?

"I'm a friend, dearie. You don't need to be afraid." The sweet, lilting voice came again. A moment later, a woman stepped from behind one of the trees. She held out her hands, as if to show she wasn't a threat.

Even in the hazy darkness, she was the most beautiful woman Elara had ever seen. Her skin was perfectly smooth, and her pale hair, an even whiter blonde than Elara's, flowed down her back. She wore a dark gown that blended with the night.

Elara might have thought her a baroness wandered away from the crowd except for the huge, translucent wings rising from her back.

"You're one of the Fae." Elara glanced from the wings to the woman's flawless face.

"As you say, dearie." The Fae woman waved a hand in Elara's direction. "But what is a beautiful girl like you doing out here instead of in the castle at the ball tonight?"

"I'm only a servant. I'm not invited to the Harvest Balls at the castle, especially not this one. High King Alexander himself is going to be there tonight." Elara felt those words down to her toes. Only a servant. Unworthy. Invisible. A nobody.

"But you deserve more. Don't you wish you could attend the ball?"

If only she could go to the ball. Wear a beautiful dress. Dance with a handsome prince. Enjoy a night where her only concern was laughing and twirling and dancing instead of working.

The woman stepped closer, her voice fluid. Gentle. Addicting in its soft, sweet tones. "You are entitled to one night. A beautiful dress. All the princes falling at your feet."

Elara closed her eyes, picturing herself in shimmering silk, sweeping across the gilt ballroom in Castle Fonthaven.

She would give anything to be noble for one evening to remember for the rest of her life.

"What if I could give you your heart's desire?" The woman's voice lowered further.

"You could? Really?" Elara's heart beat faster. This woman was Fae, right? She could do anything.

"Yes." A slow smile crept across the Fae woman's face. She held out something clear and glittering. A pair of shoes cut in multi-facets that caught the light from the castle behind Elara rested on the Fae's hands. Were these shoes made of glass?

They were the most beautiful pieces of footwear Elara had ever seen. She itched to rip her old, worn moccasins from her feet, yet something held her in place. Almost as if she was too in awe to take the slippers.

The Fae woman turned the shoes so they sparkled in the starlight. "When you wear these slippers at the ball, you will be the envy of the young women, the dream of the young men, and any man who dances with you will fall madly in love with you."

A poetic way to say she would be the envy of all the fancy nobles.

But was this too good to be true? Whoever heard of a Fae giving something to a servant? The Fae gave gifts to the nobility. That's the way the gifts and curses worked. "Why me?"

"Why not you, my dear? You're young. Beautiful. Surely you've always wondered what it would be like to dance the night away. And don't worry about being recognized. You know how the nobles are—they don't actually notice servants. You will look like one of them."

"Truly?"

The Fae woman advanced, balancing the slippers on

her palms, where they shimmered in the moonlight like crown jewels. "Trust me."

Elara studied the woman's face, its expression shadowed under the trees. It would be foolish to pass up this once-in-a-lifetime chance to live her most treasured dreams. Besides, who would deny a gift from the Fae?

The woman shrugged and took a step back as if to take the shoes. "But if you don't really want them, then I guess it's your choice."

Her choice. The first time she'd had a choice in anything in her life. After all, who said a Fae couldn't grant a gift to a servant?

She needed to act before this opportunity was snatched away just like her previous life had been. She accepted the glass shoes from the Fae, yanked off her moccasins, and slid her feet into the slippers. They were smooth and cool against her soles. A perfect fit without pinching or rubbing.

With a blast of heat and a swirl of sparks, the color of Elara's drab brown dress changed, brightening into a shimmering red. The skirt lengthened and grew, becoming fuller and swirling in a way Elara had never seen a dress do before. Fabric had been too scarce to waste on large, full skirts for the last few years.

Her scalp tingled, then hurt as her hair whipped into some sort of hairstyle on her head.

Elara smoothed a hand down the gorgeous red skirt. The silk was so soft. She patted her hair, feeling curls piled on top of her head. She glanced up at the Fae woman. "How long will this last?"

"The dress will disappear at the end of the ball but will reappear tomorrow for the next ball."

"I'll be able to go to tomorrow's ball too?" Elara clasped her hands in front of her.

"Of course, dearie." The Fae woman smiled. "What cruelty would it be if it only lasted tonight? You will be able to go to all three balls and dance with the princes and high king if you so desire. Now get going. You have a high king to charm."

The high king. Elara gripped her skirt and hurried up the riverbank and through the forest as quickly as she could. Even though the trees seemed to claw at the dress, they didn't snag it. Nor did any of the mud from the bank stick to the dress or the sparkling glass slippers.

Elara couldn't help the grin that spread over her face. She was going to the ball.

Chapter 11

Alexander

Alex strode into the ballroom in Castle Fonthaven with Princess Rosanna on his arm. As he stepped inside, it was like coming home. A swirl of people filled the room, voices rising and falling in pitch.

Gold drapes framed the many-paned windows that overlooked the winding Pohatomie River. At this time of night, the candles in the gold chandeliers reflected off the windows and bounced from the mirrors set along the top of the room.

Elegance. Society. Glittering halls. This was Alex's world, the one he'd thought lost to time a hundred years ago. None of the castles he'd seen had retained this much of the old Tallahatchia as Pohatomie.

But it wasn't exactly as Alex remembered. Beside him, Princess Rosanna wore a beaded, buckskin shirt with a dark blue skirt made from the silk Alex had brought with him to Neskahana. Across the room, most of the people wore a mishmash of silk and homespun. Well-made home-spun, but it was an odd pairing, as if there was only so much silk to go around and everyone had to use only a piece of it.

Something in him relaxed. As if, from the moment he'd left Castle Eyota to find a way to break his curse, he hadn't been fully comfortable. He'd slept in barns and cabin lofts and the forest floor. He'd ended up on a wild, frightening buffalo hunt and been nearly drowned in a waterfall, only to be dragged to the very threshold of Beyond and knelt in the presence of the Highest King. Nothing about any of that had been comfortable.

Nor had returning home, only to discover his father had been poisoned and Alex was now high king. He'd fallen prey to his curse, woken up to a war, and spent the past three months trying to rule a kingdom that, in some ways, he knew nothing about.

Yet, if walking into this glimmering ballroom felt like returning to his old self, then what did that say about him? He wasn't supposed to like his old self. He was supposed to be better than that now.

But his old self was still what was comfortable to him while the person he was trying to be settled on him like untailored homespun. Itchy and ill-fitting.

About as uncomfortable as Princess Rosanna seemed as she fidgeted and glanced at the windows as if contemplating dashing for the river and the nearest canoe.

King Cassius approached Alex and gave a small bob that could count as a bow. "Your Majesty. It is an honor you could join us for our Harvest Balls this year. We will enjoy sharing our humble celebrations with our esteemed high king."

This gathering—and the king arranging it—were anything but humble, and the twitch to King Cassius's mouth said he knew that, even as he made what was apparently a difficult attempt at saying the words with a straight face.

Alex kept his own face suitably neutral as he gave an acknowledging bob of his head. Enough to show King Cassius some honor since this was his castle and kingdom, but not enough to be construed as a bow. High kings, after all, bowed to no one, except the Highest King. "I am the one humbled and honored to be here."

King Cassius straightened and met Alex's eyes. Just long enough to show he knew Alex was being just as sincere as he had been.

King Cassius turned to Rosanna. As a princess a few spots down in the line of succession, Rosanna dipped into a curtsy first. It was a wobbling curtsy, and one that showed off the moccasins she wore underneath the silk skirt. "It's a pleasure to be here and see Pohatomie for the first time."

Her smile and her words appeared genuine, and, for a moment, the expression reminded Alex of her great-grandfather as he'd pledged he and his family would stand by Alex if he fell to the cursed sleep.

"We are pleased to have you grace our ballroom." King Cassius tilted his head. "I've arranged for a receiving line over here."

Alex took the spot next to Prince Tyrell from Monongadotte. The prince nodded his head and muttered something that was probably a greeting.

Alex didn't take the lack of a formal bow too personally. Prince Tyrell was wearing his elk antler crown, and he'd have to take it off to properly bow. The prince's red-brown beard and hair were washed and less wild than they had been yesterday, but his clothing was still an impressive mix of various animal pelts.

Prince Josiah of Buckhannock was on the other side of

Prince Tyrell, and he gave a bow along with a grin. Prince Josiah's black hair was tied back at the nape of his neck, and he wore a linen shirt paired with buckskin trousers and moccasins.

Alex glanced down at his own silk shirt, linen trousers, and leather boots. Except for King Cassius, he was overdressed compared to the other royalty here.

Then again, he was the high king. It wasn't a bad thing if he stood out.

As members of the Pohatomie nobility began lining up for their chance to greet the high king and the foreign princes and princess, Alex paid more attention to King Cassius than the people he was supposed to be charming. King Cassius was announcing each noble and their families himself instead of assigning that task to a servant. And something in his face—what would Alex call that look? Smug? Preening?

Almost as if he was showing off his people to Alex. Was he trying to rub it in Alex's face—and the face of Buckhannock, Monongadotte, and Neskahana—that his kingdom had fared better over the last hundred years than the others?

After all, even when they'd been at war, the other kingdoms hadn't been able to cut off Pohatomie as much as they had Tuckawassee. They could do without Tuckawassee's gold and gems, but Pohatomie's corn was a different matter.

Two could play this game. Whatever King Cassius was plotting, it would be a lot harder for him to pull off if Alex managed to charm Pohatomie's nobles so that they would be reluctant to stand against him.

Alex gave a small bow as King Cassius announced another family, a Baroness Hackett and her daughters

Monica and Beatrice. The older of the two, Monica, smiled at Alex, yet her gaze flicked to King Cassius. Something in her expression tightened, as if it was hard work keeping her smile in place.

Alex had to force his own face to remain blank except for a polite smile. That wasn't the first time one of the young women glanced toward King Cassius as they introduced themselves to Alex. He shot a quick glance over the crowd. They were better dressed in silk gowns and newer shoes.

Was this part of King Cassius's plot? If so, how? What did he hope to gain? Was he merely hoping Alex would fall in love with a lady from Pohatomie, as his father had, and thereby strengthen Alex's ties to Pohatomie?

Or was it merely that the more ambitious mothers in the crowd had been willing to spend a little extra if they thought their daughters had a chance to catch Alex's eye and become the high queen someday?

If that was the intention of the mother and daughters before him now, they were going to be disappointed. The girl in front of him evoked not a single spark of attraction. She was beautiful with the sweet, innocent sort of beauty that didn't seem to appeal to him.

"It's a pleasure to meet you." He swallowed back a wince. Did those words sound as stilted to her as they did to him?

She let out a breath, and something in her smile brightened. As if relieved? She hurried to greet Princess Rosanna next to him.

Well, at least he hadn't disappointed her by not being as charming as a high king should.

The greeting line seemed to stretch forever, but finally he straightened after saying how pleased he was to meet someone for the hundredth or more time that night and found no one else in front of him.

"A drink, Your Majesty." A servant held out a tray. Several glasses filled with clear, fresh water stood on the tray, winking in the candlelight.

Alex plucked a glass from the tray and nearly took a sip before he paused. Should he be worried about being poisoned here? Was that King Cassius's plan? Though, this was a rather elaborate way to go about poisoning him.

The servant—the dark-haired servant—raised his head. Daemyn flashed a glance around, then said in a low tone. "A little late to worry about it now, Your Highness, but, yes, that water should be safe to drink."

Your Highness. Daemyn used that title when he was secretly laughing at Alex. Not that Alex could blame him in this case. He was the one who'd grabbed the first glass a servant handed to him without thinking or recognizing Daemyn.

He gave a small nod. Message received. He wouldn't eat or drink anything here unless Daemyn was the servant handing it to him. "Thank you. I believe the princess may be parched as well."

Daemyn turned and offered the tray to Princess Rosanna. She took a glass, but her gaze lingered on Daemyn, even as he turned and offered the prince of Monongadotte a glass.

Alex wasn't even going to ask how Daemyn had managed to find a basic serving uniform and get himself added to the serving staff when he wasn't even from Pohatomie, much less employed at this castle.

But as Alex glanced over the crowd, a few other dark-haired servants mingled with the blonde-haired serving staff of the castle, including Rosanna's maid. Perhaps part of the Buckhannock delegation also managed to volunteer.

He should start mingling. Pairs of dancers had already made their way to the center of the ballroom as the musicians with their pipes and drums picked up the tempo and volume from the sedate, quiet music they had been playing before.

He would avoid dancing with any of the girls dressed in the finest dresses, at least for this first dance. He wouldn't want to play into any schemes—whether they were the king of Pohatomie's or some baroness's for her daughter.

Actually, he was supposed to be here with Princess Rosanna. He should ask her for the first dance, even if it felt all kinds of wrong when he knew his friend—his only friend at the moment—was courting her.

He turned to Princess Rosanna. "Would you..."

A flare of red flashed across the room. He froze, his breath catching, as the most beautiful girl he'd ever seen swept inside the ballroom.

Even across the dance floor, her bold, red dress shimmered beneath the candlelight, a bright spot against the blues and greens and browns everyone else was wearing. Her black, glossy hair was piled on her head with a few strands of curls framing her face.

He was moving toward her. He hadn't even made the conscious decision to go to her. His feet just started moving. Out of the corner of his eye, he could see a few of the other men in the room headed in her direction, and that sparked something in his chest. Like he needed to claim her first.

After all, he was the high king. He should at least greet her first.

He halted in front of the maiden, and she dipped into a

low curtsy. As she straightened, she tipped her head up, and he got a good look at her face for the first time.

For a moment, his breath caught in his throat. If he didn't know better...he shook his head. She'd looked exactly like Mirabelle for a moment there. But, no. As she sashayed closer, he could tell she wasn't. Her skin was paler, her eyes a brilliant blue. Such an odd pairing, blue eyes with black hair, yet it seemed so perfect on her.

There was a sweetness on her face that hadn't been there on Mirabelle, yet more of a spark than he'd seen on the girls he'd been introduced to that night. The combination of spice and innocence had his heart beating faster in his chest.

Was it so wrong that he longed for someone to look at him the way Princess Rosanna looked at Daemyn? The way Alex's mother had looked at his father? With that shine of love and glint of mischief and smile of understanding.

And this lady before him...something in his chest tugged at the sight of her. As if she might fill that aching place inside him.

He held out his hand. "Would you dance with me?"

She placed her hand in his. "I'd be delighted, Your Majesty."

He swept her onto the dance floor, into the line of couples preparing for a traditional Pohatomie dance.

For the first time since he'd woken up, he didn't worry about trying to be different or missing what he'd left behind. He just spun her and smiled and let a thrill shoot through him when she smiled back.

Surely nothing that felt this good could be anything but right.

CHAPTER 12

DAEMYN

After bracing himself to watch Alex sweep Rosanna across the ballroom in one of the Pohatomie slow, formal dances, Daemyn shouldn't have cared when Alex rushed off to that mystery woman, leaving Rosanna standing where he'd left her. She glanced around, as if lost and unsure what to do next.

Daemyn clenched his fingers around the tray of desserts he held. Alex was supposed to look after Rosanna tonight since Daemyn couldn't.

If only he could step out there, take her hand, and be the one to lead her into the first steps of the dance.

He only had himself to blame. He could've been out there, if he'd taken Alex up on his offer to make him a baron. If he forced himself to fully grasp the position of advisor to the high king and step out of the shadows where he preferred to stay.

Daemyn glanced at Josiah. Surely his nephew would step in.

But Josiah was staring off in the direction of Alex and

the mystery girl. As if he too was smitten at first sight. Even though the girl looked like she was probably a few years older than eighteen-year-old Josiah.

What was it about the girl? Daemyn hadn't noticed anything too special in his first glance, but he'd been more focused on Rosanna. He turned and found Alex and the girl weaving in and out of the other dancers.

The girl's long black hair swung in a braid down her back, whisking back and forth over the simple, red linen shirt over a buckskin skirt. Something like what the girls back home in Buckhannock's mountains would wear. Her skin was tanned but not a deep bronze like Rosanna's, but lighter. Also like a girl from Buckhannock.

She was a girl from his mountains. Strong. Lithe. Someone he could imagine running through the forest, hefting a spear for a buffalo hunt. The sort of girl he'd always dreamed of marrying. She was...

Not Rosanna. What was he thinking? He shook his head. He'd taken several steps forward without realizing it.

What was going on? Daemyn squeezed his eyes shut and drew in a deep breath. Something wasn't right here, though he wasn't sure what it was.

"Boy. You. The high king's servant."

Daemyn started at the sharp tone in the voice and spun. One of the footmen stood behind him. The head footman, judging by his bearing and scowl. "Stop staring and get back to work. What kind of servants does the high king employ? Have you ever worked in a castle before?"

"Sorry, sir." Daemyn let his shoulders hunch, his head hang. "Where would you like me, sir?"

"Take a tray of desserts to those along the walls." The head footman sauntered to the dessert table, met Daemyn's gaze, and swept a whole tray of frosted custards from the table onto the floor.

The music and dancing muffled the tray's clang as it hit the marble. The custards splattered, smearing across the floor for several feet in all directions.

"And clean that up while you're at it." The footman stalked away after one last glare at Daemyn.

Before honor is humility. Daemyn gritted his teeth and swallowed down any visible reaction. He sank to his knees, took the towel he'd draped over his arm at the beginning of the evening, and started wiping the custard and frosting onto the tray so he could take it to the kitchen for disposal. His towel quickly became sticky and gooey.

He kept his head down. For some reason, he didn't want Rosanna to see him like this, on his hands and knees scrubbing. Right now, he felt a whole lot more like Jadon from a hundred years ago than he did the strong, capable Daemyn she'd fallen in love with.

"Would you like some help?" Isi knelt on the other side of the gunk and held out a few more towels. "I saw what that footman did. Rosanna nearly came over to help, but I told her she needed to keep up appearances."

"Thanks. I appreciate the help." Daemyn glanced over his shoulder. Couples whirled and spun in a fast-paced dance, a blur of color and golden hair. Rosanna's dark hair caught his eye. She spun and took the hand of...the king of Pohatomie. Daemyn's chest tightened, and it took all his will-power to stay kneeling on the floor instead of marching over there and putting himself between Rosanna and King Cassius.

Not that Daemyn could be all that threatening when he was unarmed and his hands were covered in the slimy remains of custard and frosting.

Isi leaned a little closer as she wiped a patch of floor clean. "I also wanted to tell you, since you probably didn't notice with that footman distracting you. The high king went out the side door headed for the small garden with that blonde-haired mystery woman."

Alex left the ballroom? With a stranger? What was he thinking?

Daemyn put a hand on the floor, preparing to push upright, but froze. Wait, blonde-haired? He forced himself to relax as he picked up another towel from the stack Isi had brought. "Did you say blonde? You're talking about the girl who walked in late right before the dancing started? Could you describe her?"

Isi gave a small huff. "You saw her. Long, golden blonde hair all the way down her back past her waist. The most beautiful green silk dress I've ever seen. Probably green eyes to match. Perfect skin without a single freckle." Isi lifted a hand, touching the darker freckles on her already bronze skin.

Daemyn glanced around. Good. No one was in earshot. The Pohatomie servants appeared to be staying well clear of the two strangers in their midst. "Something strange is going on. Something..." How should he describe it? Whatever this was, it was almost like one of the powerful gifts. Or, perhaps, a curse. "Fae-like."

"What do you mean?" Isi wiped the last of the custard and began cleaning her hands as much as she could without water and soap.

"If you had asked me, I would've said the mystery girl had a long, black braid, red shirt, and buckskin skirt."

Isi halted and met his gaze. "That's not normal."

"Exactly." Daemyn tossed the used towels on the tray. "Can you slip out to the garden and keep an eye on High

King Alexander? Don't take any risks, but stick as close as you can. I'm going to take this to the kitchen, then see if there is some way I can talk to Rosanna."

Daemyn picked up the tray, stood, and headed for the kitchens while Isi slipped along the side of the room headed for the doors that led to the garden.

The kitchen staff mostly ignored him as he added the tray and towels to the stack of dirty dishes.

Daemyn headed for the buckets to wash his hands, but the scullery maid scowled and thrust out an arm to block him. "You can't use this water unless you're washing dishes."

Everything in him tightened with the need to hurry back to the ballroom, find Rosanna, and start figuring out what was going on.

But he forced himself to reach for one of the dirty dishes. "I'll finish this stack."

The scullery maid swept her gaze up and down him, then snorted. "Fine. I guess if the vaunted high king's manservant can humble himself to wash dishes, who am I to object?"

That was the odd part of being a manservant for the high king. Beneath the notice of the nobles, but an outsider among the servants.

Daemyn picked up the first dish with his sticky fingers and dunked the dish and both hands into the bucket. The water was still hot and mostly clean.

Washing dishes was a familiar job. He fell into the rhythm, scrubbing and rinsing quickly. When the stack was gone, his hands were clean.

The scullery maid smiled with an extra sparkle in her eyes. "You wouldn't want to stick around a little longer, would you?"

No. Not at all. He didn't even bother smiling back as he hurried from the kitchen.

When he returned to the ballroom, the tune had changed to something slower with more drums and less of the pipes. King Cassius now sat on his throne at the far end, watching the dancers with sharp eyes. Neither Alex nor the mystery girl were in sight. Rosanna was dancing with Josiah, both of them stumbling through the unfamiliar dances.

Daemyn managed to catch Rosanna's eye and gave a slight nod toward the doors that led to the garden. He turned and slipped outside without waiting to see if she and Josiah had figured out what he was trying to tell them.

Outside, Daemyn leaned against the castle's wall in the shadows formed by hedges and torchlight and breathed deeply for the first time that evening. The gardens at Castle Fonthaven wound around the outside edge of the third tower between the tower and the wall beside the river. The evening air filled with the wet scent of river and the dampness of night-bathed flowers while frogs chirruped so loudly all other noises were drowned out.

The faint gurgle of the Pohatomie River called to him, and it took everything in him to remain where he was. The river was adventure and open sky and a life free of duty. Duty that demanded he stay where he was.

The door to the garden creaked, and Josiah stepped outside, followed by Rosanna.

Josiah shut the door behind them and glanced around. "Are you sure Uncle Daemyn wanted us to follow him out here?"

Rosanna peered into the garden, facing away from where Daemyn stood. She kept her voice low. "Yes. He had that look. Something's wrong."

He had a look? Daemyn pushed away from the wall. "Over here."

Josiah jumped and spun on his heels, but Rosanna shook her head as she turned. "I should have realized you would be lurking in the shadows."

It was his preferred place. In the shadows. Invisible.

And yet how could he stay invisible as an advisor to the high king? Or married to a princess?

He shook himself as Rosanna reached his side. She rested a hand on his arm. "How are you holding up? I saw what the head footman did."

"I'm fine. You didn't look like you were enjoying the ball any more than I was." If only he could linger in the garden with her, but they didn't have time. Alex was out in this garden somewhere with that mystery girl. "Did you notice that girl who walked in late? The one Alex was dancing with?"

Rosanna's forehead wrinkled, and she frowned. "There was something about her. The moment she walked in, I got this odd urge to bash her over the head with my paddle and drag you as far from her as possible."

That was a stronger reaction than he'd been expecting. "What did she look like?"

"What do you mean? You saw her. She had glossy black braids and these stunning green eyes and was dressed in a beautiful, white buckskin dress that showed off her muscled arms."

Josiah gaped and shook his head. "What are you talking about? She had brown, curly hair and a green silk dress."

Rosanna glanced from Josiah to Daemyn. "What's going on? How did she look to you?"

Daemyn hesitated. How could he explain what he'd seen? "She looked like you. But..." He wasn't sure he wanted to tell her. Not all of it. Yet he didn't want to start keeping secrets from her. He'd lived too long with secrets. "But a Buckhannock version of you. As if you'd grown up in the mountains. But she wasn't you. That's what snapped me out of whatever it was when I saw her."

Josiah shifted. "I didn't relax until she and High King Alexander left for the garden. I was contemplating starting a fist fight with the high king."

Rosanna shook her head. "Is it a curse or a gift at work here?"

"I don't know." Daemyn found himself rubbing at his chest over one of his scars. He was getting the same sort of feeling now that he had right before someone stabbed or shot or otherwise killed him. That sick, sinking feeling that there was nothing he could do and the next few moments were going to be extremely painful. "We need to find the high king. I sent Isi to follow them."

Rosanna grimaced. "Let's go. I know Isi can handle herself, but..."

Daemyn slipped into the shadows next to one of the hedges and motioned for Rosanna and Josiah to follow. Rosanna's footsteps were nearly soundless, as if she had been practicing her sneaking. Josiah was louder, and Daemyn couldn't help but wish for Zeke at his back. Zeke would know what to do without Daemyn asking.

Daemyn wound through the garden, sticking to the shadows by the hedges and taller stands of trees. They passed a few couples kissing beneath trees or rose arbors.

At the far end of the garden, Daemyn found Isi crouched behind a stone water fountain. She pointed over the edge to a couple dancing along one of the cobbled paths next to the wall near the river. "They've been like this the whole time. Just...dancing. Nothing too suspicious besides the random urges to scratch her eyes out."

It was a slow, soft sort of dance. Alex had a hint of a smile on his face, and the mystery girl was beaming up at him as she moved in time with him.

Was Daemyn wrong to worry about this mystery girl? Maybe he'd read the situation wrong, his instincts gone paranoid after a hundred years of getting killed simply because the Pohatomie and Tuckawassee figured out he might have something to do with waking Alex from the cursed sleep.

Alex looked happy. Far happier than he had been since waking.

And why wouldn't he be when he was dancing with a girl like that? Like...

Daemyn shook his head. She wasn't Rosanna.

"I know what you mean about wanting to scratch her eyes out." Rosanna let out a long breath, as if she was trying to clear her head, reached out, and gripped Daemyn's hand so tightly it was almost painful.

There was a scuff, then Josiah stood and marched toward Alex and the girl with clenched fists.

Daemyn shot to his feet and grabbed Josiah's arm. "What are you doing?"

"Let go." Josiah shook off Daemyn's grip. "He's hogged her long enough. Just like all my big brothers. Keeping the girls to themselves."

Daemyn stepped in front of Josiah. What was this? That almost sounded like a long-buried resentment coming to the surface. "You ain't thinking right."

Josiah raised an arm, as if preparing to punch Daemyn.

Daemyn gripped Josiah's wrist and put as much

command into his voice as he could manage. "Stand down."

Isi heaved a sigh, clambered to her feet, and slapped Josiah a solid smack across his cheek.

Josiah blinked, shook his head, and lifted a hand to his jaw, something in his expression clearing. "Sorry."

"Go back inside and rejoin the ball. After you let that red mark fade. And tell Asa what happened so he can keep an eye on you and himself." Daemyn gave Josiah a small shove, staying between him and the mystery girl. Whatever her allure, it seemed to be working stronger on Josiah than it had on Daemyn.

"Everyone will just assume I tried to sneak a kiss I shouldn't have." Josiah shrugged and glanced at Isi. "I'll have to warn Zeke not to get on your bad side."

Isi winced. "Sorry. I don't make a habit of slapping royalty."

"In this case, I needed it." Josiah shook his head again, as if he was still dazed, and strode back toward the ballroom. The lights beaming through the narrow windows cast long strips of shadows across the garden, making Josiah appear and disappear as he walked through them.

Daemyn turned back to Alex and the girl. Alex seemed oblivious to the commotion, still holding the girl's hands and beaming at her. She had turned and was gaping at them.

"I should head back in." The girl yanked her hands free from Alex's grip, grabbed her skirts, and dashed past them toward the ballroom.

As soon as she was out of earshot, Isi sighed. "I'll go after her and watch her."

That left Daemyn with Rosanna in the garden. It

would have been romantic, except for Alex leaning against the wall looking forlorn and confused.

What was going on? Was this something he should worry about? Was this the work of a gift? For some reason, that didn't set right.

At least with Alex's curse, the answers had been obvious as a bear on a log. He'd known Alex must wake, and it was his duty to make sure that happened. All he'd had to do was visit the princesses and watch for the sapphire in Alex's signet ring to turn clear.

But this? He wasn't sure what his duty was in this case.

CHAPTER 13

ELARA

Elara hurried into the ballroom. The night had been going so wonderfully. Dancing with the high king out in the garden...her glass slippers had been floating on air. A night the most golden of daydreams were made of.

And then they had been interrupted, and the prince of Buckhannock had looked so angry. Elara hadn't recognized any of the others, but her skin had prickled, something whispering inside her to run away from them as quickly as possible.

She slipped along the wall in the ballroom, trying to avoid notice.

It didn't work. The women in the room turned to her, their eyes narrowing. Several of the men started in her direction.

Wearing a bright red dress probably wasn't the way to go unnoticed. But she'd wanted to be noticed tonight, hadn't she?

She just hadn't realized how uncomfortable that could be.

A grey-haired guard wearing the dark blue of Pohatomie cut in front of the horde of young men hurrying toward Elara. The guard gave a small bow. "Miss, the king requests your presence in the silver throne room."

Coming from the king, that "request" was a command for her immediate presence. But Elara was used to those kinds of requests. As a servant, she obeyed "requests" all the time. And like she always did, Elara pasted on a smile. "Please lead the way."

The guard spun on his heel and marched along the side of the ballroom. The guard, at least, didn't seem as enamored as most of the young men in the ballroom.

Elara hustled after him, avoiding the young men who kept stepping forward to ask her to dance. She followed the guard from the far doors of the ballroom, down a short stretch of hallway, then into the next set of ornate doors.

They stepped into a room with a glossy black and white granite floor. A silver throne sat on a dais. Only one side had windows, overlooking the river below. The windows were framed with black drapes embroidered with silver. The ceiling far above was covered with hammered tin polished to a bright shine.

Elara suppressed a shiver. This was the smallest of the three throne rooms at Castle Fonthaven. That should have made it feel cozy, but it was far from it with all the cold black and icy silver.

King Cassius reclined on the throne, his golden crown just as sharp as the rest of the room.

The guard stepped back outside and shut the door, leaving Elara alone with the king.

As much as she wanted to dart back out that door, she drew in a deep breath and forced herself to take one step forward. Then another. This wasn't that much different than any other time she had interacted with nobles, right? All she had to do was keep her head down and grovel, and she would be fine.

At least, that's what she hoped. There wasn't a law against dressing in fancy clothing and attending a ball above her station, was there?

A few feet in front of the dais, she halted and curtsied, low and deep, staying there with her knees bent and head lowered.

"You may rise." King Cassius's voice was cold and distant, too impassive for her to figure out any reason he'd called her here.

Elara straightened but kept her gaze focused on the first step of the dais. Perhaps a noble lady would have been comfortable meeting the king's gaze. But Elara wasn't noble. Her best hope for getting out of this trouble was to keep her head down.

"Who are you?"

Elara flinched. Was there a punishment for turning up at this ball uninvited?

But she couldn't lie to the king. He surely had ways of finding out. She was staying at the castle with the baroness and her daughters. Someone would notice her eventually.

Elara wrapped her arms around her stomach and bowed her head lower. "Your Majesty, I am a maidservant to Baroness Hackett and her two daughters."

"And how does a servant come to have such a dress?"

How could she explain that? Elara squeezed her eyes shut. She refused to apologize for the dress. It wasn't her fault. None of this was. How could anyone blame her for simply wanting to experience one ball?

But this was the king. He could blame her for anything he wanted to, and no one would protest.

She cleared her throat. "I was given it. By one of the Fae."

Silence stretched. One second. Two. Elara held her breath, her spine so stiff it might snap if she moved too fast.

Was he waiting for her to say more? Was he contemplating throwing her in the dungeons deep below Castle Fonthaven's second tower?

She sank to her knees, the red dress's skirts billowing around her. "All I wanted was one night to wear a fancy dress and dance with a prince. Or even the high king. I didn't mean anything more by it. I'm sorry, Your Majesty. I should not have come to the ball without an official invitation."

She bit her tongue before she could continue spouting apologies. It probably wouldn't do any good. King Cassius wasn't known for his mercy.

Would he toss her in the dungeons just because she'd worn a fancy dress? A dress gifted her by one of the Fae.

"It is a trespass against the crown to presume an invite where none was given. But I will overlook the error if you are willing to help me with a little matter."

Elara risked a tiny peek up at the king. His expression hadn't changed from his flat-mouthed, smooth-faced stare. "I am your servant, Your Majesty."

"As a maidservant to Baroness Hackett, you have no doubt overheard that I asked several of the daughters of the nobility to try to cause a scandal between the high king and his princess from Neskahana." The king's voice dropped, almost as if he was sharing some great secret with her. "But it seems that you are the only girl he had eyes for tonight. You caused quite the stir among all the young men tonight, much to the jealously of the young women."

Her entrance had been rather spectacular. And in this dress and those glass shoes, she was rather stunning. What had the Fae said? That she would be the dream of the young men and the envy of the young ladies. That's exactly what had happened. "People do love a mystery, sire."

"Perhaps." Something in King Cassius's eyes sharpened. "You have the opportunity to do what the simpering young ladies of the court couldn't. Cause a rift between High King Alexander and Neskahana. Make the high king appear foolish and unworthy of leadership. All you have to do is exactly what you did tonight. Dance with him and dance with him only for the next two balls."

She could do it, as long as High King Alexander remained as agreeably charming as he had tonight.

King Cassius needed her to make his plan work. All the other ladies of the kingdom had failed to make High King Alexander so much as look twice at them, much less dance with them. Only Elara had made him abandon the Princess Rosanna.

Elara dared to raise her eyes a few inches. How much could she push King Cassius? "What would I get out of this? Surely I would be rewarded for my service to the crown."

King Cassius's gaze didn't waver. His jaw didn't even harden, as if her boldness was nothing more than an annoyance. "You wouldn't be thrown into the dungeon. You are already treading on my leniency."

Elara swallowed and dropped her gaze once again. It had been too much to hope. Would she ever escape her life of servitude? Or would she always be kneeling like this, serving others instead of doing what she wanted to do?

"But, I see that you will be more cooperative if you are properly motived." King Cassius's voice was still hard, but at least it had a veneer of generosity to it. "I can make you a baroness. I would gift you with your own estate. Everything you have ever desired could be yours."

How could he know what she desired so accurately? It was what she would have asked for, if she'd dared.

Of course he knew. What else would a girl like her desire? She was a servant who had shown up uninvited to the king's ball in a dress given her by a Fae. She wouldn't have done that if she didn't dream above the place life had stuck her in.

How far could her dreams carry her? If King Cassius was willing to make her a baroness, what would High King Alexander be willing to grant her? If he became as enamored with her as he seemed, what was to stop her from leveraging that in some way? She could even—it was impossible to even dream—but what if he fell in love? She could become high queen with servants to do her bidding and her own castle with all its riches.

"Don't even think it."

At the harsh slap of the king's voice against the stones surrounding them, Elara glanced up, meeting the king's gaze full on before dropping her eyes back to his polished, black leather boots. "I don't know what you mean, Your Majesty."

"Don't think about betraying me to the high king. He may be high king, but he is in a precarious position. If I don't manage to unseat him, the Tuckawassee will surely kill him eventually. Or a rogue element from one of the other kingdoms will do it. It's only a matter of time. He won't be able to give you more than I can. Would you rather tie your future to a high king with an uncertain throne or to your king who can give you a comfortable, worry-free life?"

King Cassius was right. It was one thing to dream about becoming high queen, but that wasn't truly what Elara wanted. Being high queen would be work. And Elara had already done enough work to last a lifetime. She wanted an easy life. "Of course, sire. I won't fail you or betray you. The promise to be a baroness is all I have ever dreamed of. I don't desire more."

"Very well." King Cassius gestured. "You may go. I suggest you return to your guest rooms for tonight. You have already caused enough stir for one evening."

Elara nodded and started backing toward the doorway. It was getting late. She needed to return in time to change and pretend to be waking up from a nap when the baroness, Monica, and Beatrice arrived. She would also need to perfect her shocked and interested face for when they talked about the girl in red that claimed the high king's first dance. "Thank you, Your Majesty."

She had reached the door and was fumbling for the latch when King Cassius spoke again. "One more thing."

Elara lifted her gaze to face him. At this point, she was far enough away that it wasn't disrespectful. "Yes, Your Majesty?"

"Tell no one about this plan. Or your official invitation to the ball. It may be best to refrain from mentioning your Fae dress as well." King Cassius swept his gaze over the dress. She was too far away to read his expression, but she could feel his calculating look even across the room.

"Of course, sire." She hadn't planned to mention any of this, even without his warning.

As she backed out of the room, and the guard that had been waiting outside closed the door behind her, it struck her that the king had only mentioned the dress. He didn't know about the glass slippers, or that the slippers had been the real gift.

Somehow, Elara was glad that she had that one, small secret hidden even from the king.

She hurried through the castle, taking the back halls and stairways to avoid as many people as possible. Once she reached the rooms where the baroness was staying, she closed the door firmly behind her.

As soon as the door's latch clicked, the shimmering red silk of her dress flickered, then vanished, leaving behind the homespun work dress Elara had been wearing when this amazing night started.

Elara caught her breath, then relaxed. The Fae had said the dress would only last at the ball. Lifting her skirt, Elara stuck out a foot. The facets of the glass shoe winked at her. Good. The slippers were still there.

She trailed her fingers over the rough homespun of her dress, the fibers catching against her calloused fingers. Only a few more days, then she wouldn't have to wear fabric like this ever again if she didn't want to. Until then, she would have to get through tomorrow, counting down the hours until the next ball when the silk dress would appear, and she would once again dance with High King Alexander.

Perhaps she would have another dance in the moonlight with the chirping frogs, gurgling river, and cold breeze providing the music.

With a sigh, Elara headed for the small chamber she'd been given. It was little more than a large closet branching from Monica's room. Soon Elara wouldn't have to sleep in tiny closets. She would have her own manor house. She would have servants who would wait on her instead of the other way around.

She sank onto the hard, straw-filled mattress on the metal-framed bed, lifted a foot, and tugged on a glass slipper.

It wouldn't come off.

Chapter 14

Alexander

The rest of the night passed in a blur. Alex may have danced with Princess Rosanna at one point. He honestly couldn't remember.

But he could remember the girl, her stunning red dress, and her long, black hair shimmering.

He hadn't even had a chance to ask her name before she'd run off. Would she be at the ball tomorrow night?

He needed to see her again. She sparked something deep inside him that no one besides Mirabelle ever had.

Alex strode along the wall in the garden, listening to the river. He leaned against the cool stone but that didn't clear his head. It just brought memories of holding her in his arms.

Footsteps crunched on the gravel path behind Alex. "Sire, it's late."

Alex shook his head, let out a breath, and turned. Daemyn stood a few feet away, looking and sounding more like Jadon, the manservant, than Daemyn, an advisor and friend. Alex forced his smile to something that was less...he wasn't even sure what he wanted to call the feeling. "Actually, I think it's early, not late."

"Whatever you say, Your Highness."

Definitely a twitch to Daemyn's mouth. He was internally laughing at Alex.

And Alex was too happy at the moment to care. He leaned against the wall and stared at the stars far above, tiny, twinkling lights in a black dome. "Do you believe in love at first sight?"

Daemyn strode closer, leaned against the wall facing Alex, and crossed his arms. "No."

"And when you met Princess Rosanna? Surely you felt something that first moment you saw her?" Alex couldn't imagine Daemyn wouldn't have felt something. Alex had known from the first time he'd seen Mirabelle. And now this girl, whoever she was.

"I believe in attraction at first sight, but not love at first sight. Love is deeper than that." Daemyn glanced up toward the sky as well, as if searching for the words. "I knew Rosanna was someone I could fall in love with when I met her, but I fought the feeling, thinking I was going to die. And now, I think I'm still falling in love with her. Perhaps that's something you never stop doing when you truly love someone."

Was this merely attraction at first sight? It felt like something more.

Daemyn paused, then his gaze changed. It wasn't the soft look he'd had when talking about Rosanna. Instead it was wary, with a hint of command. "I would be cautious."

"What do you mean?" Alex turned to face Daemyn more fully. A hint of breeze whispered against Alex's face. Was Daemyn right? Should Alex be careful?

"There's something off about her. I'm not sure what it

is, but my instincts are telling me something's wrong." Daemyn's gaze didn't waver as he met Alex's gaze.

Alex pushed away from the wall. How could Daemyn think that? Maybe he should be careful, but that there was something wrong with her? That was too far.

Daemyn had to be wrong. It wasn't fair, after all. Daemyn was already courting a girl, a princess that probably should have been Alex's if things had gone differently. Why couldn't Daemyn be happy that Alex was happy?

Alex clenched his fists. "She's a nice girl. There's nothing wrong with her."

"What do you think she looks like?"

What was Daemyn talking about? He wasn't making sense. "What do you mean, what I *think* she looks like? You saw her. She has the most beautiful black hair and gorgeous blue eyes."

"Alex, she didn't—"

"Don't. Not another word." How dare Daemyn use Alex's first name, as if he could manipulate him to seeing his way by using their history and familiarity. Alex marched past Daemyn. "I don't want to hear another word against her, understand?"

Daemyn's face became blank in an instant. "Understood, Your Majesty."

"Good." Alex strode down the path. He was done with this conversation.

CHAPTER 15

ELARA

Elara hurried along the causeway, heading out of Castle Fonthaven. She kept her head down, but dressed in homespun, no one looked twice at her. She was invisible, just another servant joining the bustle.

With two more balls yet to come, the causeway teemed with both servants and nobles. The castle servants had last minute preparations, and the nobility were in a flurry over the "mystery girl" and how they had to get new silk dresses to try to compete.

Elara had to hide a smile at that one. They could try to compete, but she had a Fae dress. She would be the most beautiful one at the ball tonight.

Still, she hadn't been imagining things the night before. She couldn't get the glass slippers off. It wasn't like they were too tight or pinching. She simply couldn't get them to so much as budge from her feet. At least they were tight enough that she could squeeze them inside her moccasins to keep them out of sight.

As she sidestepped a group of servants carrying

baskets of corn into the castle, Elara stifled a yawn. Instead of sleeping in like the baroness, Monica, and Beatrice, Elara had to be up to see to their light breakfasts, then getting them ready to attend a formal lunch with the king and other Pohatomie nobility who were staying as guests at Castle Fonthaven. Then, and only then, could she finally sneak away for these few minutes to herself.

At the end of the causeway, she turned and headed for the barn and corral. Terrence was in the corral as she approached, brushing Kal. The elk bobbed his head up and down, eyes half-closed.

Kio was grazing nearby while Toho was on the far side, rubbing his forehead against the top railing. The wood creaked. If the buffalo kept that up, Terrence would be replacing that board sooner rather than later.

"Kal looks about ready to drool on your shoulder." Elara leaned against the fence.

Terrence grinned as he glanced at her. "He's way past drooling. He won't let me stop." He patted the elk's neck, then hurried away as the elk swung his head around to nudge Terrence with his antlers. Terrence dodged the antlers and ducked between the boards. As he joined Elara, Kal trotted up to the fence and stuck his head over.

Elara laughed and patted Kal's neck. "He's rather demanding today, isn't he?"

Terrence buried his hand in the elk's ruff. "So how was the ball last night? Did you get a chance to peek in and see it?"

Elara scratched the elk's neck. King Cassius had warned her to tell no one. But this was Terrence. Her best friend in the whole world. Surely she could tell him anything. After all, who would he tell? The buffalo? Besides, she wouldn't tell him about the king's part of the plot. Just how she got the dress. "Actually, I went to the ball."

"What?" Terrence pushed Kal's head aside. "How?"

"It was rather amazing, actually." Now that she had started, Elara couldn't stop the words from pouring out of her. She needed to share this with someone. It was such a wonderful night, except for being threatened by the king. "I was on my way out of the castle to see you last night, but then I stopped by the river, and this Fae just appeared. She gave me these glass shoes, and when I put them on, my dress turned into this gorgeous red silk. I caused quite the stir when I walked into the ballroom. Then I danced with the high king himself."

Terrence stilled, ignoring Kal bumping him with his nose. "That sounds like a memorable night."

"It was." Elara let herself sigh at the memories. "And I'll be able to go tonight too. I still have the shoes. They're made of glass. At least, I think it's glass. Here, I can show you."

Sitting on a nearby stone, Elara unlaced one of her moccasins and pulled it off, revealing the twinkling glass slipper.

Terrence knelt in front of her, inspecting the shoe without touching it. "Why are you wearing it under your moccasin? Isn't it fragile?"

"I don't think so." Elara shifted. She wasn't sure she wanted to admit the next part to Terrence. "I can't take them off."

"What do you mean, you can't take them off? You don't dare take them off or your feet are swollen and they're stuck?" He reached for the shoe but stopped short of touching it.

"My feet aren't swollen, and I'd take them off if I could.

They just...won't come off." Elara reached down and tugged on the slipper. It didn't budge.

"May I?" Terrence held out his hands, but he didn't touch the glass slipper until she gave a small nod. He grasped the shoe and tugged. It didn't so much as wiggle, even when Terrence tugged hard enough that Elara had to brace herself on the rock to avoid being pulled off.

Terrence's hand slipped, and he tumbled backwards. When he rolled upright, he was grasping his right hand with his left. Blood trickled between his fingers.

"Are you all right?" It was a foolish thing to say. Of course he wasn't all right. He was bleeding. But it was the first thing that had popped from her mouth. Elara scrambled from the rock to kneel next to him, reaching for his hand.

"I'll be fine." Terrence winced and gripped his bleeding hand. "That shoe is sharp."

"Sorry." Elara reached into her apron pocket and pulled out a handkerchief. "Let me wrap it."

Terrence held out his hand. He had a slice across his palm. It didn't look terribly deep, but deep enough. She wrapped her handkerchief around his hand, then tied it off. "You might want to have that cleaned and stitched."

Terrence nodded. "Yes. But, Elara? This isn't right. You said a Fae gave you those shoes? You sure?"

"Of course, I'm sure. This Fae appeared and offered me the shoes." Elara stared down at the sparkling, glass slipper on her foot. "Of course I took them. She said I would be able to go to the ball when I wore them."

Terrence nudged her knee. "What did she say? Exactly."

"What does it matter? It was something about falling in love and young women being envious and young men wanting to dance with me. Which is exactly what happened."

"And you didn't find that strange?"

Elara lightly shoved against his shoulder. "You don't think I'm pretty enough to turn a few heads with a fancy dress?"

Terrence huffed and shook his head. "You know that isn't it. But you aren't the only pretty girl at this castle. I don't like this."

Elara pushed to her feet. Why was Terrence griping at this? He was worse than a wolf on a sick buffalo calf. "What has you so upset? I thought you'd be happy for me. A Fae gave me these shoes and made all my dreams come true. I went to the ball and danced with the high king himself. Aren't you the one always telling me about the Highest King?"

"Yes, but I'm not sure this is a gift from the Highest King." Terrence met her gaze, his eyes deep brown and filled with something she couldn't name.

"How can this be anything but good? I'm happy. Wouldn't the Highest King want me to be happy?" Elara shoved away from him. It had been too much to hope that Terrence would be happy for her. He was so annoyingly content with his lot in life. He didn't have dreams. He didn't care if he spent the rest of his life tending the king's pet elk and buffalo, as if shoveling manure was the best he could aspire to.

Well, Elara had bigger dreams than that. She didn't want to be a servant forever. She was going to be a baroness and get the life she'd always dreamed about. Terrence could stay here with the animals for all she cared.

Elara spun on her heels and started to march away. A

sharp twinge shot through her right foot, as if she'd stepped on something sharp.

She sucked in a breath and stumbled. What was that? How could she have stepped on something sharp if she was wearing shoes?

Terrence appeared at her elbow, steadying her. "Are you all right?"

"I'm fine." She pulled from his grip. "I need to get back."

"You left your moccasin." Terrence held her moccasin and its laces out to her.

Trust Terrence to be sweet and helpful even when she was trying to be mad at him.

She sighed, grabbed the moccasin, and bent to shove her glass-slipper-encased foot into it. As she did, she caught a glimpse of a spot of blood inside the glass.

Her foot was bleeding. And there was no way she could get the shoe off to bandage it.

She quickly tugged the moccasin over the glass slipper and laced up the buckskin. Had Terrence seen?

No. If he had, he would've asked her about it. He would've gone all protective again.

And she really didn't want him to know about it. Because, maybe, there was a slim possibility that he might be right.

CHAPTER 16

DAEMYN

Daemyn drew in a deep breath of the cool air that filled the forest outside of Castle Fonthaven. With the sun climbing higher in the sky, the damp morning stillness was giving way to the warm stickiness of a late summer day.

Still, he wasn't ready to return to the castle, even if the castle's stone walls provided some relief from the heat.

"Ain't much happening out here." Zeke was leaning against a tree, eyes closed as if preparing to take a nap. "Sure you don't need another pair of eyes in there?"

"Yes, but I need you out here." Daemyn shook his head. "You wouldn't like it in there. It's all fancy clothes and etiquette. Ain't your kind of place."

"Ain't your kind of place neither." Zeke cracked his eyes open.

"No." Daemyn's fingers itched for his staff, the one that was back in Zeke's camp. He eyed the causeway to the castle. From here, the figures moving back and forth were a distant blur of homespun and golden hair. One of the servant girls hurried between the others, heading back to the castle. She only caught Daemyn's eye because she was limping. Not much, just a hitch to her stride, but enough for him to notice.

He didn't recognize her. He didn't recognize any of them. A girl with black hair, like he had seen last night, would stand out against all the blond-haired Pohatomie.

Except that Isi had seen blonde and Josiah brown. Which was it? Did the mystery girl have black hair, brown, or blonde? Had she worn a red dress or buckskins? How were they supposed to track her down if they didn't even know what she looked like?

"I should get back. His Majesty is sure to be awake now." Daemyn pushed to his feet and brushed off the buckskin leggings he wore with his linen shirt. "Keep your eyes sharp."

"I know. Keep a lookout for a girl with black hair or brown or maybe blonde. And anything shifty." Zeke glanced up at Daemyn, shifted against the tree as if getting more comfortable, and patted his strung bow sitting across his knees. "You watch yourself."

Daemyn nodded. "I'll let Isi know you're doing all right."

The smile left Zeke's face. "She's probably happier than a coon with a fish up there with all the silk and fancy trimmings."

"The fancy dresses make her happy, right enough, but I don't reckon she's enjoying the company. A stuffier lot I ain't never seen." Daemyn grimaced as he faced the castle. Much as he wanted to linger, he had to get back. He didn't like leaving Rosanna in there, even though she was well protected with Captain Degotaga and Isi watching for trouble.

No, it was Alex he had to worry about. Something had happened last night. Alex hadn't been himself.

Well, he hadn't been the version of him that had woken from the curse. If anything, he was more like he had been before the curse.

With one last wave in Zeke's direction, Daemyn set out for the castle. On the causeway, the others dodged well out of his way. It itched at him, being so noticeable.

Inside the castle, he took the servants' stairs to the third floor and entered Alex's rooms.

Alex leaned against the windowsill, the shutters and glass panes swung wide to let in a wisp of breeze. He glanced over his shoulder as Daemyn shut the door. "Good. You're back."

Daemyn clasped his hands behind his back and let his face go blank. After last night, he wasn't sure what his status was. Was he supposed to be Alex's manservant or advisor? "I apologize I wasn't here to serve breakfast, Your Majesty."

Alex sighed and turned. "Don't go back to that. Look, I'm sorry about last night. I'm not sure what came over me."

Daemyn released a breath. At least the new Alex was still here. "I spoke to Zeke this morning. Alerted him to watch for the mystery girl from last night."

Alex stiffened, and something in his gaze hardened. "I said I was sorry but that doesn't mean I want you speaking against her. She's a nice girl. I know you looked after my interests for a hundred years. You had to watch for enemies around every bend of the river. But the war is over. Not everyone is my enemy."

Was Daemyn being paranoid? After a hundred years of fighting, both in open war and secret battles only him and a handful of others ever knew about, had he grown so cynical he would simply assume this girl was a threat when she wasn't?

Except that there was something odd. And Rosanna agreed that her instincts didn't like this girl either. Even if Daemyn was wrong, he trusted Rosanna to be right.

But he would have to placate Alex for now. "I'm not saying she's an enemy. Just be careful, all right? That's all I'm advising."

Alex's shoulders relaxed. "I will. But, Daemyn? You have Rosanna. You're happy. Is it so wrong if I want a bit of that kind of happiness too?"

It wasn't wrong to want the happiness of a wife. A family. And, of the two of them, Alex was far more alone. Even without Rosanna, Daemyn had survived the hundred years with over a thousand relatives. Alex only had his mother. Daemyn had Zeke as both a nephew and a close friend. Alex had only Daemyn, and their friendship was rockier than the Falls of the Onohio. Daemyn had Rosanna. Alex missed Mirabelle, and Alex wasn't the type to handle being alone very well.

But something about this didn't set right. And after a hundred years, he'd learned to trust his instincts.

Those same instincts were telling him Alex was set on this. The best thing Daemyn could do was keep a watch on him and hope Alex didn't get into too much trouble.

"All right." Daemyn gave a small nod.

Alex brushed at his shirt. "Do I look presentable? King Cassius is hosting a lunch today. His nobles are going to be there, so it should be safe from poison."

It would be a good chance for Daemyn to do some more scouting around the castle, both for the mystery girl and for whatever King Cassius was planning.

As Captain Taum, three more of his guards, and Alex left for the lunch, Rosanna exited her room. She was dressed in a buckskin shirt and leggings.

Daemyn eyed her. "You ain't dressed for this highfaluting lunch I've been hearing about."

"I ain't going." Rosanna grinned. Her attempt at a mountain accent was getting better. Somewhat. "Josiah and Asa can fill us in on what happens. Having another set of eyes searching for whatever strange is going on is more important."

Daemyn matched her smile. "Sounds like a good plan."

When Captain Degotaga and Isi joined them, Rosanna gestured to them. "We're going to search the castle. Want to help?"

"Of course." Isi grinned. "I didn't get a proper tour yet."

"We would be less noticeable and cover more ground if we split up." Daemyn glanced between Rosanna, Isi, and Captain Degotaga. Daemyn knew the way he wanted this to go, but he wasn't sure Captain Degotaga would allow it.

Isi grabbed her father's arm. "I'll go with Pa. Which tower would you like us to search?"

"Take this tower and we'll search the second tower. The first tower is mostly offices, barracks, and official rooms, and I'm not sure King Cassius will let us wander around there."

Captain Degotaga gave Daemyn a hard look but let Isi lead him toward the stairs.

Rosanna slipped her hand into Daemyn's. She pointed down the hallway the opposite direction of Isi and Captain Degotaga. "This way, right?"

Daemyn smiled and set out in that direction, Rosanna's hand in his. They passed servants bustling around, but none of them looked like the mystery girl or gave off a feeling that set Daemyn's instincts on the edge.

By the time they met Captain Degotaga and Isi in Rosanna's sitting room after a fruitless morning and afternoon searching, Josiah and Asa were waiting there as well. After guiding Rosanna to a chair, Daemyn sat on the floor and rested his back against the chair's leg.

Captain Degotaga took up a position near the door while Asa took the place on the other side.

Isi flopped onto the settee. "I hope you found more than we did."

"Not really. No one even talked around us, much less talked to us." Rosanna rested a hand on Daemyn's shoulder. It was such a casual gesture. Comfortable.

And Daemyn was comfortable with it. He'd never felt this relaxed with another person. It was a new feeling, after so long on his own.

Josiah rested his elbows on his knees. "We discovered something interesting at the formal lunch. King Cassius seemed awful pleased that you weren't there, Rosanna. Even asked the high king, in a tactful manner, if the two of you had an argument, and that glint in his eye got more noticeable when the high king's answer was absentminded."

"And Stefan Vinzen nudged me at that moment, as if to make sure I took notice." Asa crossed his arms. "He might not be the most loyal of the family, but he tried today, at least."

"King Cassius wanted the supposed relationship between me and High King Alexander to fall apart." Rosanna's fingers tightened on Daemyn's shoulder. "What would he have to gain?"

"Instability." Daemyn reached up and rested his hand

over Rosanna's. "Neskahana and Buckhannock have always been High King Alexander's staunchest allies while he slept. If King Cassius could nudge Alex into ending the rumored relationship badly in front of Buckhannock and Monongadotte, Alex would offend his three most important allies."

Daemyn didn't continue. The others could see the consequences without him saying them. War could break out again, and Pohatomie gained more from war than anyone else. None of the other kingdoms could go for long without Pohatomie's corn, especially when they were fighting too much to cultivate their small patches of fertile ground.

It was much like what the king of Pohatomie had done a hundred years ago. He had ordered the bridges cut in Buckhannock and northern Kanawhee, causing chaos and fear, before letting the Tuckawassee use that fear to strike the more deadly blow of killing Alex's father. The Tuckawassee became the enemy the other kingdoms focused on while Pohatomie quietly got rich from an uneven trade balance with all the kingdoms.

"What are we going to do about it?" Josiah asked, glancing from Daemyn to Rosanna and back.

"We let King Cassius think his plan is working, of course." Isi waved at Rosanna and Daemyn. "That means you don't have to keep pretending. No reason to try to save a relationship that isn't really there."

"Good. Last night was already more pretense than I want to muster ever again." Rosanna's sigh brushed against Daemyn's hair.

Last night had been unpleasant. He would rather be back a hundred years serving an arrogant high prince than go through the torture of standing on the sidelines watching Rosanna enter a world where he couldn't follow.

He forced the thoughts away. It was time to concentrate on the mission. "Better we lure King Cassius into thinking that part of his plan is working while we try to find that mystery girl. I don't know how she fits in or how King Cassius is planning to use her, but she's part of this somehow, I think."

"*Is* King Cassius's plan working?" Rosanna's question was quiet, but with a depth of understanding to it.

Daemyn let the question hang for a moment. If he were to guess, breaking up Rosanna and Alex was only one piece. And if isolating Alex was the plan...

"Yes, it is." Daemyn glanced at the somber faces around him. This wasn't his home in the forest, but he wouldn't want anyone else besides the people in this room and Zeke to fight this with him, whatever this was. "Stay alert tonight. Whatever is going on, I reckon it's up to us to stop it."

Chapter 17

Alexander

Alex smoothed a hand over his shirt. He was wearing the best outfit he had along, a pair of fine linen pants, a silk shirt, and an embroidered tunic. The clothes were from a hundred years ago, and the cut of the shirt and tunic didn't match the current styles. But he would still be the best dressed man there, even more than King Cassius.

Would she be there again? Alex's heart pounded, and something clenched inside his stomach. He'd never felt this way before. As if his whole world revolved around her, and he might stop breathing if he couldn't see her again.

If only he knew her name.

That didn't matter. What was a name after all? It was just a label on a person. Not necessary to really know them.

And dancing with her last night, staring into her starry eyes, he'd looked deep into her soul, and she'd looked into his. Connected as if they were meant to find each other. As if his hundred years sleep had the purpose to bring him to this moment.

"Do you require any more assistance, Your Majesty?" Daemyn's voice was as bland as porridge without a decent helping of maple syrup.

Alex gritted his teeth. He had apologized for snapping at Daemyn last night. Wasn't that how this new character thing was supposed to work? Alex apologized when he stumbled into his old ways, and Daemyn was supposed to forgive him, right?

Then why was Daemyn holding a grudge like this? He had been acting strangely all day, all quiet and professional. Not like a friend, but like the manservant he'd been a hundred years ago.

It wasn't fair. Daemyn talked about forgiveness and honor, but he didn't give that forgiveness to Alex. No, with Alex he held grudges and wouldn't let things go.

Alex let the heat build inside his chest. He'd done everything right. It was Daemyn who was being stubborn.

He let out a breath and turned from the mirror. He was going to be the better person and not snap at Daemyn tonight as well. "No, I don't require anything else. You may have the evening off. You don't have to serve at the ball tonight. I'm sure the Pohatomie servants will be just fine without your help."

"If that is your order, Your Majesty." Daemyn gave a small bow.

No, not Daemyn. Jadon. The loyal manservant.

Alex brushed past Daemyn and stalked out the door. His guards fell into step around him. He ignored them. They were just silent, nameless guards.

Inside the ballroom, King Cassius and the nobility were already gathering. Prince Josiah was already there, his bodyguard nearby as he talked with Prince Tyrell of Monongadotte. Perhaps Alex should join them, but he didn't want to distract himself from finding the girl from the night before.

King Cassius waved him over and gave a small bow. "It is an honor that you once again grace us with your presence."

King Cassius wasn't sincere, not in the least. But Alex couldn't help but feel somewhat flattered anyway. One person here understood Alex's place.

Alex stood next to King Cassius as the nobility approached for another receiving line. Terribly dull, since Alex had met these people the night before. He had no wish to learn their names today any more than he had yesterday, nor would he remember them. There was only one person's name he wanted to learn tonight.

King Cassius was saying something about Princess Rosanna. Alex shrugged it away. Wasn't she supposed to be pretending to be in love with Alex? Trust her to run off with Daemyn instead of upholding her end of the bargain.

It didn't matter. If the mystery girl came again, Alex wouldn't be lonely. He wouldn't need Rosanna or Mirabelle.

More people entered the ballroom. Princess Rosanna finally made an appearance. More bland girls with their fancy dresses arrived, but Alex barely spared them a glance. There was only one girl who was important tonight.

Then there she was. Dressed in a deep burgundy dress with black embroidery along the hem. Her black hair was piled on her head with deep burgundy ribbons twined through the curls.

A hint of a breeze brushed Alex's face. Should he listen to Daemyn's warning? Yet how was Alex supposed to be careful? He couldn't be rude to her.

She didn't look like she was conspiring against him. She

was smiling as she walked toward him. A nice walk. Brisk but graceful, yet not sashaying in a seductive manner.

Surely there was nothing wrong with dancing with her one more time.

He met her in the center of the ballroom. Sparks shot across his skin as he took her hands. Something that felt this good had to be right.

That pesky breeze stirred in the ballroom again, and Alex ignored it. Someone really ought to close the window. They were getting an annoying draft.

As the music started, he whisked her into the first steps of the dance, gazing deep into her liquid, blue eyes, their depths like the color of the sky on a clear day.

Wasn't there something he had wanted to ask her? He couldn't think of what it could possibly be.

Not that words were necessary. Their hearts were beating as one, their souls meeting through the touch of their fingertips.

She was mesmerizing as she glided across the ballroom. Her skin was creamy and flawless. Her neck accentuated the perfect tilt to her head. She was the most perfect creature he had ever seen.

And he was falling madly in love with her.

CHAPTER 18

ELARA

Elara hadn't known a man could look that utterly, puppy-dog-eyed, drop-down-drooling smitten. Especially not a man looking at her.

But there High King Alexander was with a liquid look of complete adoration. Up until that moment, she wasn't sure she could've described complete adoration, but the wide-eyed, barely blinking stare he was giving her had to be it.

It was uncomfortable. Not in an awkward way, since his gaze was squarely locked on her face. But it was strange to have someone so focused on her as if about to forget his own name.

Was this what love was like? She would've thought it was something more than this staring, silent adoration.

Pain shot through her foot. She drew in a deep breath and concentrated on not limping nor showing the pain. That cut on her foot had been getting worse all day. One side of the glass slipper was tinted blood red. It wasn't dripping out of the shoe. Just...there.

"Are you all right?" High King Alexander's grip on her hands tightened, his forehead creased as if the thought of her in pain was the worst thing he could imagine.

"I'm fine. My feet simply ache." Elara kept a smile pasted on her face. Who knew all the practice she had smiling as a servant would come in handy here in this ballroom?

"Let's go to the garden. You can sit on one of the benches." High King Alexander stopped dancing and steered her toward the doors to the garden.

Elara glanced over her shoulder. King Cassius didn't seem to be looking their way, but he probably knew exactly what was going on. He'd wanted her to dance with High King Alexander, and she'd done that. Surely it would be all right to spend time romantically with the high king in the garden.

Actually, if King Cassius wanted a scandal, the high king spending time alone in the garden with Elara would cause it faster than them simply dancing in the ballroom.

Elara didn't see Princess Rosanna. Perhaps she'd left after seeing the way the high king had looked at Elara.

As High King Alexander steered her outdoors, she drew in a deep breath of the cool, night air. As the river-tinted breeze washed over her, the pain sharpened in her foot while her other foot starting throbbing.

What was going on? Why were these glass slippers—so comfortable when she'd put them on—hurting now?

She sank onto the first bench they came across. It wasn't the most romantic spot as the bench sat right next to one of the main paths. But it was convenient.

Last night had been wonderful. Dancing in the high king's arms. The stroll in the garden. She'd been floating on a cloud. But tonight? Tonight the shine had worn off. She had hurting feet, and all she could think about was making it through the rest of the night and the next ball so that she could claim the promised title of baroness.

Was that all this experience had become? Trying to survive? Her wish to attend the ball should have led to more than that, right? This was supposed to be her dream. Everything she had ever wanted in life.

High King Alexander gripped her hands and faced her. "Is this better, my darling flower?"

Wait, what? Elara blinked and shook her head. She couldn't have possibly heard him right. Was he starting to call her by ridiculous nicknames?

Her feet throbbed worse than they had been before. She kept her smile pasted on her face. What was High King Alexander saying now? He'd apparently kept talking. Something about a list of her perfections.

Elara stifled a yawn, glanced around, and stiffened. Monica strolled down the garden path, her hand resting on the arm of the prince of Monongadotte. When she glanced toward High King Alexander and Elara, her face paled.

Elara froze. Did she recognize her? Monica and Beatrice hadn't recognized her the night before, and the Fae said Elara wouldn't be recognized. But Elara made sure she hadn't gotten close to them. Surely Monica would notice her when she was only a few feet away, even in a fancy gown and hairstyle.

Prince Tyrell glanced past Elara, then his gaze snapped to her. As he was already a tall and large man, his elk antler crown made him loom over everyone around him. Tonight, he had a deep green shirt with a whole bear pelt draped over his shoulders like a cape.

He shook Monica's hand off his arm and stalked toward the bench, glaring at the high king. "You've been claiming her all night. And you kept her all last night too. Let someone else have a chance."

High King Alexander leapt to his feet, fists clenched. "She's mine."

Elara scrambled to stand, the spiked heels of her glass slippers catching on the hem of her dress. No, she wasn't. That was the whole point of becoming a baroness. So she belonged to and answered to no one. "I'm not—"

Prince Tyrell grabbed her hand and yanked her forward. "It's my turn for a dance."

High King Alexander shoved his way between them. "Don't touch her. She's mine."

With a growl, Prince Tyrell clenched his fists and charged.

Monica screamed. Elara stumbled out of the way, her throat too tight to force out a scream of her own. If Prince Tyrell raised a hand to the high king, it would be treason. It could start a war between Kanawhee and Monongadotte, at the very least.

The same dark-haired man who had been with Princess Rosanna the night before raced out of the darkness, followed closely by Prince Josiah of Buckhannock, Princess Rosanna, and their bodyguards. Several of these newcomers tackled Prince Tyrell. He roared, and lifted Princess Rosanna and another young woman off their feet as they clung to one of his arms while Prince Josiah dangled from the other.

Elara eased another step backwards. She needed to get out of here. Something was wrong. The dancing had been amazing. The nicknames ridiculous. The compliments were kind of nice.

But this was going too far. Now they were fighting over her. A war could be sparked.

This was wrong.

Elara swallowed and spun on her heels. Pain lanced through both of her feet. She stumbled but forced herself to keep moving. She didn't look back, not even to figure out what was happening with the shouts and scuffling sounds behind her.

She staggered around several hedges and past decorative trees until she reached the far corner of the garden. The path behind her remained silent. No one had followed her. They'd all been too busy fighting to notice her running away.

She collapsed next to a fountain with a statue of a swan perched on top. She clawed at her skirts until she revealed her feet. Blood spotted several places along both glass slippers.

Gripping the right shoe, she yanked.

It wouldn't budge.

She kicked her foot as hard as she could against the fountain. The glass slipper tinged, her toe ached with the impact, but not so much as a spider crack appeared in the glass.

"I don't understand. This was my dream. This was a gift. Why is it so terrible?" Elara gripped her foot, still ineffectually tugging at the glass slipper. She didn't deserve this. All she'd wanted was to wear a fancy dress and dance with the high king. "I didn't choose this."

"Oh, but you did, dearie." The Fae woman's silken voice purred from the shadows next to the garden wall. "Don't blame me when you don't like how your choices turn out."

"You gave me these slippers. Did you know they wouldn't come off? Why didn't you warn me?" Elara yanked harder on the glass slipper. Pain sliced into her palm, and she dropped her glass-encased, bleeding foot.

A shadow detached itself from the darkness, moving closer to the line of moonlight so that Elara could just make out the hazy shape of the Fae woman and her wings. "All I did was hold out the possibility of making all your wildest dreams come true, and you grabbed for it with your grubby little fingers. It isn't my fault you didn't ask questions. Isn't that just like a human. Always shifting blame."

Elara's heart was pounding louder in her ears, beating in time with the throbbing in her feet. She needed these slippers removed. Now. "Please. Take them off. Take them back."

"Save you, you mean?" The Fae woman let out a trilling giggle. "That's one thing I don't do. You see, I don't care about you. You're just pathetic dirt, a means to an end."

The Fae woman stepped from shadow into moonlight. The silvery light washed over her, and it was as if the moonlight was a dagger shredding her wings, her clothes, her hair. What Elara had thought were huge, impressive wings were nothing but tatters hanging from the woman's back. Her dress was strips of red and black. Her cheeks were hollow, and her hair was the white-green color of death.

Elara scrambled back as fast as she could on her hands and knees. This wasn't one of the Loyal Fae, as she'd assumed. This was one of the Fallen Fae.

That meant the glass slippers weren't a gift.

They were a curse.

"I'm not noble. You can't curse me." Elara gripped the edge of the fountain, not that the stone would do much to protect her. This wasn't fair. How could the Fallen Fae curse her when she wasn't even noble?

"I'm allowed to give a curse to a noble child at birth to represent the curse all you humans are born with. Those are the rules, stuffy as they are." The Fallen Fae waved a languid hand through the air. "But any human can choose a curse. It is, after all, what you're good at. Choosing curses. You can't even choose a gift if it were set right there out in front of you. It's deliciously pathetic. So much fun to have you as our little playthings. And you are just so willing."

Elara curled against the fountain. It would do no good to run, even if her feet weren't throbbing. She was stuck. Here with the Fallen Fae. In the glass slippers. In her life. There was no way to escape any of it.

"You were the perfect pawn. High King Alexander would have been alert against a curse if he had been approached directly. But putting a curse on him through you made it almost too easy. After all, love is one of the strongest bonds a human can experience. True love isn't possible—disgustingly self-sacrificial as it is—but infatuation is nearly as strong in the short term, and especially good for manipulation. His gift of intelligence needed to be neutralized, and what better way than with the curse of infatuation. It makes such a fool out of those caught in its grasp."

Elara wrapped her arms over her stomach. This curse wasn't just on her. It clutched the high king as well.

In the distance, the chimes of the clock set in the face of the first tower tolled, then began ringing out the hour. Elara counted by habit. Midnight.

A smile cracked the Fallen Fae's face. "Tomorrow night, you will dance with the high king again, and when the clock strikes midnight, the curse on him will be permanent."

Permanent? Elara shivered. What would that mean for her? Would she be stuck with the high king spouting annoying nicknames for the rest of her life? Would the glass slippers never come off?

"What does—" She raised her head and glanced around.

The Fallen Fae was gone. Disappeared into the shadows.

What was Elara supposed to do now? She'd tumbled from a golden daydream into a nightmare.

To become a baroness, all she had to do was dance with High King Alexander one more night.

But to do so would condemn him to living a life as a shadow of himself while Tallahatchia crumbled around him.

DAEMYN

Daemyn pinned Alex's arms to his sides, sidestepping a kick and leaning his head back to avoid having his nose crunched by the back of Alex's head. "Calm down, sire. This isn't the way to promote peace between the kingdoms."

"He was going to take her. She's my girl. He had no right." Alex shoved against Daemyn's arms, but he didn't have the strength Daemyn had from years of fighting and paddling his canoe.

That mystery girl again. Daemyn didn't dare look away from Alex long enough to search for her, but she'd been there a moment ago.

Why was Alex so beside himself? He had never been this way even over Mirabelle. Whatever was wrong, it was getting worse.

Daemyn couldn't fight whatever hold this girl had over Alex. But he could use it. "Fighting over her isn't going to impress her."

"It won't?" Alex stilled. He glanced around, then slumped. "She's gone."

Daemyn eased his grip, but he didn't dare fully let go until he knew Alex wasn't going to offend all Monongadotte by punching its prince. "Of course she is. She left as soon as you and Prince Tyrell looked like you were going to fight."

"You're right. I shouldn't have started anything." Alex tugged at his clothing, sounding more like himself than he had a moment ago. "It was foolish of me."

Daemyn released Alex and took in the rest of the situation. Rosanna, Isi, Josiah, and Asa had managed to calm Prince Tyrell. Though, calm might not be the right word for it. Prince Tyrell was a barely restrained, seething mass of antler and bear fur.

Rosanna shifted her grip on Prince Tyrell's arm to something that looked more relaxed and consoling than restraining. "I understand your disappointment, Prince Tyrell. I didn't get to dance with the person I wanted to tonight either. But there is some of the evening left. Why don't you go inside and enjoy the rest of it? The servants will have replenished the refreshment tables."

Prince Tyrell blinked and shook his head, the antlers he wore on his head tilting with his movement. Something in his gaze cleared. He turned to the girl he had been walking with. "I'm sorry, lass, for the ruckus just now. I don't know what came over me."

The girl blinked, wide-eyed, her hands still over her mouth as if to hold back another scream.

As if sensing the girl had good reason to be wary around him after his display of temper, Prince Tyrell gave her a small bow, then set off for the ballroom alone.

Isi approached the girl as tentatively as Daemyn might

tiptoe around a doe and fawn he didn't want to scare. "What's your name?"

"Monica." The girl's voice was barely a whisper.

Isi gestured to the bench. "Why don't you sit down for a moment? Rosanna and I will sit with you until you're feeling less shaky."

"I can't stay long." The girl was shaking as Isi steered her toward the bench. "If anyone saw me leave with Prince Tyrell, and him return alone, all sorts of rumors will start flying. Reputation is important here in Pohatomie."

Daemyn stepped out of the way, then nudged Alex back a few steps to give the girl some more room.

Rosanna sat on the bench on the other side of Monica. "I understand. Reputations can be such fickle things. Would it be all right if Prince Josiah escorted you back inside? Your reputation would be fine if another prince escorted you. I can assure you, he can be trusted."

Josiah swept into a perfect bow. "I am the epitome of the perfect gentleman."

Daemyn resisted the urge to shake his head. He wasn't sure where along his family tree the Buckhannock side inherited their knack for flair, but it hadn't come from him.

Monica smiled and took Josiah's offered hand. "Thank you, Your Highness."

As Josiah and Monica strolled along the gravel path toward the lights of the ballroom, Asa turned to Daemyn. "Do you need any more help out here?"

"No. Go back with them and keep an eye on things. Most people might not notice something went on in the garden, but King Cassius will." Daemyn glanced toward the ballroom, but the windows were set too high in the wall for him to see more than a glimpse of the gilt ceiling. "I would like to know his reaction."

"Very well." Asa marched away, his back straight, his shoulders stiff in correct posture. Odd how Josiah and Zeke seemed more like siblings than Zeke and Asa.

Isi huffed out a breath. "Well, that takes care of almost everyone. But what about him?" She jabbed a finger toward Alex.

Alex was staring into the garden, his eyes clouded as if he was daydreaming about something—or someone—instead of seeing the plants in front of him.

Daemyn let out his own sigh. He'd thought that once Alex woke, his duty would be over. But it seemed his duty wouldn't let him go. "I'll deal with him."

"Do you need help?" Rosanna touched Daemyn's arm. "He looks..."

Daemyn wasn't sure what to call Alex's expression either. Lovestruck, perhaps. But he had been lovestruck, and he hadn't ever looked like that. Love-addled seemed more like it.

"Infatuated." Isi's nose wrinkled as she grimaced again. "He looks like he could use a good dunk in the river."

She wasn't wrong. Alex needed something to snap him out of whatever this was.

Rosanna pointed at a fountain with a small, raised pool. "Would that work? We might be able to dunk his head, at least."

Alex was still staring into the distance. It wasn't a good sign that they were talking about him—and talking about dunking him underwater—and he hadn't even noticed. "It's worth a try."

Rosanna took Alex's arm. "Why don't we sit down for

a moment, Your Majesty? It looks nice on the edge of that fountain."

Alex blinked and followed her as docilely as a lamb on a lead rope. "Do you think I scared her off? What should I do to fix whatever I did?"

Rosanna patted his arm, and it looked like she turned the gesture into a nudge as she and Alex reached the fountain. Alex obligingly sat on the brickwork around the pool and fountain. Rosanna glanced from Alex to Daemyn, something in her expression almost pleading. "Um, it always helps to be nice. And courteous. And smile."

"Maybe he should write her poetry," Isi grumbled.

"Poetry!" Alex sat straighter, as if writing romantic poetry was a good idea. "I will write her a poem."

No, no he shouldn't. Daemyn could only imagine having this infatuated Alex give him a copy to read to tell him if it was any good. He wasn't sure even he was good enough at acting to say yes in that case.

He eyed the pool and the fountain. How should he dunk Alex? Simply push him backwards? Alex might resist or catch himself in time. Daemyn didn't want to be the one to cause a second near fistfight in this garden tonight.

There was nothing for it. He would just have to throw himself into the fountain pool and take Alex with him. It was the best way to make sure Alex got thoroughly soaked and hopefully wet enough to shock whatever this was right out of him.

Daemyn sat next to Alex on the fountain's wall, then peered past him to Rosanna. "You might want to step back."

"What?" Alex turned hazy, unfocused eyes on Daemyn.

Rosanna popped upright and took a few hurried steps away from the fountain.

"Wh—" Alex started to say again, but Daemyn swept a forearm across Alex's chest, grabbed a fistful of his shirt, and threw himself backwards, dragging Alex along with him.

Alex gave something of an undignified grunt and flailed, but he was too off balance and Daemyn kept his grip too firm.

Then cold water struck Daemyn's back and closed over his chest a moment before his face submerged. The back of his head thunked against the bottom of the pool.

Alex flailed again, and this time he managed to land a good blow with his elbow to Daemyn's stomach. He hunched under the blow and let Alex go.

Water rushed and gurgled as Alex surged from the fountain. Daemyn sat upright, water flowing from his face and cascading from the fringes on his sleeves. He swiped water from his eyes just before Alex grabbed the front of his shirt.

"What was that?" Alex's grip on Daemyn's shirt was tight, his eyes narrowed. "How dare you push me into a fountain? What is wrong with you? Do you think just because you're courting a princess you can get away with assaulting the high king? You are still just a manservant, and not a very good one at that. Don't bother returning to see to your duties tonight."

Alex shoved Daemyn away and stomped out of the fountain. He glared at Rosanna. "And you. You barely even count as a princess, wild thing that you are. Daemyn can have you."

With another glare at them, Alex marched away with squishing steps, taking the paths in the garden instead of heading directly to the ballroom. Hopefully he would have enough presence of mind to take the back way to his room.

Rosanna's eyes were wide, her body rigid.

Isi stood next to her, both hands clenched. "I know I'm supposed to be loyal to him, but I think I might start a war with him at the moment. How did you manage to serve him for so many years? He's insufferable."

Daemyn levered himself all the way out of the water. "He was always arrogant, but never purposefully cruel. I don't know what's wrong with him, but this isn't him."

At least, Daemyn didn't think Alex would act like this voluntarily. He had been arrogant, but when he'd been tested on their hike to Buckhannock, he had shown the depths beneath his arrogance.

And, as much as Daemyn wanted to give up and walk away, he had once journeyed all the way into Beyond with Alex. He'd heard the Highest Prince claim Alex as one of his. To turn his back on Alex would be to turn his back on someone who belonged to the Highest Prince, and Daemyn couldn't do that, no matter how tempting.

CHAPTER 20

ELARA

Walking was agony. Elara was beyond simply gritting her teeth and bearing it. She was shaking with the pain of each step, her eyes watering, her stomach heaving. She'd been in such pain she hadn't even gone to visit Terrence that morning.

But she couldn't let the baroness or her daughters see. What would Elara tell them? How could she possibly confess the trouble she'd gotten herself into?

She drew in a shaky breath and did the last button on Monica's dress.

Monica turned, her eyes searching Elara's face. "Are you feeling all right? You're awfully pale."

"I'm fine." They were all the words Elara could manage. She had to keep breathing steadily to keep her stomach in place.

"You don't look fine. You should go lay down. I can finish getting ready by myself, and I'll help Mama and Beatrice. They'll understand." Monica took the brush from Elara's hand.

Elara couldn't even fist her hand because her fingers were too weak and shaky. She took a step toward her small bedroom. Pain stabbed into the soles of her feet, as if she was walking on broken glass. She couldn't hide a whimper.

Monica was at her side, steadying her. "Maybe I should go fetch the healer."

"No, that's not necessary." Elara would've shaken her head, but that much movement would send her head spinning.

A wrinkle remained between Monica's eyebrows, but she kept her hand on Elara's arm to steady her. "My bed is closer. Why don't you lie down there?"

Elara let Monica help her toward the bed and collapsed into it. Even with her weight off her feet, the pain diminished only slightly. It was as if nails were stabbed into her feet all the way to her bones, grating, clawing. At least Elara had taken the time to hide the glass slippers inside her moccasins again that morning. She didn't have to worry about Monica seeing them.

Monica pulled a blanket over Elara's shoulders. "You rest."

Elara squeezed her eyes shut and let herself drift. After a while, Baroness Hackett and Beatrice entered the room, and they talked in low voices before they all left.

What was Elara going to do? If she went to the ball tonight and danced with High King Alexander, she would permanently curse him into infatuation with her.

But if she didn't go, what would King Cassius do? He knew who she was. He could punish her. He could punish the baroness, Monica, and Beatrice.

Why should Elara even worry about the high king? He wasn't her problem. She should just worry about herself. All she'd have to do was force herself through a few steps of the dance, then King Cassius would make her a baroness. She wouldn't have to worry about anything ever again. If war happened, it probably wouldn't touch Pohatomie. The last war had mostly concentrated down south along the borders Neskahana and Kanawhee shared with Tuckawassee.

Elara forced her eyes open and pushed herself onto her elbows. The sky outside the window was already dark, the windowsill splashed silver-white from the full Harvest Moon. Somewhere in the distance, the large clock was striking. Was it striking ten or eleven? Elara hadn't paid enough attention as it started chiming.

Either way, she didn't have much time. She eased out of bed and touched her foot to the floor. Pain tore through her legs all the way into her bones.

It would be so much easier to lie in bed all night. Surely King Cassius wouldn't blame her if she was in too much pain to attend the ball.

But then she would have to explain why she was in pain. She would have to reveal the shoes to him and the full secret of what the Fallen Fae had given her. King Cassius seemed to suspect that the Fae dress was enthralling the high king, but he might not have guessed the depths to the curse. He would surely use that against her and against the high king if he knew.

Perhaps that was a disloyal thought. As a good citizen of Pohatomie, shouldn't she be willing to confess this to her king?

She'd never been one to pay attention to the broader politics happening beyond Hackettsville besides the fact that the war had widowed Baroness Hackett and had cost Elara her father.

A war would cost more husbands, sons, fathers.

Tallahatchia hadn't even had a decent chance to try peace once again.

But why should Elara care about people she'd never met? Why should she give up her dream of becoming a baroness for strangers in far distant kingdoms? Surely it wouldn't hurt to go long enough to make herself a baroness?

She set her other foot on the floor. The pain was dimming now. Almost numbed by the thoughts running through her head. As much as it hurt, it was as if the glass slippers were leading her onward. She'd already set out on this path. There was no point in turning back now.

Opening the door, she peeked into the castle hallway. No one was about with all the servants busy at the ball. Holding her head high, Elara stepped into the hallway and turned in the direction that would lead her to the ballroom.

As she did, her dress shimmered, then changed into a ballgown. This time the dress had a deep black skirt and sleeves with a burgundy bodice. Hints of gold trimmed the edge of the skirt and the sleeves. Her hair cascaded down her back.

Elara forced herself to walk down the hallway, headed for the stairs. Thankfully the baroness's suite was on the second floor of the second tower. She wasn't sure she would've made it to the ballroom on the main floor of the third tower if she'd had to walk from the third or fourth floor.

Music drifted through the hallways the closer she got to the ballroom. Then the large doors were before her, and the guards were pulling them open for her.

She drew in a deep breath and stepped onto the marble

floor. Each step ached, but she tried to ignore the feeling of walking with nails stabbed into the bottoms of her feet.

Instead of trying for a grand entrance as she had on the first night, she crept along the wall, trying to stay unnoticed in the shadows. Across the ballroom, High King Alexander was craning his neck, standing on tiptoes. Looking for her.

Elara ducked her head and pressed herself deeper into the shadows. Could she go through with this? Could she knowingly finish the curse on the high king?

But if she didn't, she would be just as stuck as she had always been. She would remain a servant. King Cassius would probably punish her in some way for her failure. She might not even be able to get the glass slippers off.

Would the glass slippers come off once the curse was complete at midnight? Their whole purpose was these balls and cursing the high king. Surely Elara would be free of them at midnight.

All she had to do was put up with a little more pain and dance with High King Alexander one last time.

"Who are you?"

Elara jumped and whirled. She hadn't realized anyone else was occupying this section of shadow with her, but there he was, the dark-haired young man she'd seen last night holding High King Alexander back from punching Prince Tyrell. Elara shrank away from him. There was something about him that set her feet to aching worse. "I could ask you the same thing. What are you doing skulking in shadows?"

The young man didn't smile. Something about the lines in his face hinted he didn't smile as often as a young man should. "I'm Daemyn Rand, the high king's manservant. I've been looking for you."

Daemyn Rand. That name was familiar, but Elara couldn't place it. Perhaps she'd heard his name in gossip or rumors? She wasn't sure.

But she did know he was unsettling. His dark brown eyes gazed at her steadily, without the haze that seemed to come over all the other young men in this ballroom when they got near her, as if he was immune to whatever allure the glass slippers gave her.

"Why would you be looking for me?" Elara tried to smile, but she couldn't manage it. Not even a fake, pasted on smile.

His gaze didn't waver. "What hold do you have over High King Alexander? Are you a part of King Cassius's plan against him?"

They were at the edge of a ballroom filled with people and lined with guards at all the exits. She shouldn't feel compelled to answer. She should stomp away.

But he was unnerving, and she couldn't seem to force herself to move. "I...it's..." She swallowed and pressed her mouth shut. If she wasn't going to tell her own king the full truth of what was going on, she wasn't going to talk about it to a stranger who claimed to be the high king's manservant. "I can't tell you anything. Besides, even if I was a part of some plot against the high king, you can't do anything about it. You have no power to arrest me, and someone is going to notice if you try to drag me away."

Daemyn's jaw tightened, as if he wasn't happy being told that he was essentially helpless to stop anything, even if she did tell him what was going on. "Stay away from High King Alexander tonight. Whatever is causing this..." he gestured at her dress. "It isn't right."

A hint of a breeze shivered over her. His words held the

same ring of truth that Terrence's always did when he talked about the Lord of All and the Highest Prince.

Elara took a step back, away from Daemyn Rand and his too knowing gaze. Her mouth was too dry to come up with a reply.

"There you are, my love!" High King Alexander's voice came from behind her. She turned in time to spot the glare he sent in his manservant's direction before he swept her in his arms. "My heart has been in supreme agony all night, my most precious jewel, waiting for your arrival. I wrote a poem for you. Would you like to hear it?"

She opened her mouth to tell him no, but he was leading her onto the dance floor, and sharp spikes of pain jabbed the bottoms of her feet. She snapped her mouth closed against a cry of pain.

"Your nose is like a rose. I wish I were a bee that I may be near the petals of your lips, hardly daring to take a sip."

Oh, dear. It was worse than she thought. Elara swallowed back the pain from her tearing feet and tried to paste on a smile. She needed to figure out something to say before his gushing poetry turned even more foolish. His metaphors weren't even making sense anymore.

This was what she was condemning him to. A life of spouting meaningless poetry and pining after someone who didn't even like him back.

What kind of life would that be? He was supposed to be the high king, the one man who could unite the seven kingdoms and restore the peace and prosperity they had once enjoyed. All things he wouldn't be able to do like this.

High King Alexander twirled her in and out of the other dancers. Her black skirt swirled around her. Her feet tore with each step she took.

It was all she could do to breathe through the pain and try to keep the tears locked inside. Just breathe. Dance. Paste a smile on her face to pretend everything was fine.

A cold draft washed over her. She blinked as High King Alexander led her through the ballroom doors into the garden.

The garden. He must be planning some romantic moment out here. Trying to recreate the wonderful fantasy that the first night of the ball had been instead of the disaster it had become since.

Tonight, the full moon overhead cast a sharp, silver light that stabbed down at Elara. The breeze was a hard, icy thing clawing deep inside her as if to lay bare all the places she'd gone wrong in the past few days.

She should have known the glass slippers were too good to be true. Dreams were never as beautiful in real life as they were in the daydream.

The glass slippers stabbed deeper into her feet. She stumbled and barely made it to the nearest bench before she collapsed. She couldn't hold back the tears any longer. It hurt. A deep, bone-splintering sort of pain. She was about ready to find the nearest healer and plead for him to chop her feet off. Surely that couldn't hurt any worse than this tearing, shredding agony.

"What's wrong, my dearest flower?" High King Alexander knelt in front of her, clasping her hands, and gazing up at her with liquid brown eyes, as if seeing her in tears was about to bring him to tears as well. "Was my poetry that terrible?"

At least he was the sweet sort of infatuated. It would've been so much worse if he'd become pushy or tried to claim kisses that weren't his to take.

It would be so easy just to sit here and let this night play out however it did. If she didn't move, didn't say a word, High King Alexander would be cursed, and she would become a baroness. Surely she couldn't be blamed if she did nothing.

Even if she wanted to, was there anything she could do? She couldn't save herself from these glass slippers. Could she save High King Alexander? Could she stop King Cassius from enacting whatever else he was planning?

Elara squeezed the high king's hands, hoping he couldn't feel her fingers trembling. "I'm fine. Truly. It's..." She blinked, and another rush of tears spilled onto her cheeks. What could she tell him to explain?

He swiped away the tears before they could dribble from her chin. "I love you, my darling. Will you..."

No, no, no. Surely he wasn't asking...Elara tried to draw in another deep breath, but it shuddered with more tears.

In the distance, Castle Fonthaven's clock began to chime, tolling out the short melody it would play before striking the hour.

Midnight.

The breeze whipped through Elara's hair, shivered over her skin, and for a moment, the pain of the glass slippers numbed as if the breeze was soothing ice placed against her wounds.

"...marry me?" High King Alexander stared up at her with deep, earnest eyes. As if he expected her to say yes. As if three nights of balls and short dances were enough for that sort of question.

He didn't even realize how far gone he was.

The breeze brushed against her forehead, and for the

first time in what felt like far too long, she was thinking clearly.

She couldn't do this. It didn't matter what she thought of High King Alexander or her loyalties to King Cassius or her own ambitions to be a baroness. This wasn't right. It was as simple as that.

The clock started tolling the first chime to mark the midnight hour. Elara yanked her hands free of High King Alexander's and shot to her feet, nearly knocking into him. Her feet screamed with pain, but she couldn't give in to the agony now. She had to get away. "I need to go."

She pushed past him and staggered as fast as she could down the garden path.

"Wait! Where are you going?" High King Alexander's voice rang behind her a moment before his footsteps crunched on the gravel.

She couldn't let him catch her. Would it prevent the curse if she wasn't in his presence when that clock finished tolling midnight?

She had to try. She forced her legs to pump faster, sobbing as each running step stabbed the glass deeper into her feet.

The wrought iron gate to the garden was just ahead of her now. She shoved it open, and it bounced into a guard standing next to the garden entrance. The guard tumbled to the ground.

Elara didn't have time or breath to spend on apologizing. She leapt over the guard and dashed straight across the castle's courtyard.

The clock was striking three. Four.

"Wait! Stop her!"

She ran harder, tears pouring down her face and her breaths coming in sobbing hiccups. She couldn't let anyone stop her now. If the high king caught up before the last chime…

Five. Six.

The castle gates were still standing open thanks to the ball, but the guards were reaching for the handles to swing them closed.

One of the guards stepped in her path. Instead of trying to dodge, she rammed into him with a shoulder. It was such an unexpected move coming from her, a sobbing girl in a ballgown, that the guard staggered. By the time he regained his feet and grabbed at her, she had skidded between the two doors.

Seven.

All that lay between her and freedom was the long causeway and the second guardhouse at the far end.

There was more shouting behind her. She didn't even try to pick out the words from the thunder of her own pulse and the clinking of the glass slippers against the cobblestones.

Eight.

She glanced over her shoulder. High King Alexander was shoving past the guards and the mostly closed gates.

Nine.

Her foot caught, and she was headed for the cobblestones before she'd even had a thought to catch her balance. Her hands pounded into the pavement, then her elbows. She barely saved herself from smashing her chin into the stone.

Ten.

She couldn't force herself to move. Pain throbbed through her hands, down her arms, and tore through her feet.

This was as far as she could run. So close to escape, but unable to take another step.

Gentle hands reached under her arms and lifted her from the ground as if she weighed no more than a small child. She was set on her feet so gently the pain didn't worsen.

She stared into a kind face with warm eyes. Even the breeze, so sharp and cold before, danced in warm, soothing tendrils around him.

"Elara." The stranger said, and her name sounded so right coming from him that it didn't matter how he knew it.

Looking into his eyes, with the breeze steadying her, Elara could almost forget the glass slippers, the impending curse, the pain tearing through her legs. His gaze was a warmth, a contentment, she didn't know was possible, as if with him was everything good with no more need for wants and wishes.

"Wait!" High King Alexander's shout shattered the stillness, coming from far too close behind her.

Elara jumped and lurched away from the man who was steadying her. "Thank you." It was all she managed to gasp out before she started running once again.

Her left foot clinked, shards of glass slicing between her toes. But her right foot came down on cool stone.

Elara stumbled and grabbed at the billows of the ballgown's black skirt to peer at her foot.

Her right foot was bloody and sliced, but it rested barefoot on the cobblestones.

Elara glanced over her shoulder. The glass slipper lay at the stranger's feet, its glittering facets untouched by her blood. The stranger raised his gaze and met hers. Had he done the impossible and removed the shoe?

Eleven.

High King Alexander was only yards away, his gaze focused on her as if he didn't see the stranger standing right there in the middle of the causeway.

Elara had no more time. She spun on the heel of her bare foot and raced down the causeway. It was difficult to run with one shoe on, one shoe missing, but she couldn't afford to stop now, no matter how she lurched and tottered.

She burst past the two guards beside the open gate at the end of the causeway. Neither of the guards even looked in her direction, as if they didn't see her. Perhaps they had fallen asleep at their posts.

Elara threw herself into a stand of brush a few feet away and curled in a patch of shadow.

Twelve.

High King Alexander shoved between the gates. He turned in all directions. Still looking for her.

Elara tried to calm her breathing, staying still as she possibly could in the underbrush. If he hadn't been so frantic, he might have been able to spot her there only a few feet away or he would've noticed the bloody footprint she'd left on the grass at the end of the causeway.

High King Alexander rounded on one of the guards and grabbed his shirt collar. "Did you see a girl run this way a moment ago? A girl with black hair and blue eyes and the most stunning red dress?"

Wait, black hair? She was blonde. And she was wearing a black dress.

What did High King Alexander think he saw when he looked at her? It was unsettling to have him talk about her and yet get a major detail like her hair color wrong.

The guard shook his head. "I didn't see anyone, sir."

"She just ran by. How could you possibly have missed her?" The high king shoved the guard away from him. "You are a useless, pathetic pair of guards. I'll have King Cassius punish both of you for this."

High King Alexander wheeled and marched toward the castle. The two guards looked at each other, then one of them raced after the high king as if he thought he would have to defend himself before King Cassius.

Elara released a shuddering breath. She'd gotten away. She fisted her fingers in her skirt, then stilled at the feel of the coarse homespun beneath her fingers.

Her dress was once again the basic blue homespun she'd been wearing earlier. She sat on the ground and stuck her feet out. Her right foot was a bleeding mess while her left foot was still trapped in the glass slipper. She tugged on the slipper, but it wouldn't budge.

"Why won't it come off?" Elara yanked on the slipper, but it wouldn't move. Whatever had caused the other slipper to come off wasn't working on this one. "The ball is over. High King Alexander wasn't cursed. Why is it still stuck?"

"He's still cursed." The Fallen Fae's voice was a shivering whisper while the Fae woman herself was a deeper shadow in the darkness. "I said the curse would be permanent. Not that it would be broken. You should try to listen better, dearie."

"But the other one came off. Why didn't this one?" Elara glared at the Fallen Fae, trying to hide the way her skin was crawling. Why hadn't she noticed how cold and dark the night was around the Fallen Fae? It wasn't even the good kind of icy the way the breeze had been earlier.

The Fallen Fae glanced at Elara's bare foot, and something shifted in her eyes for a moment before she shuddered. As if drawing herself together, she shrugged. "It won't make a difference. The high king is still cursed. He will search for you, and when he places that shoe back on your foot, the curse will be permanent. On him, and on you. Those glass slippers are never coming off."

ALEXANDER

He must find her. He had to find her. He simply couldn't live without her. She was his whole world. The breath in his body. The blood pumping through his veins. She was his sun. His moon. His everything.

Something was niggling at the corner of his brain, but Alex shoved it away. He didn't have any time to waste dwelling on anything and anyone but her. He had to find her, no matter the cost or how long it took.

King Cassius had guards he could send to search for her. Alex would have to ask him for aid. He would beg on his hands and knees if he had to.

He marched back across the causeway, barely glancing at the guard following him.

In the center of the causeway, a glass slipper glittered in the moonlight. Alex halted and knelt in front of it. He hadn't paid it much attention when it had fallen from her foot, but now it was his last link to her.

He picked it up and cradled it to his chest. Besides the

girl who had run away with his heart, this glass slipper was the most precious thing in the world to him.

Would he ever see her again? What if he never found her?

The ache inside him was too great. He leaned over and kissed the place on the cobblestones where his beloved had stood moments before, looking at him with such an aching expression in her eyes. What had been wrong? Why wouldn't she let him fix it?

All he wanted to do was protect and cherish her. He would worship the very ground she walked on if that was all he had left of her.

"I will find you." It was a promise he'd keep even if it took the rest of his life.

With the glass slipper pressed to his heart, Alex stood and strode the rest of the way down the causeway and through the main gates of the castle.

After crossing the courtyard to the third tower, Alex flung the doors to the ballroom open. Inside, the music had already hushed. Groups of people were standing, talking. Probably discussing his beloved's dash from the garden.

Why had she run? He'd just proposed their hearts' desire.

He shoved that thought away. She must have had a reason. He simply had to find her, and all would be well. He would solve all their problems once they were together.

"King Cassius. I require your assistance." Alex strode across the ballroom, ignoring the groups of people. They were nothing to him unless they knew where he could find his love's whereabouts.

"Gladly, Your Majesty." King Cassius gave him a bow as Alex stopped a few feet from him.

King Cassius always had been the most accommodating king. Alex couldn't remember why he had ever thought he disliked the man. Alex held up the glass slipper. "I need to find the girl that fits this shoe."

The smile dropped from King Cassius's face for a moment, and he blinked as if Alex's request had somehow startled him. "Do you possibly know her name or have a description? Surely many girls in my kingdom will fit that shoe."

He didn't know her name. Shouldn't he know her name? That niggling was back in the corner of his mind.

No, why did it matter if he knew her name? Their hearts were linked. "Only my beloved will fit this shoe. I will try it on every fair maiden of your kingdom until I have found her."

A smile returned to King Cassius's face. "Of course, Your Majesty. It shall be done. I will send a company of guards and my seneschal with you. They will see to it that you have my people's full cooperation."

"Thank you." Alex gave King Cassius a nod. Such a good king. Alex would have to make sure King Cassius was rewarded for his loyalty.

"Sire." Jadon strode from the crowd. He glanced at those circling them, then lowered his voice. "What are you doing? This isn't like you."

How dare Jadon question him? Jadon was just a manservant. He shouldn't even be standing here in the ballroom. "I know what I'm doing."

"No, you don't. Don't you understand how this looks? Whatever makes you think it's a good idea to try a shoe on every girl in Pohatomie to find a girl whose name you don't even know?"

"I love her." Alex turned to Jadon. "What do you even

know of love? Surely you've never truly been in love if you have to question why I'm doing this."

Jadon crossed his arms and glared back.

Princess Rosanna stepped to Jadon's side and rested a hand on his arm. "You know that's not true."

King Cassius glanced between them, and his smile grew. "Now this is unexpected. I'd begun to suspect, but to have the princess of Neskahana fall in love with a mere manservant...your parents must be so devastated. He's far beneath you."

"Daemyn's not—" Rosanna glanced up at Jadon and snapped her mouth shut. Jadon was giving her a look, as if begging her not to say anything more.

"Are you truly going to put up with such insubordination, Your Majesty? You are the high king. You shouldn't let your manservant question your decisions." King Cassius's voice was low. An older and wiser king giving his humble advice to his overlord. "Especially not in front of this crowd."

King Cassius was right. How dare Jadon question Alex in front of all these people? And he'd tossed Alex into a fountain the night before, claiming it was for his own good.

Jadon was the one who had been acting strangely. Was he no longer loyal?

"I'm your advisor." Jadon took a step forward and gripped Alex's arm. "Alex—"

How dare Jadon lay a hand on Alex? And call him by his first name, much less a nickname. Alex ripped his arm free from Jadon's grip. That settled it. Jadon needed to be taught a lesson. He couldn't be allowed to step above his station like this. Alex pointed at Jadon. "King Cassius, throw this man in the dungeon immediately."

Chapter 22

Daemyn

For a moment, Daemyn could only stare at Alex. Even when he had been at his most arrogant, Alex had never ordered Daemyn thrown into the dungeons.

Daemyn opened his mouth to protest, to say something—anything—to snap Alex out of this. But he stopped himself. He had been warning Alex for the past three days and nothing he said had reached him.

"Very well." King Cassius motioned to the guards standing behind him. "You heard the high king. Arrest him."

The guards stepped forward. One yanked a long knife from a sheath at his waist while the other brandished a spear.

Rosanna stepped forward as if she planned to intervene somehow. Josiah, with Asa at his heels, also rushed forward.

Daemyn met Rosanna's gaze and shook his head. He

didn't look away until she halted and nodded, though her hands remained clenched.

As the guards grabbed Daemyn's arms and tied his hands, he glanced toward Josiah.

Josiah halted, crossed his arms, but didn't try to interfere. Asa's shoulders sank, but he remained at Josiah's side.

At the far side of the ballroom, Daemyn caught sight of Stefan. He too looked torn about helping. Daemyn gave him a tiny shake of his head and quickly looked away before King Cassius figured out who he had given a signal to. Stefan would be put in a precarious position if King Cassius realized he was distantly related to Daemyn.

Pressure built in Daemyn's chest. He wanted to resist the tightening rope around his wrists. But he couldn't. Not here.

Instead, he faced Alex, then bowed as low as he could with his hands tied behind his back. "Sire."

Without giving Alex a chance to respond, Daemyn straightened and marched toward the door. The guards had to trot to keep up. If there was nothing he could do about being arrested, then he was going to go willingly, meekly.

Just before the ballroom doors, the guards managed to catch up and grab his arms so that they could properly march him into the corridor instead of chasing after their prisoner.

Daemyn tensed, listening for the sound of the ballroom doors closing behind him. As soon as the doors were closed, he'd knock aside these guards and escape. He knew this castle almost as well as those who lived here. Once he was locked in the dungeon, escape would be next to impossible.

Instead of the doors closing, another set of footsteps followed. A sure, confident stride.

"Bring him to the black throne room. I wish to speak with him." King Cassius's voice was crisp. Confident.

Not a good sign.

Daemyn jerked his arm free from one of the guards, then rammed his shoulder into the other, slamming the guard against the wall.

The guard slumped, gasping for breath.

Daemyn took off down the corridor. He just needed to find the nearest servants' staircase, then lose the guards amid the warren of the upper rooms.

"Guards." King Cassius raised his voice, but it wasn't a panicked shout.

More footsteps pounded behind Daemyn. Two more guards rounded the corner ahead of him. With his hands behind his back, he didn't have any way to defend himself.

He dodged a long knife one of the guards was thrusting at him and rammed his shoulder into another guard.

The corridor was too narrow. There were now seven guards surrounding him. He had nowhere left to run.

He tried to dash through an opening between two of them, but one raised his spear and rammed its butt end into Daemyn's stomach.

Daemyn hunched under the blow, struggling to catch his breath. He couldn't give up. If he let them take him, he'd be locked in the dungeon. A dark, small dungeon.

Something smashed into his back, and he went down to his knees, tensing his muscles to prepare for the coming blows. A kick spiked pain along his ribs, and he tumbled onto his side on the floor, unable to stop his fall with his hands tied behind his back.

More kicks. More spear ends thumping into him. Daemyn lashed out when he could, but there wasn't much he could do besides curl into a ball, keep his stomach muscles tensed to protect his internal organs, and take the beating.

He tried to keep his breathing even, concentrating on that instead of the blows and the pain. How many times over the past hundred years had he breathed through the pain and told himself to take it? That seemed to be his lot in life. He'd had to take Alex's orders starting when he was ten. He had to take all his deaths during the hundred years while Alex slept.

Hands dragged him to his feet. Daemyn coughed and tasted blood. He didn't resist as the guard hauled him the rest of the way to the throne room. They forced him to kneel on the black and white granite tiles.

King Cassius strode past him and sank regally onto the silver throne. "It can be a delicate matter to start a war without the blame falling on you. But starting wars is a long-held, family tradition, as you well know. You were there, after all."

Daemyn went still, and it took everything in him not to flinch. Not this again. King Cassius more than suspected. He knew Daemyn's secret. How many times had he been killed after someone said something similar?

And this time, he was no longer indestructible. If King Cassius decided to have him killed to "test" a theory, Daemyn would actually stay dead this time.

His chest ached at that thought. Now that he would stay dead, he didn't want to. He wanted to live this time around. He wanted to grow old naturally and marry Rosanna and raise a family.

He should've let himself relax and truly live these past

three months. He'd been so uncertain, and yet now, none of his hesitation seemed important.

Daemyn needed to talk King Cassius out of ordering him stabbed or gutted or shot or whatever method of death he chose to test his suspicion. "Yes, I'm Jadon Rand. I'm also Daemyn Rand. But that doesn't matter anymore. High King Alexander has woken from his cursed sleep. You have no reason to kill me."

"Don't I? You have caused a great deal of trouble for both Tuckawassee and Pohatomie for the past hundred years. I know a great number of people who would like to see you well and truly dead. I can name at least one major in the Tuckawassee army who would love to kill you yet again." King Cassius leaned back in his silver throne, his golden hair and even more golden crown stark in this room of silver and black.

Daemyn couldn't let King Cassius's words make him flinch, even if they sent a pain far deeper than the aches of his beating.

He didn't want to die. He wanted Rosanna. Children. A life. Something more than endless wandering and gritting his teeth under the orders and rules at Castle Eyota. He wanted smiles and laughter and a joy he wasn't even sure he knew how to feel just yet.

Rosanna's brother Willem had been right. Daemyn shouldn't have held back. He should've loved Rosanna with every breath in his body when he'd had the chance, instead of making her patiently wait for him to get his head and heart sorted out.

Daemyn met King Cassius's gaze and refused to look away. "If you don't want to be blamed for starting a war, you can't kill me. I might not be important, but I have powerful friends who will not take it kindly if you are responsible for my death."

"I know. It is a pity, really. I would like to kill you now. I have a feeling you will be much less trouble dead than alive." King Cassius leaned forward. "But I can't keep my hands clean if I order your death directly. If I simply follow the high king's orders and throw you in my deepest, darkest dungeon, it won't be my fault if you're forgotten there and left to die."

A dark, confined place. Like one of the coal or iron mines of Buckhannock. Daemyn fought to draw in a breath past his constricting chest. He couldn't be locked up in a place like that. Where he couldn't move. Couldn't breathe. Couldn't see the sun and feel the breeze.

King Cassius smiled, as if Daemyn's emotions were playing in his eyes. "It actually doesn't matter if you're dead or alive or even if your friends manage to rescue you. The damage has been done, and it was even better than I had planned. The high king seems determined to make a fool of himself. At this point, the best thing I can do is step out of his way. Even if you could stop Neskahana and Buckhannock from going to war on your behalf, assuming you are important enough to them, the rumors about the high king's foolishness will persist. The seven kingdoms will never be united, and tensions are very profitable for Pohatomie."

"Very profitable for you and a few of your select follow-ers. I didn't see the average citizen of Pohatomie getting rich."

King Cassius waved a hand as if that was a trivial matter. "Exactly. Without the high king, my ancestors and I have been able to raise Pohatomie to a powerful place among the kingdoms. They need us far more than we need them."

"Perhaps. But none of the seven kingdoms are self-sustaining. That's why we need each other." Daemyn shook his head. In their greed, so many of the kings had ignored that fact, even when their kingdoms suffered and the smugglers grew rich while decent folk starved or went without basic goods. "Whether you like it or not, we are all Tallahatchia, and Tallahatchia has always been at its strongest under a high king who sees how each of the diverse kingdoms work together."

"And you believe that boy out there can do that?" King Cassius gave what would have been a snort if he'd been less concerned with appearing regal. "Perhaps, long ago, the high kings reigned like that. But the high kings themselves are greedy, using their position for their own prestige. And who suffers the most when the high king wants to keep everyone happy by lowering the cost of food? Pohatomie. Who is told that we are just the simple farming kingdom with no place of status among the other six kingdoms? Pohatomie. No, I will not let our place among the kingdoms be diminished again."

Could Alex become the high king he needed to be to hold Tallahatchia together? Maybe. Eventually. He had the intelligence, if he learned the wisdom to apply it. He was making progress, both in the last few weeks before his curse and in the months since.

But Alex as he was now? His mind nearly stolen from him by whatever this was. No, this Alex wasn't capable. And it didn't look that promising that Alex had succumbed to this so quickly.

King Cassius smiled. "Even you doubt him. Do you think anyone will stand with him without you at his side?

Neskahana and Buckhannock are only loyal because of you. None of them are loyal because of him."

How strong were the pledges of Neskahana and Buckhannock? Would those kings honor the promises their ancestors made to Alex before his cursed sleep? Rosanna's father had when sending Rosanna to wake Alex, but now that Alex was awake and real instead of a story they could imagine to be greater than he really was?

Daemyn didn't know. And there was nothing he could do about it while tied, beaten, and kneeling before King Cassius.

King Cassius relaxed against his throne. "While this verbal sparring has been entertaining, I have guests to attend to and a high king's mad-cap mission to aid. Guards, take Daemyn Rand to the Pit."

The Pit? Daemyn swallowed, his muscles tense with the urge to fight the guards. But there were too many. It would just result in another beating.

King Cassius's slow smile crossed his face once again. "I think you're going to like the Pit. I've heard it has the ability to make even the toughest man go insane before he dies."

Chapter 23

Elara

Elara gripped her knees, shivering, and rested her head on her arms. Her stomach was hollow, her chest tight. What she wouldn't give for a taste of the warmth she'd felt around that stranger.

What should she do now? She didn't dare return to the castle, not even to slip into her room so she could leave with Baroness Hackett, Monica, and Beatrice in the morning. High King Alexander would turn the castle inside out looking for her.

Terrence would know what to do. He would help get her out of here before High King Alexander thought to turn out the guards to search the nearby forest.

Elara crawled through the underbrush on her hands and knees for several yards. She wasn't ready to push herself onto her injured feet just yet. Branches scraped against her face. Roots dug into her knees, and dirt gritted against her hands.

Was she leaving a trail of blood spatters from her

injured foot? Would Terrence get in trouble for helping her?

She had nowhere else to go. No other friends she could turn to.

And Terrence would tell her to come. He was that good of a friend who would want her coming to him when she was in trouble rather than trying to deal with it on her own.

It would take too long if she crawled the whole way down the hill. Any moment now the high king would have the guards scouring the mountainside. She wasn't sure why they weren't pouring from the castle already. Surely the high king realized she couldn't have gone far.

Unless this curse had taken away that much ability to be logical.

Elara grabbed a sapling and used it to pull herself to her feet. It took everything in her not to scream at the pain tearing through her left foot, the one still trapped in a glass slipper. Her right foot throbbed, and it couldn't be good for her open wounds to have dirt ground into them every time she took a step.

But she had no choice. Her dress wasn't much cleaner, nor did she have anything on her to cut a strip from her hem. Sturdy homespun that she was wearing, it wasn't going to just tear by yanking on it with her hands.

One more step. All she needed to do was take one more step. Then one more.

She wasn't strong enough for this. The walk down the hill to Terrence's shack was too far, her strength too small. Her head already spun. Tears dripped down her face, and she didn't bother to swipe at them.

She tripped, falling to her hands and knees. She couldn't go on. She just couldn't. She was all alone in this forest, and Terrence didn't even know she was in trouble. No one did. The Fallen Fae was right. Elara was just as trapped in this curse as the high king.

She let herself sink the rest of the way to the ground and gave in to the sobs. She had tried, but she wasn't strong enough.

"Miss? I was under orders just to watch, but you look like you need help."

Elara choked on a sob and managed to raise her head.

A shadowed figure moved away from a tree, stepped into the moonlight, then sank into a cross-legged position a few feet away from her. He was carrying a staff in one hand while an unstrung bow and a quiver of arrows peeked above his shoulder. His appearance wasn't doing anything strange in the moonlight, so he wasn't a Fallen Fae. Probably. She didn't exactly trust her own judgment on that.

She scrubbed at the tears on her face, wincing at the gritty feel of her fingers. "Who are you? What do you mean, you're under orders? Whose orders?"

The young man eyed her, but he didn't move from his seated position, though he remained tense. "I'm Ezekiel Rand. And I reckon you're the person I'm supposed to be looking for."

Looking for her? Who else was after her? Elara pushed upright, but she didn't try to get to her feet. She was in no shape to run from him.

Rand. Why did that name sound familiar? She squeezed her eyes shut, trying to get her mind to cooperate. Her mouth was dry, her head dizzy. She concentrated on taking deep breaths to keep from fainting.

Rand. Daemyn Rand. That's where she'd heard the

name earlier tonight. He'd also said he was looking for her. "Are you related to Daemyn Rand?"

"Yes." Ezekiel didn't move, but he went tense, his fingers tightening on the staff. "Why?"

"I met him tonight." Elara pulled up her knees to her chest. She should have listened to his warning. She should have stayed away from High King Alexander. Instead, she'd made everything worse.

Daemyn Rand said he was just High King Alexander's manservant. But servants often knew more about what was going on than they let on. They tended to have connections. And this Daemyn was cautious enough to have a relative stationed outside the castle watching for her.

How much had Ezekiel seen? Had he seen the Fallen Fae? Did he know about the curse? "How did you figure out I'm the one he told you to look for?"

Ezekiel's gaze remained steady. "I was to watch for something strange, and I'd say it's a heap shifty to see a black-haired, curly-haired girl in a green dress come racing down the causeway chased by the high king, hunker in the bushes, and appear later with blonde hair and wearing homespun. It was a mighty convincing transformation, I'll give you that. In the moonlight, it even looked like some of your facial features changed."

Elara hadn't changed her hair color. And her dress had been black and burgundy.

But Ezekiel wasn't the first person to describe her differently than she saw herself in the mirror. This was a Fallen Fae's handiwork she was dealing with. All of it was deception. Even the truths the Fallen Fae had told her had been meant to deceive.

Was it true that the curse would be permanent if High King Alexander put the other shoe back on Elara's foot?

She wasn't sure what was truth or a lie or a truth twisted into a deception anymore.

She couldn't risk it. That had seemed more like a taunt to remind Elara of her helplessness than an attempt to deceive her. But surely it wasn't the whole truth. Just enough of the truth to turn it into a shadow of itself.

Was there any way to stop it? Elara needed to get out of here, and she needed to get to Terrence.

Would Ezekiel let her go? If he was anything like Daemyn Rand, then he was suspicious of her. She had been tricked, but she hadn't been exactly innocent in this. She'd willingly taken those glass slippers. She'd gone to this third ball knowing what it would do to High King Alexander.

She straightened her shoulders. If she was at fault, then she should be the one to fix it. Somehow. "I didn't mean for any of this to happen. Not like this. I know you don't believe me. But trust me. I need to get out of here before High King Alexander comes looking for me. Really, really bad things are going to happen if he finds me. I have a friend. The king's buffalo boy. I need to get to him."

"And if I let you go to him, will you tell me the full truth of what is going on?" Ezekiel's gaze had that same unwavering steadiness as his relative Daemyn. It was disconcerting, even in the haziness of the moonlight.

Should she tell him? She had planned to tell Terrence but he was the king's buffalo boy. He didn't have too many more options than she did.

But Daemyn Rand had seemed like someone who thought he had the ability to affect what was going on. If anyone knew of a way to fix this, he would.

Besides, who else did Elara have to trust? She had to trust someone with the truth before it was too late for herself and for High King Alexander. She wasn't going to trust King Cassius. He would be overjoyed at this situation.

Elara drew in a deep breath and nodded. "I'll tell you and Terrence the truth together."

"All right, then. Let's go." Ezekiel leapt to his feet and held out a hand to her.

She braced herself for the rush of agony and let him pull her to her feet.

It wasn't enough. Pain clawed deep, and she cried out, dropping back to her knees. She'd thought she could push through for just a few more steps, but she was done. She simply couldn't go any farther.

"Are you all right?" Ezekiel knelt in front of her, his eyes flicking over her until his gaze dropped to her feet. "You're injured. Why didn't you say something?"

It hadn't occurred to her that he couldn't see her foot bleeding in the shadows cast by the trees around them. She grimaced and didn't hold back the tart reply. "You just assumed I'd thrown myself to the ground to sob my heart out due to some overwhelming emotional trauma?"

"Um, kind of. It sure as shooting appeared that way from a distance." Ezekiel held out the wooden staff. "Hold this."

She grabbed it by reflex, holding it out of the way as Ezekiel put one arm beneath her knees, the other behind her back, and hefted her from the ground. Being carried wasn't the most comfortable position to start with, and it was even more awkward when she was pressed up against some stranger's chest.

At least he looked about as stiff and uncomfortable as she felt. "Where to, miss?"

She gestured with the staff, nearly whacking Ezekiel's

head. "Down the hill in that direction. There's a shack behind the barn. That's where Terrence lives."

Ezekiel heaved her a little higher and set out down the slope. Elara had to grab the front of his shirt to keep herself steady and concentrated on not crying out when he accidentally jostled her. Thankfully, Ezekiel didn't talk. This was awkward enough without adding small talk.

He carried her toward the barn, then followed her directions around back to where Terrence's shack had been built against the barn, as if he was just another one of the animals, and not a very important one at that. Terrence had never seemed to mind, though.

The shack was dark. He probably slept. She would've felt bad waking him, but she was desperate.

Ezekiel stopped, and Elara thumped the door with the wooden staff.

"Do you reckon he's home?" Ezekiel shifted his grip on her.

"He should be. I didn't see him in the corral with the elk and buffalo, and that's the only other place he goes." Elara thunked the staff against the door, harder this time.

A light flickered to life. A soft thumping, then Terrence's voice, "I'm coming."

The door opened, and Terrence stood there, holding a candle. His dark blond hair was tousled, his trousers and shirt rumpled. He was barefoot. "What do you...Elara? What happened?"

"It's a long story. Can we come in?" Elara tucked her feet against Ezekiel. Hopefully Terrence wouldn't notice the blood until after they were inside. She didn't want to have to explain right that minute.

Terrence glanced from her to Ezekiel Rand, and something in his expression cooled, though Elara couldn't guess why. He stepped back and held the door open. "Of course."

Ezekiel turned so he could stick her head inside the door first before easing her feet in next. At least he was taking care not to bash her feet against the door posts. That was more care than she would've expected from a stranger.

As soon as he got inside, Ezekiel set her down on the nearest chair. The shack was so small the kitchen table with two chairs on either end took up most of the room. Terrence's bed, complete with rumpled blankets, ran the length of one wall while the fireplace filled the other end.

Terrence shut the door, then worked his way between the wall and the table until he could reach the lamp. While he opened one of the glass doors and stuck the candle inside to light the lamp's wick, he glanced between Elara and Ezekiel again. "Elara, what's going on? Who's he?"

Ezekiel leaned against the wall beside the door, gripping the wooden staff once again. He didn't seem inclined to answer for himself, so Elara sighed and turned back to Terrence. "He's Ezekiel Rand. He found me in the woods as I was trying to get here. I need help."

She pulled back her skirt and stuck out her right foot, showing him the still bleeding gashes that stretched along the sides and sole of her foot.

Terrence nearly fumbled the candle as he hastily set it on the table next to the lamp. "What happened?"

Elara stuck out her left foot. The glass was tinted blood red everywhere except the glinting, spiked heel. "You were right about the glass slippers. They weren't a gift. They were a curse."

Terrence knelt in front of her and gently picked up her right foot. "I'll let you explain in a minute, but first, this needs tending. Are you feeling lightheaded?"

"A little." Elara slumped against the back of the chair. She was safe here. Terrence would know what to do, and he'd help her.

Terrence raised his head to peer past her. "Ezekiel. That's what you said your name was? Could you fetch a bucket of fresh water? There's a well to the side of the barn."

"Call me Zeke." Ezekiel pushed away from the wall, hesitated, then produced a small pack. After digging around for a moment, he held out a metal flask. "Here. It's a stiff moonshine for cleaning that wound. It'll hurt worse than fire, but it's better than infection."

"Thanks." Terrence took the flask. "While you're out, could you also fetch the bandages from the barn? They're on a shelf just inside the doors. I don't keep much for medical supplies in here."

Zeke nodded and went outside, leaving the wooden staff leaning against the wall in his place.

Elara sank lower in the chair so she could rest her head against the back. "Kind of surprising you don't have supplies in here. You're always getting hurt."

"The barn is closer when I'm with the animals. Besides, I need to keep bandages and liniment on hand if they get hurt. They're more important than I am." Terrence's mouth twitched with a small smile, though it faded as he looked down at her foot. A lock of his hair fell across his forehead, reminding Elara of when they were both younger.

Things had been so much simpler then. She and Terrence had played for hours whenever her father traveled to the castle as Baron Hackett's guard. Those had been some of the best days of her childhood.

She closed her eyes as Terrence built a fire in the fireplace. As it had been so warm lately, he must've allowed the fire to go out and had probably been eating cold meals rather than heating up the shack.

Once he had a fire going, he set out a basin and a few cloths.

The door opened, and Zeke stepped inside, carrying a bucket of water in one hand and a stack of white linen bandages in the other. He nudged the door shut behind him with a foot.

"There's a kettle by the fire." Terrence knelt in front of Elara, set a basin beneath her foot, and uncapped the flask. "I...um..."

While Zeke crossed the room and poured the water into the kettle, Elara stuck out her foot. This wasn't a time to be awkward. "Please, don't worry about it."

Terrence grasped her ankle with one hand and poured the moonshine over her foot.

Elara yelped and yanked her foot free of his grasp, more by reflex than conscious thought. The moonshine continued to stab into the wounds, even after he'd stopped pouring.

Zeke sighed and joined Terrence kneeling on the floor. "I apologize for this, miss."

Elara gripped the seat of the chair and nodded, though the movement sent the room spinning.

Zeke leaned an elbow on her knee and grasped her ankle with an iron grip. With his mouth pressed in a line, Terrence poured the moonshine over her foot again.

"Ow! Ow! Ow!" Elara jerked, but Zeke pinned her down.

"There. All done." Terrence set the flask aside and clambered to his feet.

Zeke's grip relaxed, but he didn't let go. Elara couldn't

figure out why until Terrence returned and poured steaming water from the kettle into the bowl that had caught the moonshine dripping from her foot.

Elara gritted her teeth and squeezed her eyes shut. This torture wasn't over yet.

Zeke's grip clamped on her ankle again. "Scrub all the dirt from those gashes. It ain't going to help her none if those wounds ain't clean."

Elara braced herself as water splashed and dripped. Terrence must be getting one of the rags wet.

Warm, wet cloth touched her foot. It stung but didn't hurt as much as the straight moonshine had.

Until the cloth started scrubbing hard and firm against the tender, raw gashes.

"Owww! Ow! Stop!" Elara jerked, but Zeke wouldn't let her go. She bolted upright. She had to make them stop.

Spots danced in front of her eyes. The room swirled. She would...

SOMETHING cold and wet splashed her face, somewhat soothing. But then the cold water splashed her neck.

Elara yelped and opened her eyes.

Terrence was leaning over her, a dripping rag in one hand. Zeke, the firelight reflecting in his brown hair, peered over Terrence's shoulder.

Elara blinked up at them. She was lying down, and the thing beneath her was too soft to be the floor.

She was tucked into Terrence's bed, his blankets drawn over her and his pillow soft beneath her head.

Terrence let out a breath and sank back on his heels. "You're awake. Good. I was getting worried."

"What happened?" Elara thought about pushing onto her elbows, but it was rather comfortable to lie there. Her left foot still stabbed with pain, but her right foot felt better. Still throbbing. But a better sort of throbbing than before.

"You passed out." Zeke stepped back. "Blood loss and pain, probably."

"Zeke managed to catch you, so you didn't hit your head." Terrence twisted the damp rag in his hands. "At least we were able to finish cleaning and bandaging your foot while you were out."

"How long?" Elara peered past them into the room. It was still hazy with darkness, lit only by the lamp and the candle. The strip around the door still showed dark, so it must be still night. Still, it was hard to tell in Terrence's windowless shack.

"Quarter of an hour, at most." Terrence stood, but continued to twist the rag in his hands. "The glass slipper still won't come off."

"Thanks for trying. I'm not even sure why the other one came off. It just sort of happened." Elara would've liked to continue to lie there, but if it had only been a few minutes, then maybe there was still time. She needed to explain what was going on and hope they could figure out a plan. She tried to push onto her elbows, but her head spun again.

Terrence was at her side in a moment, supporting her back. "Are you sure you should try to sit up?"

"I don't want to be lying down while I explain." Elara gripped his shoulder and used him to pull herself upright. He was nicely solid. The steady presence she'd always had in her life, even as she'd lost her parents, and he'd lost his.

"Let me prop you against the headboard at least."

Terrence tugged at the pillow, then helped her scoot back until she could rest her back against the bed's headboard. He tugged one of the folded blankets from the end of the bed and propped it behind her as well, giving her somewhere soft to rest her head.

"This will help." Zeke held out a tin cup filled with water. "I have experience with injuries and blood loss."

"Thanks." Elara took the cup and sipped. The cold water soothed her tongue and eased her throat. Another sip, and the muddiness in her head cleared somewhat.

Terrence pulled one of the two chairs next to the bed. "When you're ready, can you tell us what happened?"

It would have been so much easier to put off the telling. But she'd already lost so much time as they'd tended her foot. If she were to do the right thing and warn someone about the curse, she couldn't put it off any longer.

Elara started at the beginning, explaining how she'd gotten the glass slippers and what the Fallen Fae had said. Looking back now, it was easy to see how the Fallen Fae had told Elara exactly what she'd wanted to hear.

She mentioned how wonderful that first night was, though she kept that part short, and spent more time making sure she repeated everything King Cassius had said. He had warned her not to tell anyone of his plot, but at this point, Elara wanted to hold nothing back from Terrence. And this seemed like information Zeke should know if he and the high king's manservant were going to do anything to help High King Alexander.

Zeke's jaw tightened as she talked, but he didn't interrupt. At least both he and Terrence seemed to understand that she needed to get through this explanation before they started asking questions.

She told the second ball in a rush and explained

meeting the Fallen Fae again and realizing what would happen if she went to the third ball.

"And you still went?" Zeke halted long enough to glare at her before he began pacing across the small space alongside the table once again.

Elara looked to Terrence. Surely he would understand. Or at least, wouldn't condemn her.

Terrence reached out, as if to pat her shoulder, but drew his hand back. "It's all right. Keep going."

Elara couldn't keep going. Not with the lump that was filling her throat. Had she ever told Terrence how much his friendship meant to her? Even now, when she'd messed up more than she'd ever thought possible, he wasn't turning her away.

She cleared her throat. She couldn't dwell on that now. She had yet to tell them the most important part.

It was too embarrassing to admit the full truth of why she'd gone to the ball tonight. She wasn't ready to admit that she'd gone simply because she'd cared more about becoming a baroness than what was the right thing to do. Terrence's gaze didn't waver, but Zeke's glare said he'd picked up on her motivations even with her attempts to gloss over them.

But his glare disappeared as she mentioned the stranger she'd met briefly on the castle's causeway. Terrence, too, straightened, his eyes widening.

"And then I went to start running again, and the glass slipper just came off." Elara shrugged and stared down at her hands. "I don't understand why."

"The Highest Prince." Terrence whispered the name and met her gaze. "The Cursebreaker."

And this was a curse.

The curses the nobility were given at birth always had a

cursebreaker. It was meant to symbolize the Cursebreaker. Did that mean this curse too could be broken?

Perhaps there was a way to escape this curse and the glass slippers. This was the truth the Fallen Fae hadn't told Elara, wanting her to despair.

But there was hope. There was the Cursebreaker.

"Then High King Alexander was there, and I kept running. I hid until he was gone, but then..." Elara swallowed. No turning back from the explanation now. "That Fallen Fae came back and told me the curse wasn't broken. Just delayed. If High King Alexander manages to find me to put the other glass slipper back on my foot, the curse will become permanent. On him and on me. I'll never be able to take the slippers off, and he'll be cursed to be madly infatuated forever."

Elara stared at her hands, waiting for their response. Laying out the last few days like that, it didn't put her in a favorable light. She had gotten them into this mess by taking the glass slippers, and she wasn't sure what she could do to fix it.

When she looked up, Zeke was heading to the door. He grabbed the wooden staff. "I need to warn—"

Footsteps crunched outside, then the door rattled under a firm knock. "Buffalo boy! Open up! I have orders from the king."

Elara stiffened. Had they managed to track her here already? Surely it was too dark outside to notice the blood trail she might have left. Would they notice Zeke's tracks where he carried her?

Zeke pressed himself between the wall and the door so that when the door opened, he would be hidden behind it. When neither Elara nor Terrence moved, Zeke motioned, though Elara wasn't sure what he wanted them to do.

As the door thumped again, Terrence jumped to his feet. He glanced at Elara, then around at the room, before he made his way to the door. He opened it only a few inches, which blocked Elara from view with the door and with his body. "What is it?"

She winced. What if the guards insisted on searching the shack? There wasn't a good way to go about explaining this.

"King Cassius requests you ready the elk cart immediately." A deep, male voice said from outside the door. It sounded somewhat familiar. One of the castle guards, perhaps? "It seems the high king wants to leave in the middle of the night to go off and search for this girl that supposedly fits in this glass shoe he found. Gone off his rocker, if you ask me, but what can our king do but give him what he wants. He's the high king, after all. A pretty worthless one, but that's how it is."

"I see. I'll see to it right away. Will the high king need me to drive the elk cart? You know how touchy they are about a new hand on the reins." Terrence was all poise, as if he didn't have the very girl the high king was searching for in his room.

"I'd assume so. I'd pack a bag for several days, if I were you. The high king seems downright set on this. Had his own manservant thrown in the dungeon when he tried to talk sense into him."

Behind the door, Zeke stiffened, his grip whitening on the wooden staff.

"I see. Let His Majesty King Cassius and the high king know that I will have the elk ready in half an hour." Terrence ducked his head, then shut the door.

For a minute, none of them moved while they listened

to the crunch of boots on dirt until the sound faded into the night.

When another few moments passed with no more sounds from outside, Zeke stepped from his corner. "All right. Here's the plan. Terrence, you're going to go with High King Alexander. Do your best to keep him from doing anything foolish and keep him away from here as best you can. I'm going to sneak into Castle Fonthaven and see about rescuing Uncle Daemyn and passing the information about the curse to my friends there."

Uncle Daemyn? The Daemyn Rand Elara had met in the castle hadn't looked old enough to be Zeke's uncle. But big families had a way of making the generations go a little wonky. And she'd gotten the impression that the Rand family was a big one.

"And you." Zeke turned to Elara. "You're going to hide here until my friends and I come back for you. We can get you out of Pohatomie and hide you from High King Alexander while we figure out what will break this curse."

"What if you're caught sneaking into Castle Fonthaven? Or trying to rescue your relative? Or sneaking back out?" Elara gripped the blanket spread over her tighter. "I can barely walk on my own now. And King Cassius isn't going to let you just waltz into the dungeon."

"Stay here for as long as you can, then see if you've rested enough to try to make it to the border with Buckhannock. Do you have any friends who can help you?" Zeke rubbed the staff, shifting his feet toward the door as if he was itching to be on his way.

Did she have any other friends besides Terrence? She'd never bothered to make friends with the other servants. She'd spent too much time internally disdaining Monica and Beatrice to salvage the friendship that they'd had as children.

Would the baroness help her? Elara couldn't be sure. Baroness Hackett was loyal to King Cassius, mostly. But she hadn't been thrilled about King Cassius's plan to use Monica to trap High King Alexander.

Baroness Hackett might not help her, but Monica would. Could Elara consider Monica a friend? And did Monica see Elara as a friend in return? She had always called her a friend, but that was an easy thing to say to a servant. It would be less easy to say if that same servant came begging for help hiding from both King Cassius and High King Alexander. It would be treason against two kings.

"Maybe." Elara couldn't look at either of them. Was she really this alone in the world? She'd never felt terribly alone, probably because she'd been too focused on her ambition to one day become wealthy to care if she didn't have any other friends besides Terrence.

"Good. I have a castle wall to scale before daylight." Zeke didn't even glance in their direction as he yanked the door open and disappeared into the night, shutting the door firmly behind him.

Terrence stared a moment before he shook himself and glanced at Elara. "Um, well, I need to pack. And go. Sorry about leaving you here alone."

Elara gestured. "I understand. Really." And it was probably less awkward being left here alone than if he'd stayed with her. Terrence was her closest, oldest, dearest, and, well, only friend, but it did seem a little weird to hide out in his shack just the two of them. When they'd been children, she wouldn't have thought anything of it. But now, being adults complicated things.

Terrence nodded, reached under the bed, and pulled out a leather bag. Walking to a chest of drawers, he began stuffing clothes into it. "There's plenty of dried meat and a fresh loaf of bread in the cupboard. You should have enough food to last for a few days, at least. I'll leave a fresh bucket of water so you won't need to go outside except to sneak to the privy. There shouldn't be anyone around. No one but you ever comes to the barn except the occasional guard with orders from the king, and they won't have any reason to be here knowing I'm gone."

"I'll be fine, Terrence. Don't worry about me." Elara leaned against the blanket he'd propped behind her. "Worry about yourself. It's not going to be easy trying to keep the high king from doing anything too crazy. He was spouting horrible poetry about my nose earlier tonight. Whatever this curse is doing to his brain, he isn't thinking clearly."

Terrence nodded, then paused with his leather bag gripped in his hand. "Are you going to be all right, Elara? We barely know Zeke Rand, much less his friends. How do we know we can trust them to look after you?"

Elara let out a long breath. How did they know they could trust Zeke? He had helped her. But as she was learning, everyone had an agenda. Everyone deceived for their own ends.

"I'm not sure he has my best interests in mind, but I think he's loyal to the high king. At least, his uncle is the high king's manservant. That has to count for something." Elara rubbed her fingers against the blanket. It was an even more rough homespun than her dress. "I'm not sure I have a choice but to trust him. I can't stay here. Either King Cassius or High King Alexander would find me."

Terrence swallowed and stared down at the bag in his

hand. "If you leave, we might never see each other again. You'll flee the country. Who knows how long you'll have to stay in hiding? Last time, it took a hundred years to end the cursed sleep. How long will it take to break this curse? It might never be broken."

Elara stilled. It hadn't even occurred to her that her exile could last that long. She hadn't thought beyond getting away.

Could she do it? Leave everyone and everything she'd ever known and put her trust in strangers to protect her? Was that what her life had become? Instead of becoming a baroness, she would lose everything.

Did she have to lose everything? Yes, she'd made mistakes. She'd taken the glass slippers. But was it fair that she would have to give up everything and leave?

Perhaps there was a way she could stay. Elara let the plan unfold in her mind. It was worth a try. "I'm going to stay here tonight, but tomorrow I'll watch for Baroness Hackett to leave, and I'll go home with her. Monica will hide me, if necessary. The high king can't stay in Pohatomie searching for me forever. Perhaps you could even plant the idea in his head that I've fled the kingdom. He will move on, and I'll be safe to remain here."

"King Cassius still knows who you are and where you live." Terrence met her gaze, and he didn't sound like he was trying to talk her out of her plan. More like he didn't dare hope it could work.

"Yes, but he got what he wanted. Everyone is already talking about how High King Alexander is a few acorns short of an oak tree. There's nothing else he could want out of me." Elara sat straighter. This could work. She wouldn't have to leave.

"All right." Terrence looped the strap for the leather

bag over his shoulder. After blowing out both the lamp and the candle, he headed for the door. In the doorway, he paused, nothing but a silhouette outlined by moonlight. "I'll do my best to keep High King Alexander away from Hackettsville. Stay safe, Elara."

"You too." Elara managed to call out just before he shut the door, leaving her in the darkness of his tiny shack.

She wiggled deeper into the blankets, wincing each time she moved her feet, and lay down. The pillow smelled of Terrence, a mix of the musty smell of elk and buffalo and the soap sold in Fonthaven.

For a moment, she was tempted to cry again. But she'd done enough crying that night already.

Would this plan work? Or was she cursed to the pain of wearing the glass slippers for the rest of her life?

CHAPTER 24

DAEMYN

It was a darkness so complete he wasn't entirely sure he was awake. Perhaps this was a nightmare, and all he had to do was blink and he'd be free of it.

Daemyn squeezed his eyes shut and tried to take a deep breath. His ribs burned. Definitely bruised. Maybe hairline cracked. Hopefully none were broken all the way through.

His wrists and arms hurt, and it took him a moment to realize his hands were chained above his head with his whole weight dangling on his arms.

Gathering his strength, he tried to get his feet underneath him to relieve the pressure. But he could only touch the floor when standing on his toes, and even then he couldn't take all the pressure from his wrists.

Even apart from the ache of his weight hanging from his arms, places all along his arms, legs, back, chest, and face throbbed from the second beating the guards had given him after hauling him from the throne room to the dungeon. He tasted blood and smelled it when he dragged a breath through his aching nose.

Were his eyes swollen shut? Was that why it was so dark? It felt like he had his eyes open, but he couldn't see even a hazy outline of a wall or a door.

How small was this cell? His breath caught in his chest.

No, he couldn't think about it. It couldn't be that small. Perhaps it was huge and that's why he couldn't see the walls.

He leaned back. His shoulder blades struck cold stone right away. Leaning, his right shoulder brushed a wall. When he shifted the other way, his left shoulder struck the wall. Kicking out, his toe bumped the wall facing him before he'd even had a chance to gain momentum for his kick.

His heart pulsed louder in his ears. His breathing came harder, faster.

He was in a cell barely big enough for him to fit inside. The ventilation shafts for the Buckhannock mines were bigger than this.

Not that Daemyn had ever crawled into one of them, even as a child. He didn't—couldn't—do tight, dark spaces.

This was the Pit. The place where people were forgotten. Abandoned to die.

The walls were growing tighter, narrower. He could feel the press of stone, the weight of it on his chest.

He had to get out. Now. He needed light and space to move. Not darkness. Not this confining, suffocating hole.

He wrapped his hand around the chain and tried to pull himself up. He could raise himself a few inches, but he couldn't twist his other arm enough to get a good grip on the chain.

He tried to bring his knee up to wedge himself with his back against the wall and his feet against the other. But he couldn't maneuver his knee high enough. His feet slipped against the smooth stone.

He was trapped. He couldn't climb his way out. He couldn't move. He couldn't even take the weight from his hands and arms.

Darkness. Stone. Pressing. Harder. Tighter.

His breaths were hot and clinging in front of his face. How much air was in here? Was he suffocating already?

He had to get out. He shoved against the stone, yanked on the chains. Kicked. Clawed.

His breathing was faster. Raw and sharp in his throat. Pulsing louder in his ears.

Darkness. Stone. Pressing. Tight. Tight. Tight.

He couldn't breathe. Couldn't move. Too tight.

Out. *Out*. Now. He needed out.

He was eight, standing at the edge of a mine in Buckhannock, his father's hand firm on his shoulder. He'd wanted to dig in his heels. It was dark in there. Too much stone before him. Around him. Over him.

The light from the entrance faded and snuffed out entirely as they turned a corner and went deeper in. The earth itself swallowing them whole.

"Someday you'll work here." His father's voice was deep, booming in the depths of the mine. "We're miners, Jadon. We know the earth. We might be poor, and it's a humble job, but with the strength of your two hands, you can provide for your family, and there is honor in that. Before honor is humility."

The earth was pressing down on him. It was as if the weight of all the layers of rock and dirt above him sat on his chest. He was shaking. "I can't."

His father knelt in front of him. So strong, the muscles in his arms thick from wielding a pick ax against the solid rock. "There ain't nothing to be scared of down here."

He trembled, his breathing faster and faster. He tore from his father's grip and raced for the mine entrance, tumbling into the sunlight choking and crying.

He'd cried again at nine when that earth his father hadn't feared had swallowed him, spitting out his broken, barely living body. Then there had been weeks, months, of healing. None of it had truly been enough.

As the oldest, it was his job to provide. His job to take his father's place in those mines and scrape out a living.

He just couldn't do it. The darkness. The stone walls crushing him.

Then a royal messenger had arrived on their doorstep. The high prince had chosen him out of all the boys born on the high prince's birthday to serve as his manservant, should he and his parents accept the honor.

They hadn't wanted him to go. Perhaps his mother would have stood firm if she had been less desperate between trying to raise six children and nurse their father back to health.

He'd gone. And every night that first year as he cried himself to sleep for homesickness, he'd told himself it was better than the mines. Every taunting word from another servant about his mountain speech or his backward ways or his uselessness as a servant had been better than facing the darkness below. He'd endured Castle Eyota, endured High Prince Alexander, because he'd no other choice.

There had been times, during the hundred years, when he'd fought until death because dying at the end of some Tuckawassee long knife or arrow was better than being thrown in their dungeon.

And still he'd ended up here. This was death the way death was feared. Darkness. Abandoned. Alone.

Daemyn slumped against the chains holding him, shaking. Something wet was drooling down his arms, and he smelled blood. His wrists throbbed. As did his knees and toes from trying to fight the stone walls.

How long had he been down there? Hours? Minutes? Seconds?

He needed to get a hold of himself. Losing himself in the past, in panic, wasn't going to help his situation.

Easier said than done. The darkness was breathing down the back of his neck, wrapping fingers around his throat, smothering his mouth, sending flashes of imagined light spearing across his eyes.

He drew in as deep a breath as he could manage and let it out slowly. Another deep breath. Another slow exhale. Until his shaking was more a tremble than a shudder and his pulse had calmed from a thunder down to a drum beat.

The darkness around him was making him think of death, but this was not his death. He had died—well, mostly died—nine times. He had never fully, truly died because then the Highest Prince would've opened the door in the WaterVeil, and Daemyn would've entered Beyond in an instant, so quickly he wouldn't have even noticed the dirt of his former life being swept away on the threshold.

All those times over the hundred years, Daemyn had glimpsed what his final, true death would be. Not darkness. Not utterly forsaken.

But a door flung wide open. A beckoning hand taking him through. A light welcoming him with warmth.

Light. Daemyn squeezed his eyes shut, as if the darkness behind his eyelids could somehow shut out the intense darkness of this pit. He remembered light. Not the weak light of the sun or the cold light of the moon.

But *light*. Found only in the throne room of the Lord of All with the Highest Prince's declaration of *mine* still ringing in the breeze, giving him entrance.

That was Daemyn's end. Whether he escaped or was rescued or spent the last days of his life in this forsaken, black pit. It would not last forever. He would step from this darkness into that light.

A hint of coolness brushed his face. No more than a wisp of a draft, perhaps imagined more than real. But it carried memories of a turquoise pool, a forest of jeweled trees, and a song in a language unknown.

He leaned against the wall, easing some of the pressure from his arms. But he didn't open his eyes. If he kept his eyes closed, perhaps he would remember light instead of being crushed by the stone around him.

There was no escape for him. He had to come to terms with that. Not on his own. He couldn't move enough to climb the chain that bound his hands, nor could he lift his feet high enough to push himself up the tight shaft. The walls were too sheer for him to even dig his toes in and give his arms a rest.

Even if he managed to climb the shaft, what then? There must be some solid stone or iron trap door barred above him. Nothing he could open from the inside.

He was truly and helplessly trapped.

In the stories told around campfires, the hero was never trapped. He always found a way out. Being helpless was portrayed as pathetic. Weak.

Daemyn knew better. There were times people couldn't rescue themselves. When the only option left was to wait for rescue.

Waiting had its own kind of battle against fear and panic and despair. There was no shame in that.

He couldn't depend on Alex to come to his senses and order King Cassius to release him. Daemyn didn't know what had happened to Alex, but he wasn't thinking like himself.

At least, he hoped not. He didn't think Alex would send him to this pit on purpose.

He had to trust that Rosanna, Zeke, Isi, Josiah, and Asa would rescue him. He had to either believe that or start preparing himself to die down here.

Would they be able to rescue him? He had shown Rosanna the back way into the dungeon on their first day here. Would she be able to lead the others through the winding maze that was Castle Fonthaven to get to the tallest tower?

King Cassius would be alert for them to try something. He would have all entrances to the dungeon guarded. Would he think to guard that one too?

Should they even try a rescue? It might be what King Cassius was hoping. After all, it wouldn't be good politically if a princess of Neskahana and a prince of Buckhannock were caught breaking into Pohatomie's dungeon to rescue a prisoner the high king had ordered thrown in there.

It could even be the spark that set off the war.

Almost he wished he had a way to tell them not to even try. To leave him down there because the risk to them and to Tallahatchia was too great. He wasn't worth starting a war.

Almost. Because he didn't want to die in this pit.

No, he didn't want to die at all.

He wanted to live. Not just the pretense of life that so

much of the past hundred years had turned into. He'd been so focused on pretending to be what everyone expected him to be. Pretend to be the perfect manservant. Pretend to be his own son after killing off a previous name and version of himself. Sometimes he was pretending to be forty years old. Sometimes seventeen. Until somewhere along the way, he'd forgotten how to simply *be*.

Be Daemyn Rand. Be the man who loved Rosanna and loved all his many nieces and nephews across the country. Be someone who remembered how to laugh and smile and relax without worrying whether he was acting too much like a former version of himself. Be a man who lived the way the Highest King commanded.

If he ever got out of this pit, he was going to stop holding back. Stop pretending and start living. Embrace this life he'd been given and live it wholeheartedly.

And he was going to stop seeing the hundred years of not aging as a burden he'd had to endure. Yes, it had been hard. But it had also been a gift. It had given him a hundred years' worth of experience, yet he still had the sharpness and energy of a twenty-one-year-old mind and body.

If he'd been as wise as he'd thought he was, then he would have treated life as short and time as fleeting. Of all people, he should know just how fast a hundred years could fly by. Instead, he'd been like every other young man, seeing time as something he had in abundance.

Yes, he was just like every other young man. Fumbling through a romantic relationship and just trying to figure out who he was and where he belonged in life.

Rosanna's brothers had been right. Time was a gift from the Highest King, and Daemyn needed to stop wasting it.

DAEMYN SHOOK and struggled to catch his breath. How many panicked bouts had he fought off now? He couldn't remember. If he'd ever thought being forced to face his irrational fear of tight, dark spaces would cure the panic, he'd been wrong. So very wrong.

Sweat trickled between his shoulder blades, down his spine, and along his face and neck. His hands had long since grown numb, and his shoulders had gone from screaming in agony to a pain too intense to even register. The back of his throat stabbed from thirst and shouting.

He needed to keep a hold on himself. Rosanna was going to rescue him. And when she did, he couldn't have her find him wild with panic and clawing pathetically at the walls. He needed to be calm. Calm. Ignore the walls smothering him. Ignore the way his eyes were dancing with lights and colors that weren't really there thanks to the oppressive darkness.

Was that voices he heard? The tromping of footsteps?

He tried to still his breathing and his heart enough to listen. There was a faint rattle and the creak of rusted hinges.

Was it there? Or just another hallucination? It could be nothing but his mind playing yet another trick on him.

Or it could be Rosanna searching the dungeon for him. Would she think to look here? Daemyn didn't know what this Pit looked like from the outside, but it might be nothing more than another stone in the floor or a tiny, iron square.

Gathering his strength, he stood on his tiptoes and shook his arms, rattling the chain and striking it several times against the stone walls. "In here! Rosanna! Zeke! In here!"

His voice felt both loud and oddly muffled inside this shaft. Could anyone even hear him on the outside? Or was his voice as trapped inside this suffocating prison as he was?

Iron grated on iron, far closer than anything he'd heard or imagined he'd heard before. This sound had to be real. Was it Rosanna? Or a soldier King Cassius had sent to make sure Daemyn was still in the pit?

"In here!" Daemyn rattled the chain again. Even if it was one of King Cassius's soldiers, Daemyn would endure any taunting or further torture if it meant he would get a glimpse of light, even torchlight.

Voices, louder now, though still too indistinct for him to recognize the words or the people who were doing the talking.

A squeak and groan of iron came from above him. An outline of orange light appeared around a hatch several feet above his hands. With a grating sound, the hatch opened the rest of the way and torchlight poured into the shaft.

Daemyn blinked up at it, unwilling to look away even to give his eyes a chance to adjust.

The torch was held directly over the shaft, then partially blocked by a head. A long black braid fell over her shoulder as she peered down into dungeon pit.

Daemyn wasn't sure if he wanted to laugh or just sag against the wall. All he knew was that he didn't want to hold back anymore, and that's probably why he found himself smiling—or as much as he could smile with his bottom lip swollen and his cheek puffy with a bruise. "Are you here to rescue me, Princess?"

Rosanna let out a sound that was a strangled mix of a sigh and a laugh. "You do look like you're in distress."

As Daemyn's eyes adjusted, he could make out Zeke peering over Rosanna's shoulder. The chain attached to the manacles on Daemyn's wrists ran the length of the shaft and disappeared through a hole in the iron hatch. It must be attached to a crank to either raise or lower the person in the pit.

Zeke shook his head as he knelt across the hole from Rosanna. "How did they even get you in there? It ain't near big enough to squish you inside."

Daemyn grimaced and shifted as much as he could at the end of the chain. "I don't know. I was unconscious for that part."

Rosanna handed the torch to Zeke and lay on her stomach. "How badly are you hurt?"

He could put weight on both of his legs and neither of his arms was in more pain than the other. He took as deep a breath as he could manage with his arms pulled taut over his head, and pain shot across his ribs. Painful, but not excruciating. He'd been mostly dead enough times to know the difference between injuries that healed and those that killed. "Sore, but I'll live. They weren't trying to kill me with their beatings."

"Beatings? More than one?" Rosanna reached into the hole, as if she wanted to clasp one of his hands, but her arms weren't long enough to reach him.

He probably should've kept that to himself. But it was time to be honest with Rosanna, of all people.

Still, he wasn't going to tell her the details he could remember of the two beatings. Especially not while he was still stuck in this pit. The walls were closing in on him, and he needed to get out before the darkness overwhelmed him again. "I'll be fine. Zeke, stop gawking and get me out of here."

Zeke handed the torch back to Rosanna and knelt mostly out of sight behind the upright hatch. "It ain't going to be pleasant. I got to crank you up by your hands."

"At this point, I don't care if you yank me out by my hair." Daemyn stood on his tiptoes as high as he could and grabbed the chain with one of his hands. His grip was tenuous, his fingers numb and the muscles in his arm stretched tightly for too long. "I'm ready."

There came a clanking sound, and the chain jerked upward. Daemyn's hand slipped, and he fell for an inch before he was halted by the manacles. He sucked in a breath as the manacles dug deeper into his skin. The bones in his hands ached under the pressure until they felt about ready to snap. He gritted his teeth. If a few broken bones were what it took to get out of here, then so be it.

Inch by inch, the cranking gear raised the chain. Daemyn watched as each link tipped over the edge of the opening and disappeared through the hole in the hatch. Each disappearing link brought him that much closer to the surface and freedom and wide-open spaces.

When his hands were six inches from the top, Rosanna propped the torch against the wall, leaned over the pit, and grasped Daemyn's arm. Her touch was nothing but a vague pressure since his arms were so numb. She heaved upward as much as she could.

Zeke stopped cranking, grabbed Daemyn's other arm, and joined Rosanna in hauling Daemyn up and out.

As his shoulders cleared the sides of the pit, Daemyn gathered what little strength he had in his shaking arms and leveraged his body the rest of the way from the hole to sit at the edge of the pit, his legs still dangling inside.

When Rosanna lowered his arms, it was both a relief

and pain. Tingles shot down his arms, throbbing with needle-like jabs in his fingers.

Zeke pulled out his lock picking tools, a flat piece he could insert to give himself leverage on the lock and a pick with a bump on the end.

Daemyn forced a hint of a smile to his face. Hopefully it would distract Zeke from the way his hands were shaking. "I regret teaching you to pick locks less than I used to."

"I reckon you only got your bad influence to blame." Zeke set to work on the first manacle. It clacked open in less than two seconds. The locks on a set of manacles weren't the most complicated. Zeke had the other off in another few seconds.

He was free. The shaking was growing worse, as if his body was just now coming to terms with how easily he could've died in that pit.

It was agony to move his arms even a few inches, but Daemyn did it anyways. He wrapped his arms around Rosanna and held her as tight as he could manage, resting his forehead against her shoulder.

She was real. And she was here. Solid and warm. Not darkness. Not stone. Not his imagination playing tricks with him.

He loved her. It was such a deep-down love, he couldn't have put it into words better than that simple phrase. Because she was Rosanna. His prison-breaking princess.

No holding back. Not this time. "I love you."

Her arms tightened around him, and he felt more than heard her small laugh. "I love you too."

He could've stayed like that all day, holding her. But this was probably awkward enough for Zeke, and Rosanna hadn't mentioned it, but Daemyn was growing all too aware of how sticky he was with sweat and dried blood. He probably didn't smell all that great either. He forced himself to pull back. He would wait to kiss her until after he'd had a chance to clean up.

Rosanna's mouth had a quirk at one corner as she brushed at his hair with the back of her fingers, but her smile faded as her gaze focused on his wrist. She grabbed his hand and gently pushed back the end of his sleeve. Blood crusted around his wrist where the manacles had torn into his skin. Dribbles of dried blood ran down his arm nearly to his elbow.

Rosanna traced her fingers over the wounds. Could she guess what it meant? How long and how often he had fought the chains to tear his skin so deeply? "You never told me you didn't like tight spaces."

Daemyn met her deep brown eyes. Was that a note of hurt in her voice? He swallowed and tried to ignore the pressing weight of stone around him. "It ain't something I like to tell."

"You aren't indestructible. Or invincible. And that's all right. You're allowed to have flaws, you know." She took his hand in both of hers and rubbed at his skin. "Your hands are like ice."

The tingling pain was growing worse. He twitched his fingers, and pain shot through them. He rubbed his other hand against his leggings. "How long was I down there?"

It could've been days for all he'd been able to keep track, but his better sense told him that the hours would've stretched into what felt like days.

"Nearly a day." Rosanna switched to his other hand, rubbing with firm, steady motions. "I wanted to come sooner, but King Cassius was guarding us worse than a mother bear over her cubs."

Zeke pulled out his canteen, uncapped it, and held it out. Daemyn tried to take it, but his fingers still felt too thick, throbbing too painfully to register the sensation of the canteen's metal.

Kneeling, Zeke held the canteen for Daemyn and tipped water into his mouth.

The water was warm with a metallic aftertaste. But it soothed Daemyn's raw, dry throat and settled into his empty stomach. He hadn't even realized just how thirsty he was, and it took restraint to keep from snatching the canteen from Zeke.

Zeke pulled the canteen away. "You can have more later. Let that settle first."

Daemyn tried to collect his thoughts. He'd spent enough time inactive in that pit. He had to put himself back together and move on. He'd done it after being mostly dead nine times. Surely spending a day in dungeon pit was no different.

He planted a hand against the floor and managed to get one foot underneath him, then the other, before tottering his way upright. Both Zeke and Rosanna reached to him, as if to steady him, but he waved them away. He needed to stand on his own, at least for a few moments.

"What's the plan for getting out of here?" He propped himself against the wall and waited for his legs to adjust to bearing his full weight once again.

"We sneaked in through that secret passage from the tallest tower. If you're up to it, we're going to sneak out the same way." Rosanna stepped closer and wrapped an arm around his waist. "Isi and Josiah are waiting for us in an unused room on the sixth floor of that tower so we can plan. Asa and Captain Degotaga are currently guarding our sets of rooms like normal to make it look like we haven't left."

Daemyn wasn't sure he wanted to know what they would've done if he couldn't climb the nine sets of stairs to the tallest tower.

Not that he was positive he could make it up all those stairs with the way his body was aching.

But this was what he'd always done. Pushed through pain and kept going, whether it was before or after dying. He could do this because he had no other choice.

Rosanna gave him a smile and held out a hand. "Come on. We'll do this together."

Daemyn slipped his hand into hers and clasped it as tight as he could manage. But she squeezed tightly back and tugged, urging him forward.

This time instead of pushing on alone, he had Rosanna on one side and Zeke on the other. He wouldn't have to watch them move on with their lives, grow up, grow old, while he stayed the same. This time, he got to age and grow old and *live* right alongside them.

It was such a heady sort of freedom he would've laughed out loud, but then they would really think he'd cracked his kettle for sure.

CHAPTER 25

ALEXANDER

Alex cradled the precious glass slipper in his lap as the elk cart bounced over the rutted track. Behind him, his guard captain and King Cassius's seneschal clung to the bench seat while a squad of King Cassius's soldiers and all of Alex's guards jogged along the trail.

Alex gritted his teeth as the pair of elk pulling the cart surged forward. They were a decently matched pair, one of a kind, it was said, to be trained to pull a cart like this. But they were still prone to prancing off-step.

The king's white buffalo was also trained to pull a cart, but buffalo were more reliable when led at a walk. They tended to have only two speeds: a plodding walk and a full-on, reckless charge.

Alex couldn't risk the glass slipper. It was his only link to the girl who held his heart. Every time he gazed at the glass slipper, his heart beat faster, and his chest grew tight.

He had to find her. He couldn't live like this, too sick to eat, too tense to sleep.

"We're coming up on Logansville. It's a small farming village. Do you wish to stop, Your Majesty?" The blond-haired young man driving the cart asked as he heaved on one rein and slapped the other to convince the elk to swerve around a large rock in the center of the road.

The elk didn't cooperate fast enough. Alex gripped the edge of the seat with one hand while clasping the glass slipper to his chest with the other. The cart's wheel hit the rock, and Alex was flung into the air. Only his grip on the seat kept him from pitching over the side. He thumped down onto the hard wood.

In the back of the elk cart, King Cassius's seneschal and Alex's captain bounced into the air before landing on their wooden bench, Alex's luggage rattling by their feet.

This was worse than shooting the Falls of the Onohio.

That thought sent an uncomfortable twinge into his chest. Like he had something he should be sorry for.

Had he really given the order to have Daemyn locked in the dungeon? Alex shook his head, trying to remember that part of last night clearly. His only clear memory was his beloved racing away, leaving this glass slipper behind.

His beloved. He had to find her.

Jadon had been in the way. He hadn't understood. He hadn't listened. He deserved to spend a few days in the dungeon.

Alex would have him released. It wasn't like he was planning to leave him in there forever. As a manservant, Jadon should know better than to voice his opinion in front of his betters. A good manservant should be silent except when asking for clarification on an order or saying "yes, sire."

The elk cart jounced around a bend, and there in a valley next to the Pohatomie River was the small village of

Logansville. Stands of corn with beans twining up their stalks and squash growing at their bases filled the hills surrounding the town.

The elk's driver drew the cart to a halt in the town center. Alex should probably learn the young man's name, but surely he wouldn't have to put up with this discomfort for that long. He had to find the love of his life as soon as possible.

As the townsfolk peeked from their homes and shops, gawking at the elk cart, Major Vinzen, King Cassius's seneschal, stepped onto the side of the town's well and unfolded a piece of paper. "By order of High King Alexander, King Cassius requests that all unmarried young ladies present themselves in the town square."

Alex scanned the gathering crowd, searching for hair as black as a crow's wing and eyes the deep blue of a morning sky. Would she be here?

As the young women began to step out of the homes and shops, glancing around and behind them as if uncertain what to do, Major Vinzen and the other guards instructed them to line up before Alex by the fountain.

Alex knelt on the cobblestones and motioned to the first girl. "Take off your right moccasin."

"What?" The girl stared.

"What, Your Majesty." The guard nudged her. "Sit."

She swallowed, perched on the edge of the fountain, and tugged off her low moccasin.

Alex lifted her foot and tried to slip on the glass slipper. The glass slipper wouldn't even fit over the girl's toes.

He released her. "Nope. Next."

The girl grabbed her moccasin, hopped from the well's short wall, and dashed off without even bothering to put her moccasin back on.

The next girl's feet were too small. The next too large.

It took an hour, but Alex tried the glass slipper on every girl in the village, and the glass slipper refused to fit any of them.

He climbed back into the elk cart, his heart heavy with unbearable longing. He needed to find her. No matter how long it took.

Chapter 26

Elara

Elara peeked around the corner of the barn at the castle causeway, leaning all her weight on her right foot. Crowds of the nobility that had come for the balls were leaving while extra guards had been stationed both at the castle gate and the end of the causeway, inspecting each person with more scrutiny than usual.

She'd intended to sneak out of Terrence's shack in the early morning and find a place to hide in the thick brush near the river, but after staying up well past midnight, she'd overslept. Without windows, Terrence's shack had remained so dark she hadn't realized it was mid-morning until she'd cracked the door open.

Neither Zeke nor his friends had returned, and Elara didn't feel quite as bad about following through on her plans behind his back. He'd said he'd return before dawn, and it was now nearly noon without any sign of him.

Elara scanned the crowd on the causeway again. There. Baroness Hackett, with Monica and Beatrice pressed close behind her, waited several families back in the line.

Between Elara and the castle lay an open, rocky hillside. There was no crossing that in the daylight. How was she going to sneak from her current position to meet them at the canoe without anyone noticing her?

She grimaced and eased some weight onto her left foot. Spikes of pain shot through her leg all the way to her hip, sending tears into her eyes. It was going to be nearly unbearable to take the long way around through the forest at her back. But did she have another choice?

The crowd stirred at the far end of the causeway by the castle's gate. A moment later, the crowd parted, cramming to either side of the causeway, while a squad of ten guards trotted down the center.

What were the guards doing? Surely they weren't for her. King Cassius couldn't possibly know she was still there, nor could he connect her to Terrence. Who would have told him the maidservant of Baroness Hackett was friends with the king's buffalo boy? Even if anyone had noticed, it wasn't the sort of thing that would stick in people's memories.

At the end of the causeway, the squad's commander barked orders, and the guards peeled off in pairs, scattering in all directions.

They were searching for something or someone. Even if they weren't searching for her, she didn't dare linger where she was.

There was nothing for it. She had to hike through the forest to circle around to the canoes.

Elara eased backwards, using the barn's wall for support. When she was out of sight behind the barn, she turned and hopped past Terrence's shack. She'd straightened the bed and did her best to hide any evidence that she'd been there before she'd left, but she wasn't skilled at tracking. She didn't know what sort of signs a guard might be able to read in the dirt that she couldn't.

Her footsteps turned into a crackling rustle as she entered the trees behind the barn. This early in the fall, the leaves overhead were still green with only the occasional leaf showing a hint of orange at the tips. The foliage provided shadows, though she still felt exposed.

Elara hobbled into the forest until she could no longer see the castle or the barn, though the faint sounds of people's voices carried into the trees.

The sounds would keep her from getting lost. As long as she could hear the castle noise, she wouldn't hopelessly wander this forest.

The trees clustered so tightly in places she felt like she was shoving her way through a wall of wood and leaves. The ground beneath her wasn't flat, but constantly dipped and turned, with roots and rocks that caught the heel of the glass slipper even inside her moccasin. She hobbled with the pain and the lopsided height difference caused by the single glass slipper.

She had to keep going. If she could get to the baroness, scramble into a canoe, and arrive at Hackettsville, she would be safe. She would have a moment to rest and figure a way out of this mess.

Ahead, the trees thinned. Had she reached the river already?

She tottered forward, peering through the trees, but halted before she stepped from the forest.

The castle's causeway lay directly across the open space from where she stood. She had only gone about half the distance.

Something crashed in the trees to her left, between her and the river. A pair of the guards, searching.

Elara set out once again, this time more slowly. If she stuck to this patch of forest, perhaps she could slip past them. All she needed to do was join the flow of nobility on the trail from the castle causeway to the river.

Only a few more steps. She gritted her teeth, trying to keep the tears from clouding her vision as she glanced around the forest surrounding her. Surely she could keep going for a few more steps.

"Halt!"

The shout came from behind her. Elara stiffened. Should she try to run? Pretend she didn't hear?

No. She couldn't outrun them, and running would only make them more suspicious. Drawing in a deep breath, she pasted on her best, deferential servant expression and turned.

Two guards strode from the forest behind her. They hadn't drawn their long knives or brandished their spears yet, so they didn't see her as a threat.

"Miss, what are you doing in the forest?" One of the guards halted a few feet away from her while the other took a few steps to the left as if to get between her and the castle should she try to flee.

Elara ducked her head, as if to show the guards proper respect. "I am meeting my lady and her daughters this morning to aid them in their return to our home."

"Where is your home?"

Had King Cassius given them instructions to look for a servant girl from Hackettsville? Elara didn't want to lie, but she didn't want to give them the truth either. "A small town upriver. Nowhere important, really."

The guard's eyes narrowed. Perhaps her evasive answer had been a tad suspicious. "Where were you last night?"

What could she say? She couldn't tell them she'd been at the ball, danced with the high king, then fled to the forest.

"In the forest." That was partially true, at least. She had been in the forest for some of the night. Elara shifted a few steps backwards, nearly tripping at the stab of pain from her left foot. "Please. I need to meet my lady. She will be furious if I'm late."

It was a common enough complaint for a servant. Nothing suspicious there.

The second guard gave a small snort and waved at her. "Let's stop wasting time. She's obviously not the one we're looking for. She's hobbling so much she can barely walk. She can't possibly have been dancing last night."

They were looking for her. Why? Had King Cassius realized there was something deeper going on with her Fae-given dress? Had he decided that having her on hand would be a way to have power over High King Alexander?

Either way, she didn't want to get caught. Would the guards be watching for her to join Baroness Hackett? King Cassius knew she worked for her.

"Have you seen anyone this morning, miss? A girl with a fancy glass slipper and a ball gown, perhaps?"

At least they didn't realize the glass slipper was stuck to her foot nor that the ball gown was more an illusion than a real dress. Elara shook her head. No, she hadn't seen a girl wandering around in a ball gown.

"You may be on your way, miss." With a nod, the guard turned and strode toward the castle, the other soldier trailing him.

When they were out of sight, Elara let out a long breath and sagged against a tree. That was close.

And it told her one thing. She couldn't join Baroness Hackett, Monica, and Beatrice at the castle docks. King Cassius would have a guard stationed there, watching for her. She had to take to the forest and parallel the river. The men paddling Baroness Hackett's canoe would be going slowly as they worked their way upriver. If Elara moved fast enough, she might be able to meet them at one of the points where they swung in close to the bank and wave them down.

If that didn't work...Elara stifled a groan and squeezed her eyes shut against her watering eyes. She would just have to walk all the way to Hackettsville. She'd crawl if she had to.

ELARA CRAWLED onto a rocky point jutting out into the river. It felt like she'd walked miles and miles from Castle Fonthaven, but it was probably no more than a mile. If that.

But she could go no farther. Her left foot felt like it was shredding down to the bone with each step while the wounds on her right foot had reopened and started to bleed.

She tucked herself into a hollow in the rock where she would be out of sight from the river.

Had the baroness's canoe already passed? Elara didn't think so, but she hadn't been able to keep the river in sight the entire time she'd been hiking. To save time, she'd cut straight through the forest in places where the river curved.

Voices and rippling sounds carried from the river. Elara peeked her head over the edge of the rock.

Three canoes worked their way up the river in a tight clump. Two young men each, probably guards, paddled the canoes while two young ladies sat in the center canoe, a middle-aged man in the canoe farthest from Elara, and a woman who was probably his wife in the canoe closest to her.

Not the baroness but one of the barons from farther up river. Elara rested her head against the stone beneath her again. The rock was warm, the sun beating down from the clear sky above. If she lay here much longer, the heat was going to become unbearable.

The baron and his brigade of canoes moved upriver and disappeared around a bend.

Elara closed her eyes. It was tempting to yield to the exhaustion weighing on her. But she couldn't give up now. Terrence was depending on her to get herself to safety at Hackettsville.

Another set of rhythmic splashes came from the river. Elara gathered her strength and lifted her head.

This time, it was a large, dugout canoe. The kind made from burning a large tree and chipping at the ash until it was hollowed out. Canoes like it were often used to transport goods or people on the rivers.

And Elara recognized this one. She pushed herself upright and waved both arms.

The farmer in the bow of the canoe noticed her first and pointed. In the center of the canoe, Monica started, glanced at her, then waved back nearly as wildly as Elara had.

Within a few minutes, the two farmers from Hackettsville who had come that morning to fetch their baroness and her daughters home from Castle Fonthaven had the canoe pulled along the lee side of the rock.

"Elara!" Monica popped out of the canoe and hugged Elara before she even had a chance to brace herself. "You're all right! We were so worried when you weren't in our rooms when we returned from the ball. What happened? How did you get here?"

Elara patted Monica's back. Over Monica's shoulder, she caught sight of Beatrice's wide eyes and Baroness Hackett's pinched forehead.

They had all been worried about *her*. Their maidservant.

All those years of resenting them for their status, and it hadn't been like that at all. They were truly worried about her, and Monica was hugging her as a friend.

Would it be enough? Would they help her once she told them the truth? They could lose their home, their status, everything if they helped her.

Elara pulled out of Monica's hug. "It's a long story, but I need help. I'm running from King Cassius, and if he or the high king finds me, the high king could be permanently cursed. I understand if you don't help me. I'll hide out in the woods if I have to. But I don't know where else to go."

"Of course we'll help. Won't we, Mama?" Monica turned to the baroness.

Baroness Hackett glanced from the two farmers paddling the canoe, then to her daughters, before looking at Elara.

Elara hunched beneath that gaze. She shouldn't have asked for their help. She'd served them so grudgingly, grumbling how unfair it was that they had so much while she had so little. But here she was, having messed up everything, asking them to risk all they had for a mere maidservant they had taken in after her parents died.

Baroness Hackett straightened her shoulders. "I would like to hear the full story once we reach Hackettsville, but I've had a feeling something more has been going on. Hurry into the canoe, and let's be on our way."

They were going to help her. Elara swallowed at the lump that filled her throat. She didn't deserve this gift of their friendship.

DAEMYN

By the time they climbed the nine flights of stairs and gone down two more, Daemyn was shaking and gasping for breath. He had to lean on Rosanna to stay on his feet while Zeke scouted ahead. When it was safe, Zeke led them down a deserted hallway, paused before a door, and knocked three times, then twice, then once.

The door cracked open, and Isi stuck her head out. "Good. You're back. And you got Daemyn."

She flung the door wide and stepped aside. "I'll fetch a tray from the kitchen and let Pa know you're all safe."

She slipped outside as Zeke, Daemyn, and Rosanna entered the room, and Zeke shut the door behind them.

"Uncle Daemyn!" Josiah jumped to his feet. "You don't look so good. What happened?"

"Guards ain't paid to be gentle when they throw a body in the dungeon." Daemyn glanced around the spare room. It was all but empty with a few random wooden chairs piled in one corner and a low table in the center. At least it had a few rugs both rolled against the wall and spread out on the wood floor. A good place to hide from King Cassius's notice.

Daemyn headed for the rug that looked softest and eased onto it, lying on his back. It was tempting to close his eyes and let himself rest.

But there was still so much to do. He needed to find out where Alex was and what was wrong with him and what their current situation with King Cassius was and if a war was about to start at any moment. "What happened after I was tossed in the dungeon?"

Rosanna knelt next to him and picked up one of his hands, inspecting the wound around his wrist. "These should be tended. And you should rest."

It was so tempting to simply close his eyes. But something in him was pulled taut from the *not knowing* of the hours he'd spent in the dungeons.

From the glimpse through the shutters he'd gotten in the tallest tower, it was still early evening. They had a few hours before they'd attempt whatever escape plan they devised for getting out of this castle. He could rest once they had their plans in place.

"You can tell me what's been happening while my injuries are being tended." Daemyn grimaced. "I suppose you're going to want to inspect the bruises."

Zeke sat on his other side and set down his pack near Daemyn's head. "I ain't letting you die of some bleeding inside because you were too almighty stubborn to let me do my job."

Daemyn groaned, forced himself to sit up, and tugged his shirt over his head. His skin prickled, and he tried to appear relaxed as he set his shirt aside and lay back down. It was uncomfortable, having his scars uncovered. They were scars from wounds a man shouldn't be able to live through.

It didn't help that his scars were now joined by purple and blue splotches across his chest, stomach, and arms. He probably had bruises all down his back and legs too.

Rosanna took Daemyn's hand and rested his arm across her lap. "Zeke, can you pass me that canteen?"

Daemyn gritted his teeth and tried to ignore how stiff his insides were at being the center of attention like this. At least Josiah was sitting a few feet away, watching but not crowding. Daemyn focused on one of the beams running along the ceiling. "All right, I'm cooperating. What's been happening?"

"I found the mystery girl." Zeke poked at one of the bruises, and Daemyn did his best not to flinch. "It turns out she's a maidservant who got tricked by a Fallen Fae into putting on a pair of glass slippers that cursed the high king to fall madly in love when he danced with her. This girl, Elara, ran from the third ball before the curse could become permanent at midnight."

A curse to fall madly in love. That explained why Alex had been acting so strangely, how the girl's appearance had been shifting depending on who was looking at her, and the odd behavior of those around her.

Was that why he had been able to resist its pull? His heart already belonged to Rosanna.

But Alex still hadn't been himself after she'd left the ball. If anything, he'd been more frantic. More irrational. He'd been clutching that glass slipper to his heart as if it was the only thing he cared about. "The curse didn't break, did it?"

"No." Rosanna scrubbed at a line of dried blood on his arm. "According to what the girl told Zeke, one of the glass slippers came off when she briefly met the Highest Prince, and Alex found it. If Alex finds her and puts the glass slipper back on her foot, then the curse will take full effect."

If Alex had already been out of his head enough to toss Daemyn into the dungeon, how much worse would he be under the full, permanent effect of this curse?

Any progress Alex had made toward peace in Tallahatchia would be lost. In some ways, this curse would be worse than when Alex was sleeping. At least, as a sleeping high prince, he could be turned into a legend people could hope for. A high king out of his head with infatuation was just a pathetic figure no one respected.

"Right after you were thrown in the dungeon, he left to search for her." Rosanna wrapped a strip of cloth around Daemyn's wrist.

"Hopefully, he won't find her." Zeke started washing the blood from Daemyn's other arm. "She was headed to a friend's shack. The king's buffalo boy, as it turned out. He was called away to drive the elk cart for the high king, and he promised to do his best to sidetrack him. I left Elara in his shack, but I ain't sure she stayed there. She seemed twitchy as a squirrel."

Daemyn nodded and tried to ignore Rosanna's fingers as she spread balm over his bruises.

"There." Rosanna sat back on her heels and swiped her fingers on a cloth.

Daemyn rolled upright, grabbed his shirt, and tugged it on before either Zeke or Rosanna changed their mind about being finished tending him.

"Here. Let me get the bruises on your face." Rosanna dipped her fingers in the balm again and reached for his face.

He froze while her gentle, but firm touch sent bursts of pain across his bruised cheek and jaw. "Does it look as bad as it feels?"

Zeke snorted as he packed up the rest of the supplies. "Worse, I reckon. You got two black eyes and one side of your face is more colorful than a rhododendron."

"It isn't so bad. At least your nose is still straight." Josiah grinned. "I reckon Rosanna will still like you well enough."

Rosanna cleaned her fingers on the rag again, then swept a glance over Daemyn's face, a quirk to the corner of her mouth. "I suppose I'll keep him. At least there ain't any gushing blood this time."

This was the moment he was probably supposed to say something. Something witty or romantic or just something. Anything. But his mind had frozen. It wasn't even a tangle or whirling. Just frozen as a deer catching a whiff of danger on the wind and being unsure which direction to run.

A pattern of knocks sounded on the door, then Isi breezed inside, balancing a tray piled with food on one hand and closing the door behind her. "I got as much food as I dared. The Pohatomie cooks are probably going to be gossiping for weeks how Rosanna has the healthiest appetite of any princess they've ever seen."

"Not a bad thing to be known for." Rosanna grinned as she stood and took the tray from Isi. "Did you get any of those scones they were serving at the balls? King Cassius may be a conniving traitor, but he does hire good cooks."

Daemyn relaxed as their banter covered his lapse. He needed to sleep while he could. Escaping Castle Fonthaven that night wouldn't be easy. And probably painful.

"JUMPING off the castle wall was the best plan you could come up with?" Isi hissed as they huddled near a side door of the third tower.

Daemyn grimaced. He wasn't exactly looking forward to it either. "Zeke and I could climb down the castle walls —at least, I normally could. But the rest of you would need a rope, and that would take too long. The guards would notice."

"And they won't notice a bunch of large splashes?" Rosanna crouched at Daemyn's side. Captain Degotaga hadn't been happy about either Rosanna or Isi going, but Rosanna hadn't left him much choice, and Isi had to go along if Rosanna went.

"We just have to be quick." Zeke reached over his shoulder yet again, checking that his unstrung bow and arrows were secured.

It probably wouldn't be that simple, but Daemyn wasn't going to correct him. They'd find out soon enough when it came time to take the leap from the castle wall. It looked a lot higher from up top.

"Is this what adventures with Uncle Daemyn are like?" Josiah pressed in closer. "I've been missing out on the fun."

"You're a prince." Zeke nudged Josiah with an elbow. "Asa made me promise I ain't allowed to let nothing happen to you. And I ain't about to get my big brother mad at me."

Trying to ignore his nephews, Daemyn studied the movements of the guards on the wall top. They'd have to time this correctly. The guards were wary, but they were watching for movement from outside the castle, not within it. At least until someone realized Daemyn had escaped the dungeon. Then this castle could be crawling with soldiers.

Daemyn focused on the guards. Once they turned and started in the other direction, it would be time to move. "Remember, jump where I tell you. And make sure you jump a ways out from the wall. Either keep your toes pointed as you go into the water or dive with your hands stiff in front of you."

"We know. You've told us at least three times already." Josiah sounded like he was rolling his eyes.

"Four times." Zeke's voice held something of a laugh.

"I wouldn't have to repeat it if I knew my nephews actually listened to a word I said." Daemyn didn't take his eyes away from the guards. They were nearing the moment when they'd spin on their heels. In three. Two. One.

The guards clapped their heels together, whirled, and marched in the other direction.

There was something to be said for the kingdoms like Neskahana and Buckhannock that had felt the effects of the war. They, at least, knew how to properly set a guard pattern. The guards on Castle Fonthaven's walls were mostly for show.

Daemyn eased to his feet, and the others behind him fell silent as shadows. He crept onto the stone steps leading to the wall top, his moccasins muffling his footsteps. His staff was a solid weight in his hand, even as his ribs ached.

When the guards were about halfway down the wall, Daemyn reached the section of battlements where the river ran deep without boulders beneath. He patted that section and motioned.

Zeke nodded and helped Isi onto the battlements. Isi glanced down, and her face whitened. When Josiah clambered up beside her, he looked a bit green beneath his bronzed skin.

Daemyn couldn't blame them. He'd jumped from this wall before, and even he wasn't looking forward to making the jump again.

Rosanna glanced at Daemyn, drew in a deep breath, and joined the others. It was crowded with the three of them on there, but as soon as the first jumped and splashed into the river, the guards would be alerted. They'd need to dive one after the other.

Raising his staff, Daemyn faced the Pohatomie guards. They were nearing the end of their march along the wall and would be turning back in a few moments.

Behind him, there was a faint scuffing sound, a drawn-in breath, then a few heartbeats later, a splash. A surprisingly small splash. That would be Rosanna, if they'd stuck to the plan. Of Isi, Josiah, and Rosanna, Daemyn counted on Rosanna to be the one brave enough to take the leap first.

The guards stiffened, glancing around. Not wary yet. Probably wondering if that was a fish or something more.

Another noise behind Daemyn. A much larger splash. Isi or Josiah?

This time, the guards whirled, their hands reaching for their long knives. As their gazes focused on Daemyn, they shouted and charged forward.

A small stifled shriek. Then a splash. Now that was Isi.

"Uncle Daemyn?" Zeke's voice came from behind him, tense and ready.

"Go." Daemyn stepped forward, using his momentum as he jabbed his hardwood staff into the first guard's chest. The guard collapsed, gasping.

A splash marked Zeke's entry into the water.

As the second guard charged, Daemyn whipped his staff up and took him under the chin. The guard fell to his knees, gripping his jaw.

Boots tromped on the stairs to the wall top. Daemyn glanced over his shoulder. At least five soldiers were racing up the stairs, headed for him.

No more time to delay. Daemyn rolled onto the battlements, pressed his staff against his side so that it wouldn't punch into him when he hit the water, and launched himself from the battlements.

Cold air rushed past his face as he dove head first toward the river. The water was dark and slick below, the moon a shimmer on the surface.

Then he plunged into the water, cold smacking hard into him. He angled himself as he went in deep. The current caught him, and he swam with it for several minutes, the river's cold fingers working through his buck-skins, shivering against his skin. When his lungs began to ache, he kicked to the surface.

Shaking the water from his eyes, he glanced around. He was thirty feet into the center of the river. Forested hills bordered both sides with the castle reflecting on the water well behind him.

A few shadows bobbed in the river ahead. Daemyn could only count three heads, but that didn't mean the fourth wasn't hidden in the shadows.

Daemyn lodged his staff beneath his body, then stroked across the river toward the bank where they planned to meet. His ribs ached with each pull against the water, and he had to grit his teeth at each deep breath. When he felt the mush of the silt bottom, he used his staff to lever himself to his feet.

A figure splashed into the river out to him, her black braid swinging. "Your ribs survive that jump all right?"

"I'm fine." Daemyn tried to keep the strain out of his voice, though he didn't protest when Rosanna took his arm over her shoulders. "Was that enough adventure for you?"

"That was scarier than the shooting the Falls, that's for sure." Rosanna's voice held a trace of a laugh.

"If you like that, there's some cliffs we can jump off in Kanawhee. Not as tall as the castle wall, but a little safer to do multiple times." Daemyn squished toward the bank. "And a waterfall you can jump from in Buckhannock."

"Sounds like we'll have to visit there next." Rosanna glanced up at him, the moonlight shining in her eyes and grin.

The night was warm, even standing knee-deep in the river with their buckskins dripping wet. The bullfrogs along the banks croaked loud enough to cover most other sounds in the night. Daemyn had the urge to lean down and kiss her, right there in the swirl of river and moonlight. Since arriving in Pohatomie, they'd had so little time to be themselves like this without their roles of princess and manservant getting in the way.

Rosanna's grin faded. "I think...I think everyone is watching."

"I know." He didn't want to care. It would've been nice to be bold enough to take advantage of the moment and kiss Rosanna.

But they were in the middle of a castle escape. They had miles to travel and a curse to stop. Sure, a kiss wasn't going to take long. But this wasn't the time to get all distracted over kissing either. Zeke and Josiah would never let him live it down.

Having an abundance of nephews could be a hassle at times. Even if he didn't know what he would do without them.

"Later." He whispered and pressed a quick kiss to her hair before putting some distance between them.

"I'll hold you to that." Rosanna lightly swatted his back, then set off for the riverbank once again.

With his arm still slung over her shoulder, Daemyn kept pace with her, the silt glopping at his moccasins with each step.

As they neared the riverbank, Zeke reached out a hand, grinning. "Took you long enough. Need a hand in your old age?"

He wasn't about to dignify that with a reply. Sometimes it was best not to encourage them. He took Zeke's hand and let him pull him up the steep, muddy bank from the river while Isi held out a hand to Rosanna.

Daemyn gestured into the forest with his hardwood staff. "Lead the way to this shack."

Zeke strode into the shadows beneath the trees as they circled around the castle, headed for the corral and barn. Daemyn took the rear, watching their back and preventing the others from seeing just how much he hurt.

After several minutes of hiking, they approached the shack. It was dark, though late enough that even if that girl was still there, she was probably asleep.

Zeke knocked, then stuck his head inside. After a moment, he huffed out a breath. "I left her right here."

"You were a random stranger telling them what to do." Daemyn leaned on his staff. His ribs ached. The bruises all along his body throbbed. His face felt like it was misshapen with swelling, even if the dunking in the cold river had helped.

All he wanted to do was lie down and rest. But Alex was about to be cursed. King Cassius would be searching for them soon. He had no choice but to push himself forward.

"Where would she go?" Rosanna walked around the shack, looking under the pillows on the bed and pulling out a few drawers. "I don't see a note."

"If she were smart, there ain't none." Zeke stepped from the doorway.

"Any ideas where she went?" Josiah bounced on his toes.

"She said something about being a maidservant." Zeke's forehead wrinkled, then cleared. "To the baroness of Hackettsville."

Hackettsville was on the Scionee River, upstream of Castle Fonthaven.

Daemyn glanced over his shoulder, to where the walls of Castle Fonthaven now blazed with lights. "We had better fetch our canoes before King Cassius sends out his guards."

An all-night canoe trip, fighting the current the whole way. Daemyn leaned on his staff to ease his throbbing ribs. This night just kept getting longer and longer.

CHAPTER 28

ALEXANDER

Alex slumped on the bench, clutching the precious glass slipper to his chest. They were working their way down the Scionee River back to the Pohatomie, stopping at the small farming villages. He'd tried the slipper on every eligible young lady he found, but so far nothing.

Was he ever going to find her? He couldn't give up, but the task before him appeared so insurmountable. How was he supposed to find his dearest love among all the maidens of Pohatomie?

As they rounded a bend in the track that followed the river, a wooden manor house came into view, tucked into the trees, with a small town near the river.

Would this be the place? Surely his beloved couldn't live much farther from Castle Fonthaven than the circle he'd done. If he didn't find her here, then he'd have to check the other side of the river, then start circling farther from the castle.

The turn off for the manor house approached, yet the buffalo boy didn't slow the elk. Instead, the cart rumbled right past the rutted trail as if the boy didn't see it right there.

"What are you doing?" Alex waved over his shoulder at the manor house. "We need to stop."

"Um, not there." The buffalo boy stayed focused on the elk. "There's no one eligible there."

"You don't know that." Alex tightened his grip on the glass slipper. It was warm in his hand. And something tugged deep inside him. She had to be here. Their hearts were so deeply connected he could sense it. "Turn around. We need to stop."

"I don't think that's a good idea, Your Majesty." The buffalo boy showed no signs of slowing the cart.

Alex braced himself against the seat. This called for drastic measures. He wouldn't let a little thing like a stubborn buffalo boy stand between him and the darling of his heart. "I order you to turn this cart around immediately. I'll jump out and run back if I have to."

"Your Majesty, that wouldn't—" The boy glanced at him.

Alex shoved to his feet, gripping the back of the bench to keep his balance as the cart jounced over yet another root. The ground blurred beneath the cart's wooden wheel as the elk dashed along. Would it hurt when he hit the ground?

It didn't matter. Alex had to find her. He planted his foot on the side, took a deep breath, and braced himself to jump.

"Fine." The buffalo boy tugged on the reins, slowing the elk pair. But there was something in his gaze.

How well did Alex know this buffalo boy? Not well. He hadn't even bothered to learn the young man's name. He could be a traitor for all Alex knew. Was he conspiring to keep Alex from his true love?

As the elk cart slowed by a gentle, grassy slope that led down to the Scionee River, Alex leapt before anyone had a chance to stop him. He landed with a jolt, fell, and tumbled. When his momentum slowed, he rolled to his feet and dashed toward the manor house without bothering to brush himself off. What did it matter if he arrived grass-stained and dirty?

Alex's guard captain jumped out and fell into step behind him, glaring as if the captain wasn't sure Alex would listen if he gave him a lecture on jumping from moving transportation.

Alex kept jogging, and the squad of soldiers that had been running behind the cart closed around him to provide protection. In some ways, striding up to the door with the guards was probably more dignified than bouncing up in that monstrosity of an elk cart.

The manor house itself wasn't much to look at. It was more like a glorified cabin rising in two stories up the river-bank from the Scionee. Behind it, hills flowed into the distance, covered in places with dense patches of trees and open with farm fields in others.

A small field stretched behind the manor house. The corn stood in dry, brown stalks at this time in early fall, the beans that had twined their way up the stalks during the summer all harvested. But the huge leaves of the squash covering the ground beneath the cornstalks were still green while the orange of pumpkins and yellow of gourds peeked between the leaves.

A quaint picture, if Alex had ever seen one. At least it wasn't completely backwoods.

With a glance at Alex, his captain pounded on the door. "Open up in the name of His Majesty High King Alexander."

Alex cradled the glass slipper to his heart. This was it. He could feel it. He was about to be reunited with his love.

CHAPTER 29

ELARA

Elara froze at the pounding on the door, the shout, the words that iced into her stomach. Her hands stilled on the skirt she was mending. He'd found her. Terrence hadn't been able to stall him for long. Only two days.

It wasn't enough time. High King Alexander couldn't be near giving up yet.

Elara raised her head and glanced around the room. Baroness Hackett's mouth was pinched, her skin pale, as her quill pen hovered in midair over the report on the manor's harvest she was reviewing.

Beatrice curled on a stuffed chair near the fire, hugging her knees, her eyes wide.

Monica peered out the window, and her face whitened until it was nearly the same gray as the cloudy sky above. "He's here. And he has a whole squad of King Cassius's soldiers as well as his own guards."

It would be unthinkable to attempt to fight them off. Four women with no fighting skills, all the manor's farmers out in the fields or tending their own homes. Nor would Baroness Hackett sacrifice herself or her daughters for Elara. She wasn't worth that, even if the baroness said she would protect her. It was one thing to say it. Another thing to carry through on those words when faced with the high king himself.

They would have to let him in. They had no choice.

Baroness Hackett set aside her quill and rose to her feet, her face smoothing. "Monica, take Elara to the attic and lock her in, then join us in the parlor while we host the high king." The baroness turned to Elara. "I'm sorry. The attic only locks from the outside, otherwise I'd have you lock yourself in there. I trust you will stay quiet?"

"Yes, milady." As quiet as a possum. "Thank you for hiding me."

Baroness Hackett inclined her head, pausing as if she was going to say something. But a firm knock pounded on the door again, the shout more insistent this time. The baroness straightened. "Go."

She swept from the room. Beatrice glanced at Elara before she scurried after her mother.

"Come on." Monica grabbed Elara's arm and tugged her out the door.

She limped after Monica as fast as she could. Her right foot ached every time it touched the floor, but her left foot screamed as the remaining glass slipper bit deeper with each step.

Instead of following the baroness down the stairs, they raced for the far end of the hall where a ladder was attached to the wall, a trap door above it.

Elara climbed the ladder and pushed the trap door open. She heaved herself through the opening and rolled onto the dusty floor.

The attic was dark, only a few hints of light showing through some of the eaves where the chinking had come loose. A few random pieces of furniture and trunks tucked into one corner, none of them large enough to block the trap door, while bundles of drying corn dangled down the center from the peak of the roof.

Monica's head and shoulders popped through the opening. "I'll come get you as soon as it's safe."

She shouldn't delay Monica, but Elara sat facing her. "Why are you doing this for me? It would be a lot safer for your family if you just handed me over to the high king."

"Mama told you. It's our duty to make sure the high king isn't cursed again, and to keep our king from committing treason against the high king as much as we can." Monica went up a few more rungs and sat on the edge of the hole facing Elara. "Besides, you're almost like family, you know. We all feel bad that you felt desperate enough to take those glass slippers in the first place."

Elara winced at another throb from her left foot. "It wasn't your fault."

The truth of those words sank into her. No, it wasn't the fault of the baroness, Monica, or Beatrice. They had always been kind to Elara. Monica confided in her like a friend.

It had been Elara's fault that she'd taken their kindness and turned it into jealousy. It would've been one thing if they'd mistreated her. But they'd done nothing but reward her generously for doing the job she'd been hired to do.

"Maybe not. But I should've noticed. You're my friend, Elara. I should've seen that something was wrong." Monica glanced down the hole. "I hear their voices. I have to go before anyone comes looking."

Elara nodded. Once Monica was back down the hole,

Elara swung the trap door closed after her. The lock clinked, sealing her in.

A week ago, she would've sat there and stewed at being locked in the attic. Now she breathed a sigh of relief and tiptoed as quietly as she could with her lopsided, painful gait across the room to the furniture.

She tucked herself behind an old, musty padded chair, huddling as far back as she could in the darkness. Surely no one would find her here. Who would think to search the attic for another girl hidden away?

CHAPTER 30

ALEXANDER

Neither of the girls before him was the one he was searching for. Alex kept his polite smile in place as the baroness introduced her two daughters, as if he didn't remember them from the ball. Not that his memories of them were all that clear. They were the sort of blonde-haired, blue eyed, innocent girls that blended together with all the other vaguely pretty girls he'd met both at the ball and in the past two days in the surrounding villages.

Alex motioned to a chair. Might as well get this over with. "If you would please have a seat?"

The oldest girl sat and promptly stuck out her foot, almost as if she was trying to hurry him along.

Alex slipped off her moccasin, set it aside, then carefully eased the glass slipper onto her foot. Her toes wouldn't even squish inside, and she'd have to cut off a few toes to come close to fitting.

"Looks like it doesn't fit." The girl popped to her feet

262

and snatched her moccasin before he could put it back on. "Beatrice, your turn."

The younger girl hurried over to the chair with her head down, sat, and stuck out her foot without looking at Alex.

Alex slid her moccasin from her foot and tried the glass slipper. This girl's toes fit inside, but her heel stuck over the back. She'd have to cut off her heel to get anywhere near having the glass slipper fit.

Alex stood, holding the glass slipper to his chest. "I'm afraid the slipper fits neither of your daughters."

Something flashed in the baroness's eyes, but she smiled and waved toward the door. "Let me show you to the door, and you can be on your way, Your Majesty. I understand this quest is important, and I wouldn't want to keep you any longer."

He needed to continue his quest to find the girl who would fit this glass slipper, but something was twisting inside his chest. He'd been so sure she was here.

The glass slipper caught the light in his hand. It almost felt like it was tugging on his hand, wanting to be united with the second slipper that must still be in the girl's possession.

"Are you sure these are the only two girls in your household?" Alex turned to the baroness.

If he hadn't been looking at her, he might have missed the look in her eyes. Behind her, the younger girl glanced at the older one, her eyes wide.

This was more than Alex's instincts. He'd been right. There was something going on here.

"There is another girl here, isn't there? I demand to see her at once." Alex took a step closer to the baroness, keeping his head held high. He was the high king. He was to be obeyed. "Don't lie to me."

Baroness Hackett dipped into a curtsy. "She's just a maidservant, sire. I didn't think she would be important enough for your royal majesty."

"I gave the order for every eligible young lady to be present. Even the maidservants." Alex glared at the baroness. Why would she keep Alex from the girl he loved?

The baroness was jealous. That had to be it. She wanted one of her own daughters to marry Alex, and she would've been angry when her maidservant claimed his heart instead. Had she mistreated her?

The glass slipper in his hand tugged again. Yes, that had to be it. This was why his love had been so afraid. She feared the baroness. For good reason. This baroness must have locked Alex's true love in a room, which was why she hadn't come to him the moment he arrived.

He stormed from the room and up the stairs, following the tugging of the glass slipper and his heart. The baroness, her oldest daughter, King Cassius's seneschal, and Alex's guard captain trailed behind him. The baroness was still sputtering inane excuses. Trying to cover up her crime, undoubtedly.

How badly had she mistreated the girl Alex loved? She must have been a cruel woman to work for. Her daughters were probably worse. They might look beautiful and innocent, but their hearts were dark and ugly.

He stalked down the hallway, checking each door and peeking inside. No one was inside any of the rooms, which were mostly bedrooms and sitting rooms with the occasional linen closet thrown in.

At the far end, a ladder was nailed to the wall with a trapdoor at the top. Alex tried the trap door. Locked.

Did they have her locked in the attic? How cruel was this baroness?

Alex spun on his heels to find her, her daughter, Major Vinzen, and Alex's captain of the guard all waiting in the hallway behind him. The daughter had her hands twisting in front of her, staring at the ceiling and biting her lip. Even the baroness had a pinched look to her face.

Yes, they didn't want him poking around the attic. Which was precisely why he needed to check there.

He held out a hand. "The key."

The baroness hesitated, then glanced at her daughter. "It will be all right, Monica. Give it to him."

The daughter, Monica, swallowed and fished in a pocket for a moment before she pulled out a small key.

Alex took it from her and inserted it in the lock on the trapdoor. He was on his way to rescue her. She just needed to hold on for a few more moments.

CHAPTER 31

ELARA

Voices came from below, indistinct and muffled, and the key clinked in the lock.

Elara shrank deeper into the darkness in the pile of furniture. It had only been a few minutes. High King Alexander couldn't have left already.

That meant he was the one on the other side of that trapdoor. Had the baroness and Monica turned Elara over to him willingly? Or were they being forced?

What should she do? Perhaps if she stayed still long enough, he wouldn't find her here. All she had to do was hold still for a few more minutes.

Her left foot ached, begging her to move from her cramped position. But she gritted her teeth and didn't so much as twitch a finger.

The trapdoor banged open, and the ladder creaked under the weight of someone climbing.

"Miss." High King Alexander's voice called into the attic. "I'm here to rescue you."

Rescue her? He was the one she needed rescuing from.

Elara held her breath and huddled in the shadows. What had compelled him to check the attic? How had he even guessed she was here?

"Don't be afraid. You can come out now. The cruel baroness won't hurt you ever again."

Cruel baroness? What gave him that idea? The baroness had been trying to help.

But High King Alexander wasn't in his right mind. He was most of the way cursed, and that had to be why he wasn't seeing things the way they truly were.

The floorboards creaked as he strode across the attic, headed toward her hiding place. Of course he was searching this corner. This pile of furniture was the only place in the entire attic where she could hide.

The glass slipper on her foot flashed. With a whoosh, her homespun dress changed into a black ball gown. The width of the skirts pressed against the chair in front of her, puffing around its edges.

Of all times for the slipper to decide to change her dress. Elara pressed both hands over her mouth to keep her groan muffled deep inside her. Why did this glass slipper have to make things so difficult?

High King Alexander's face appeared over the top of the padded chair. A smile burst onto his face, and his eyes filled with warmth, as if she was the most precious thing in the world to him. "I knew I'd find you, my darling."

Her muscles coiled with the urge to bolt. But where could she run? She was trapped in this attic. In this corner. With the glass slipper on her foot.

Had she ever had a chance to escape High King Alexander and this curse? Or had she been trapped from the moment she'd taken those glass slippers? No escape. No rescue.

High King Alexander held out a hand. "You're safe now. It's all right."

The tenderness in his voice clogged her throat. Because his concern for her wasn't real. It was the curse making him fall madly in love with her.

She had no choice. She took his hand and let him pull her to her feet. He led her to the trapdoor, his hand warm and strange around hers. Her skin crawled with the urge to tug her hand free, but she didn't.

He let go at the trapdoor, went down the ladder first, then looked up at her with a smile. "It's all right. I'll protect you."

Who would protect her from him? From the curse?

She was trapped. Perhaps she should make him drag her from the attic kicking and screaming. It would be difficult for him to force her down that hole.

But what good would it do in the end? He could just slip that glass slipper on her foot up here if he wanted to. He had guards to help him force her to leave. And it would cause the baroness more trouble if she tried to prevent the high king and his guards from taking Elara.

It would be better to keep some of her dignity. Perhaps if she played along, she would have a chance to get away from him and hide in the forest.

Elara limped the last few steps to the trapdoor. It took several minutes to wedge the ball gown's skirt through the hole. Annoying glass slipper. Why couldn't it have waited until she was back in the second story before transforming her dress yet again? There wasn't even a ball tonight.

High King Alexander smiled and took her hand again. "Shall we, milady?"

Elara could only manage a small nod. Over the high king's shoulder, she met Monica's gaze. Monica wrapped her hands over her stomach, her eyes wide. Elara gave a small shrug of her shoulders and tried to convey how much she was sorry for this whole mess.

The high king led Elara down the hallway. She tried to keep up, limping and wincing. After the dash to the attic, her left foot was shredding. It was amazing she wasn't leaving a trail of blood with every step.

High King Alexander glanced down at her with scrunched eyebrows. "Are you all right?"

"I'm fine." She shook her head, but the movement sent a swirl of dizziness through her head.

"You aren't well." High King Alexander swept her up in his arms, still gripping the glass slipper in his hand. "I should've realized you would be weak with the way they have been mistreating you."

"But they haven't been—" Elara started to say, but High King Alexander was already turning, his gaze hard.

He motioned toward Baroness Hackett. "Arrest her for her mistreatment of this girl."

Monica pressed both hands over her mouth, eyes widening. But Baroness Hackett stood with her back straight, her face serene, as the high king's guard captain tied her hands, glancing from the high king to Elara as if he knew this wasn't right.

"Please don't arrest her. She didn't hurt me. Please." Elara gripped the front of his shirt. Surely this curse made her have more influence on him. Would he listen to her?

High King Alexander's grip tightened on her as he started down the stairs. "I understand it's troubling to see her arrested. I've heard how captives can sometimes grow to sympathize with their captors. But you'll heal once you are free."

Baroness Hackett wasn't Elara's captor.

High King Alexander wasn't her captor either. It was the glass slippers and the curse that held her and all of them prisoner. It was the curse deep inside her that she'd fed for so many years with her jealousy and discontent.

And she couldn't rescue herself from any of it.

High King Alexander carried Elara to the front parlor and set her down in a padded chair near the center of the room.

King Cassius's seneschal strode in after them, followed by Baroness Hackett, her hands tied behind her back and the guard captain steering her with an arm.

Beatrice's eyes widened, and she jumped to her feet. "Mama!"

Monica hurried forward and grabbed Beatrice, hugging her tightly.

Elara turned away, focusing on her hands in her lap. She'd caused their pain. Baroness Hackett was the only parent they had left, and Elara was the reason they could lose her. Would the high king have her thrown in the dungeon like he had his manservant? Surely he wouldn't go so far as to have her executed.

There was noise coming from outside. Elara lifted her head and tried to peer out the windows, but she couldn't see outside because of the angle where she was sitting.

Baroness Hackett's gaze strayed to the window as well, but Elara couldn't read her expression to know what she was thinking. The high king's captain tightened his grip on the baroness's arm.

High King Alexander knelt in front of Elara, as if the other people in the room didn't matter to him. He slipped her moccasin from her right foot. His jaw tightened at the sight of the bandages, but he didn't comment on them.

Elara didn't try to explain. He probably thought it was

more proof of supposed cruelty on the part of the baroness and wouldn't believe Elara if she said it was from that glass slipper he was preparing to slip on her foot. He held up the glass slipper. "You, my darling, are the love of my life. I've known from the moment I first saw you in that ballroom that you stirred my heart."

Elara gripped the arms of the chair. Could she bolt from the room? Was that rising commotion outside more guards arriving? Had King Cassius sent reinforcements to make sure High King Alexander tracked her down?

She hadn't even been able to walk down the stairs without help. Would her left foot hold out if she tried to run? Probably not.

There was nowhere to go and no strength to get there. All she could do was brace against the chair as High King Alexander grasped her ankle and moved to slide the glass slipper onto her foot.

CHAPTER 32

DAEMYN

The river flew beneath Daemyn's canoe, the paddle solid in his hands. Had Alex already found the maidservant Elara? Was he already too late to stop yet another curse from falling on Alex?

In the prow of the canoe, Rosanna stroked strong and sure. Beside them, Zeke, Isi, and Josiah paddled their canoe, a small wave curling from the prow.

They curved around a bend, and the banks of the Scionee River opened into farm fields with a log cabin style manor house on the eastern bank. A crowd of men gathered in front of the manor's door, while off to the side, a young man stood beside a pair of elk harnessed to a small cart.

Daemyn leaned into the paddle, turning the canoe toward the eastern bank. Rosanna dug her paddle in as well, helping him guide the canoe across the current. Within moments, he ran the canoe to ground on the sandy shallows in front of the manor. He didn't try to properly pull the canoe to the dock that jutted into the river. There wasn't time.

How long had Alex been here? Had he put the slipper on her yet? If he was already cursed, how long would it take to break this curse? He wasn't sure he could handle another hundred years waiting for yet another cursebreaker for Alex.

Daemyn scrambled from the canoe and splashed into the river, the water soaking his moccasins and leggings to his knees. He grabbed his staff from the canoe and dashed from the river. Rosanna, Josiah, Zeke, and Isi would follow as soon as they could.

As he sprinted up the hill, the guards in front of the manor house closed ranks, their spears bristling outward.

Daemyn skidded to a halt, gripping his staff. He didn't want to fight these men. They were merely following orders, and he didn't want to be the cause of a war by killing any of them.

Stefan wasn't outside with King Cassius's men, and Daemyn wasn't sure that was a good or bad thing. The way Stefan's loyalties were torn, he might not be willing to give the order to have King Cassius's soldiers stand down, not even for Daemyn.

Off to one side, Alex's small knot of guards stood, their hands on the long knives at their waist as if torn between attacking Daemyn and standing down. Captain Taum, their leader, wasn't with them, probably inside with Alex.

Daemyn would need their help if he had a chance of getting past King Cassius's squad of soldiers. As running footsteps crunched behind him, Daemyn faced Alex's guards, meeting their gazes one at a time. "You know me. You know how my family served the high king. Let me pass."

Sauk, a man whose long, black hair was streaked with gray, stepped forward. "I know. But High King Alexander had you thrown in the dungeon. I doubt he would want you to enter."

"He is partially under a curse, and if you don't let me pass, he could fall fully into it." Daemyn eyed King Cassius's guards in case any of them decided to attack while he talked with Sauk. Zeke and Josiah stepped forward, long knives in their hands. Isi had drawn a knife while at Daemyn's side, Rosanna gripped a rock, hefting it in her hand as if feeling the weight before she threw.

Sauk glanced over his shoulder at the other men, his stance shifting as if he was uncertain what he should do.

It was good enough. Daemyn didn't have more time to waste trying to convince him. "Try not to kill anyone."

Without waiting for the others, Daemyn lunged toward King Cassius's soldiers and whipped his staff up, catching three of the spears brandished toward him and lifting their points out of the way. Before the soldiers could recover, he whirled the other end of the hardwood into a soldier's side.

His ribs ached, his bruises throbbed, but he wasn't going to let that minor pain stop him. He'd fought through much worse.

Spinning away from a spear jabbing toward him, he cracked his staff into a man's arm, causing him to drop his spear.

Zeke plowed into the soldiers as well, his knife a blur. Josiah was on Zeke's other side, fending off a spear with his long knife.

A rock whipped past Daemyn's head and clunked into the shoulder of a man who had been about to thrust his spear at him. Daemyn felt the hard line of a smile tug at his face. Isi and Rosanna were at their back, making sure no one circled around them.

With a shout, Sauk led Alex's seven guards into the fight, attacking King Cassius's men as well.

Daemyn didn't have time to subdue every guard standing between him and the door. He drove his staff into another man's stomach before whipping it up and cracking a man across the jaw.

Behind the knot of fighting men, the young man who had been standing near the elk and cart slipped along the wall of the manor, headed for the door as well. He wasn't armed, and Daemyn didn't think he was a threat.

Dodging between two of the guardsmen, Daemyn raced for the door, batting spears out of the way. A rock clacked against a guard's knee, and he stumbled out of Daemyn's way.

Then he was at the manor's door. He yanked it open and dashed inside, Rosanna at his heels.

A staircase was immediately in front of him, but to his right a large opening led into a parlor filled with people.

A girl was sitting in a chair in the center of the room. She had to be the maidservant Elara, but she looked like the mystery girl with black hair, this time in a blue, silk dress.

Alex knelt in front of her, a glass shoe in one hand, the girl's foot in his other.

"Don't." Daemyn lunged forward and knocked the glass slipper from Alex's hand with the end of his staff.

The slipper spun away and clattered against the floor, undamaged even after the force Daemyn had put behind the blow.

Alex's head snapped up, and he glared. "What are you doing, Jadon?"

Daemyn flexed his fingers on his staff. "This is a curse, sire. I can't let you do it."

Alex lunged to his feet, drawing the old-fashioned dagger belted at his side. "You were always jealous of me. You don't want me to be happy. It wasn't enough to steal the princess who woke me. You have to go and make sure I never have happiness."

Behind Alex, Captain Taum stepped forward, one hand still on the arm of a middle-aged woman who had her hands tied behind her back.

Stefan shifted, frowning. Daemyn wasn't sure he would stay out of this or make sure Alex was cursed since that was what his king would want.

Rosanna stalked around Daemyn and brandished a stone in her hand. Her stance was poised, her voice almost a growl as she glared at the others in the room. "Anyone who takes another step is going to regret it."

Daemyn eased a hand from his staff. Perhaps he'd been approaching this wrong. He'd tried to be the manservant. The advisor. Maybe he should try appealing to Alex as his friend. "Alex..."

"That would be High King Alexander to you." Alex's eyes hardened. He plunged the dagger toward Daemyn's chest.

Daemyn barely had time to raise his staff, catching Alex's forearms and pushing him back. His ribs burned with the effort, but he gritted his teeth, breathed past the pain, and shoved hard enough to make Alex stumble.

Taking a step back to gain more space, Daemyn rammed the end of his staff into Alex's stomach. Hard.

Probably harder than necessary. Definitely harder than he should.

Alex had fallen for a curse yet again, and once again, it

became Daemyn's problem to fix the mess. Alex had ordered him thrown in a dungeon. At times, it seemed like his life hadn't been his own since the moment he'd agreed to become Alex's manservant at the age of ten. Too young to fully realize what he was getting into besides a desperation to take care of his family and avoid the mines.

If he let it, this spark would simmer. He let out a long breath, forcing his shoulders to relax, mentally taking that flame of anger and snuffing it out.

His life wasn't his own. But it wasn't Alex's to dictate either. It had been painted before time began on the wall in the Highest King's halls. This was the work the Highest King had given him to do. He had been given a duty to serve. *Before honor is humility.*

He had come all too close to becoming hard and bitter during those hundred years. That wasn't who he wanted to be. He wanted to smile and laugh and remember that a life worth living had joy along with the sorrow.

Alex straightened and charged forward again, dagger flashing in his hand. Daemyn blocked, hooked a leg behind Alex's knees, and shoved. As Alex went down, he followed the motion, using his staff to pin Alex's dagger hand to the floor.

Before Daemyn had a chance to fully pin him, Alex lashed out with a foot, catching Daemyn in the ribs.

Pain flared through his chest. He gasped and fell backwards.

Alex pounced, swinging with his knife. Daemyn let go of his staff. Its length was useless here on the ground, and he grabbed Alex's wrist, trying to wrench the knife away from its downward trajectory.

Daemyn twisted, trying to get the leverage to push Alex off. His bruised muscles shook with pain, his aching ribs making it difficult to get a decent breath. Lack of sleep and paddling most of the night and day weakened his muscles.

If this had been a real fight, he would've pulled out his own knife.

Except that this was a real fight, at least to Alex. In his cursed state, he was trying to kill Daemyn.

And Daemyn couldn't fight to kill him in return. None of the others in the room could help either. Rosanna shifted, as if she wanted to help, but if she moved, Captain Taum would likely join the fight on Alex's side. He had no idea why Daemyn had just attacked the high king.

Alex's dagger eased closer to Daemyn's face.

Daemyn had died a number of ways in the last hundred years. Getting stabbed by Alex was not the way he wanted to die a final time.

CHAPTER 33

ELARA

Elara sat frozen in the chair. Should she try to run? Probably. But she couldn't force her muscles to move.

Daemyn Rand was wrestling on the floor with the high king. The high king had a dagger and stabbed at him. Daemyn rolled, and the two of them became a blur of movement Elara couldn't decipher.

The high king wasn't going to stop fighting. Not while he was under this curse.

The glass slipper lay on the floor a few feet away from her, its facets winking in the late afternoon sunlight streaming through the windows.

Monica had pushed Beatrice against the wall and was standing in front of her, as if trying to shield her younger sister. Baroness Hackett eased away from the high king's guard captain to stand closer to her daughters. The captain had a hand on his long knife, but he hadn't drawn it. King Cassius's seneschal was also tense, as if he was thinking about interfering in the fight as well.

But neither the seneschal nor the guard captain moved. Not with Princess Rosanna standing there, a rock poised to throw in her right hand and a second rock in her left.

The front door burst open again, and Terrence darted inside. He glanced around the parlor, his gaze latching on her.

Elara huddled in the chair. It had been bad enough facing Terrence in his shack and admitting how she'd messed up. But this was worse. She'd tried to run. She'd tried to fix this.

And still she was in trouble. There was nothing Terrence could do to help.

The high king let out something like a growl and tackled Daemyn again, sending him to the floor. Daemyn let out a muffled cry of pain.

What was Elara going to do? The sounds of fighting still came from outside. If she tried to run, she might end up right in the middle of a battle. But if she stayed, the high king would continue fighting until he put the glass slipper on her foot.

Terrence picked up the glass slipper, glancing from Daemyn and High King Alexander as they fought to where she huddled in the chair. He squared his shoulders and knelt in front of her.

"What are you doing?" Elara stared down at Terrence's blond hair.

"I don't want to inflict this glass slipper on you again." Terrence held it in both hands. Streaks of blood showed on his palms and fingers, as if he'd already managed to cut himself on the slipper's sharp edges. "But the high king won't stop fighting until this is back on your foot, and I trust that the Highest King will provide a cursebreaker for this curse too."

"No, Terrence, don't..." Elara placed her hands on his shoulders, trying to push him away. She couldn't let him do this. What would happen if he placed the slipper on her foot instead of the high king?

His shoulders were solid beneath her hands. He wouldn't budge for his pair of elk or the buffalo he cared for. He didn't give an inch under her hands.

He cradled the heel of her right foot in his hand and slid the glass slipper into place. Even through the bandages, the slipper's sharp edges dug into her skin.

But when Terrence raised his head, it was the look in his eyes that stabbed her. They filled with the same utter devotion she'd seen in High King Alexander's gaze in the past few days.

Terrence took her hand in his and gazed up at her as if she was the most precious thing in the world to him. "I love you."

No, no, no. Elara choked on a sob. Not Terrence. It was bad enough that she'd destroyed the high king. Been a pawn for King Cassius. Cursed herself with these slippers.

But to steal Terrence's mind as well? He was her best friend. How could she do this to him? He didn't deserve to spend the rest of his life groveling at her feet.

"Elara..." Terrence reached for her other hand, still gazing at her with that look in his eyes.

She couldn't do it anymore. She couldn't lose him too.

Yanking her hands from his, Elara staggered to her feet and lurched around him. Both of her feet tore with agony, and this time blood spilled around the edge of the left slipper and dripped onto the floor.

She needed to leave. Perhaps if she ran deep enough in the forest, no one would find her, and she wouldn't hurt anyone again. It seemed she destroyed all those around her.

She'd lost her father to the war. She'd lost her mother shortly afterwards. She'd hurt the family who had taken her in and given her a job so she could take care of herself. Now she'd cursed her best friend.

The front door was still blocked with knots of fighting people. Elara raced through the manor and skidded into the back door, hitting it with her shoulder. She fumbled with the latch until it snicked open. After flinging the door aside, she stumbled down the steps and sprinted across the back lawn. The glass slippers sliced into her feet, her bones, her heart, with each step.

A field spread across the hills behind the manor house while the forest rose into the distance on the far side. Safety, so far away.

Elara plunged between the dry stalks of corn, their leaves grating against her arms and rustling against her black ballgown. She stumbled over the branching vines of the squashes and pumpkins covering the ground while the dry bean tendrils reached for her face and hair.

The field stretched for all directions around her, the scattered stalks of corn rising higher than her head.

She tripped, her toe catching in a vine, and sprawled onto the ground, her hands pressed in the dirt. Her breath came out a sob. Tears streaked hot and wet down her cheeks. Pain radiated from her feet into her whole body, her head pounding, her hands shaking, her stomach churning.

As much as she wanted to be strong enough to run and never look back, she couldn't. Both feet bled. It took all her remaining strength to drag herself upright and sit on a nearby pumpkin, its sides a mottled orange and green.

Was there truly no escape for her? Were these glass slippers going to kill her as she slowly bled out?

There was no way to save herself from the curse of

these slippers. She couldn't run far enough nor was she strong enough to make them let go of her feet. She couldn't even save those who had been caught in this curse with her.

Utterly helpless. That's what she truly was. She'd schemed for so long about how to save herself. From a servant's life. From these slippers. From High King Alexander. None of it had done any good. Instead of saving herself, she'd destroyed her own life and the lives of everyone she hadn't even realized she'd cared about.

She hunched over, wrapped her arms around her knees, and sobbed. She was broken, her chest filled with jagged pieces of glass. What a horrible person she must be to selfishly choose this.

The dry cornstalks rattled as a breeze swept down from the mountains, over the forests, and through the field. Its cool fingers wrapped around her feet, soothing some of the pain, before brushing against her face.

"Elara."

The name was a call deep inside her chest as it was spoken on the breeze with all the tenderness of a father claiming a child as his.

When she lifted her head, the stranger from the castle causeway was kneeling in front of her. Yet, he wasn't a stranger. Not anymore. Had he ever truly been a stranger to her? Or had she simply been blinded to the reality he revealed to her now?

He was the Highest Prince. The Cursebreaker.

A circlet glinted against his hair, and there was something powerful about him even as he knelt in the dirt. Yet she couldn't exactly put her finger on what about him felt that way.

"Why do you weep?"

Elara scrubbed at her face, gritty dirt smearing across her cheeks. Why did she cry? For a moment, she couldn't pick just one reason. Why wouldn't she cry at this moment?

She sniffed back a line of mucus and tried to surreptitiously swipe her nose on the back of her hand. Here she was with ugly, puffy eyes, dirt-covered face, bleeding feet, and a running nose while the Highest Prince of All knelt before her. As if she needed any more reminders of how much of a mess she was.

She hugged her arms over her stomach and stared at the glass slippers, now red with her blood. "I cursed my best friend. He was just trying to help me."

"Why do you believe he is cursed?"

"He put the slipper on my foot and looked at me the way High King Alexander has." Elara rubbed her arms. "Like he was in love with me."

"Is he not?"

Elara blinked, something in her chest fluttering. Terrence hadn't danced with her while she was wearing the glass slippers. The wording of the curse specified that the young men that danced with her would fall madly in love with her.

He hadn't been under the influence of the curse when he'd put the glass slipper on her foot. The emotion she'd seen in his eyes...it had been real.

Was Terrence in love with her?

He'd always been her best friend. Always there for her. Always giving her advice when she asked, lending a shoulder to cry on when she needed. Their relationship was so comfortable, so close, she'd never paused to think that, for him, it had deepened into love somewhere along the way. He'd done such a good job of hiding it, treating her like he always did instead of pressuring her into a change she might not want.

Her heart beat harder, faster in her chest. What did she feel for Terrence? In that awful moment when she'd thought Terrence had been cursed, it was as if all the sunshine in her world had been snatched away.

Elara hugged herself tighter. Was it possible she was in love with Terrence? She'd thought love was all the romance. The glittering ball gowns. The swoony feeling as she'd danced in High King Alexander's arms in the garden in Castle Fonthaven.

But true love had to be more than that. Maybe love was what she had with Terrence. Even in the glass slippers and ballgown while the high king perceived her appearance according to his own dreams, Terrence had held that slipper in his hands and seen *her*.

Perhaps true love was a reflection of this moment as she huddled on a half-ripe pumpkin while the Highest Prince knelt before her in the dirt. It was the breeze caressing her hair and filling her with strength even as the Highest Prince's gaze laid the truth of her and the curse inside her bare for her to see. It was a trust that even as the Highest Prince saw the worst of what was inside her, he still had chosen to love her from before he'd laid the foundations for Tallahatchia's mountains.

Reaching down, Elara tugged on a glass slipper. Still stuck.

She should've known. Terrence wasn't cursed. Perhaps the curse on the high king had been broken when Terrence put the slipper on her foot. But the curse on her went deeper. Deeper than the glass cutting into her feet.

Because some part of her still clung to the slippers and the dreams they represented. The reality had turned into a nightmare, but the dreams of silks and princes and dances still lingered. A part of her might even take the slippers all over again just for that taste of the life she had wanted. "Why was I not given more? It's not fair that others have so much when I have so little."

Something in the Highest Prince's gaze turned stern, all stone and burning embers and mountains immovable. But his voice was gentle. "If you were not content with the abundance you were given, how could you have been content with more? The things you desire would make you happy for a moment, but they would not make you blessed. Be content knowing I will not give you more abundance than you can handle in me."

Elara hung her head as his words settled into her. She was not like Monica and Beatrice. With their wealth, they had looked after her. Given generously. Done much.

If she had been in their place, would she have been as generous? Or would she have been stingy and arrogant, lording the things she had over those around her.

In dreaming of silk dresses and castles and a romantic dance with the high king, she'd nearly missed the bounty she'd already been given.

No wonder Terrence had remained merely her friend instead of revealing the depth of his feelings for her. She'd spent her time with him talking about how she wanted riches and grandeur and a prince to sweep her away. He had nothing to offer her but the life she already had. Days of hard work followed by evenings in a small cabin. Homespun dresses and worn moccasins.

But it would be a life of laughter and true happiness. If Elara could be content and find joy in where she had been placed.

It wouldn't be easy. Not when the cursed slippers still

clung to her, as if knowing deep down she was the same, cursed girl who felt entitled to more than she deserved.

The breeze gave her the strength the look up. His gaze was warm. He was the Cursebreaker, and he was her hope. She couldn't rescue herself from this curse nor the curse inside her, but he could. He'd already planted the seed of wanting the curse to be removed. Now there was only trust. "I can't remove these glass slippers."

"No, you cannot. They must be broken." He reached forward, as if to cradle her foot in his hands.

She drew her foot back. As much as she longed to be free of these slippers, she hesitated. "Why? Why are you doing this? Saving me?"

He held up his palm. There, in gold letters as if engraved in his skin, was her name. *Elara.* "You were chosen for this moment. That I could be your Cursebreaker."

She was his, her name written where it would not be forgotten. Even though she was a servant, to him she was never invisible.

Perhaps that was the secret to contentment. Knowing that serving him was better than riches or silk.

When he gently picked up her left foot, the glass slipper slid free easily. The Highest Prince held the glass slipper in both hands before he crushed it. Glass splintered, spearing into his hands. Blood welled around the shards stuck in his palms.

Elara let out something like a squeak, and her hand twitched forward a few inches, and she wasn't sure if the twisting inside her came from seeing him hurt or aching over the slipper's destruction. As if, even now, she wanted to snatch the slipper back.

The Highest Prince eased the second glass slipper from

her right foot. He shattered this one too in his hands, glass embedding into his skin. And still her name glittered gold on his palm, shimmering beneath a coating of blood.

Her feet throbbed, the gashes exposed and raw.

Water swished, and Elara blinked at the basin of water that was now beneath her feet. She couldn't say where it had come from. It was simply there, as if it had been there the entire time without her noticing.

The Highest Prince dipped a white cloth into the water, wrung it out, then dabbed her bleeding feet. The water soothed the ache, washing away the last lingering shards of glass from her wounds.

When the wounds were washed, the Highest Prince wrapped a white bandage around each of her feet. Even though his hands bled, the bandages remained unspotted. Clean.

She was free. She drew in a deep breath, and it tasted of earth and dry cornstalks and the deep running Scionee River. It was time for new dreams. New hopes. New desires.

When she opened her eyes, the Highest Prince was gone. The basin was gone. The glass slippers were gone.

But her feet were bandaged, her heart healing.

Elara ran her fingers over her homespun dress. It wasn't silk. It wasn't a beautiful ball gown. But for the first time in her life, she was content.

CHAPTER 34

ALEXANDER

Alex held a dagger in his hand, its tip only a few inches from Daemyn's chest. Daemyn's hands were locked around Alex's wrists, his fingers painful as steel manacles. Daemyn's breathing was coming in gasps, his face twisted as if in pain, while Alex's knee pressed to Daemyn's chest, pinning him down.

What was he doing? Alex gaped and stilled. As if realizing he was no longer fighting, Daemyn's grip loosened.

Alex stumbled to his feet, the dagger slipping from his hand to clatter onto the wood floor. Something shook deep inside him, his stomach churning at the sight of a thin line of blood standing out along Daemyn's sleeve.

Alex had done that to him. He'd done...he pressed a hand to his temple, trying to sort out the blur of memories tumbling through him. His hand, pointing at Daemyn. *Throw this man in the dungeon.*

What had he done? Alex staggered back another step, staring at his hands, then up at Daemyn. He had traces of two black eyes while a bruise spread across his cheek. By the way he pressed an arm to his chest, he was in pain. As if he'd taken a beating.

Alex remembered enough of their recent fight to know the bruises hadn't come from him. It must have been King Cassius's guards when they had thrown Daemyn in the dungeon.

Thrown in the dungeon. Beaten. On Alex's orders. Each bruise. Each broken bone Daemyn might or might not have. It was all Alex's fault. Again.

Alex wanted to crumple to his knees right there, but there were too many eyes in the room. The king's buffalo boy kneeling on the floor in front of a chair. Princess Rosanna facing Alex's guard captain and King Cassius's seneschal. Baroness Hackett with her hands behind her back with her daughters huddled on either side. He couldn't break here.

He stumbled from the room, headed for the outside door.

"Your Majesty, don't—" Daemyn's voice was only steps behind him. Too dutiful to allow Alex to dash off without a guard.

It was only then Alex had a vague memory of a squad of King Cassius's guards following him. He probably shouldn't run out into the middle of them. He wasn't sure how safe they were.

The door flung open, and Zeke stepped inside. "Uncle Daemyn! Are you..." He halted, glared at Alex, then turned to Daemyn. "Outside is secure."

Alex spun and headed for the back door. It was standing a crack open, probably after the girl's retreat. When Alex stepped outside, he didn't see any sign of her. Good. He wasn't ready to face her yet. He wasn't ready to face himself at the moment.

He sank onto the back step, the stone cold beneath him. He propped his elbows on his knees and rested his head in his hands, digging his fingers into his hair.

This had been a curse. The truth lay raw and aching before him. This was worse than the hundred year's sleep. Now, as then, it had been his choice. Then, as now, he'd ignored the good advice of those around him to continue in his own stubborn way.

But last time, he'd been so arrogant he hadn't known better. This time, he knew the allure of a curse. Deep down, he'd known what he was doing was wrong. There had been so many moments along the way when he could've stopped giving in to the curse.

He'd been so lonely he hadn't cared. He'd let himself be convinced that this was real and right.

He'd thought himself better. But at the first test, he'd fallen right back into his old ways. Worse than before, even.

Was it possible to hate himself this much? Like he wanted to tear himself in two, shedding the arrogant, disgustingly weak, horrible part of himself. Why had he thought he could build a friendship with Daemyn? Or find a romance with a stranger like the girl he'd thought himself in love with? He didn't like himself. Why would anyone else like him?

Behind him, the door creaked open. Someone sank onto the other side of the step.

Alex didn't look up. He didn't have to. He groaned and tightened his grip on his hair. As if the pain of tearing hair from his scalp would make up for what he'd done. "I'm sorry."

Those words were hardly enough. But was anything? Nothing Alex could say or do could make this right. Maybe if he offered to have himself thrown in the dungeon.

But Daemyn wouldn't ask for that. Though, by the ache in Alex's ribs, Daemyn hadn't held back earlier. Not that he blamed him. He deserved it.

"I know." Daemyn drew in a deep breath, as if steeling himself to say something he wasn't going to like. "I—"

"Don't. Just…" Alex raised his head but couldn't look at Daemyn. He was going to be his usual, deferential self. Even if he didn't feel like it, Daemyn would do what he was supposed to do and tell Alex all was forgiven.

Alex didn't want to hear it yet. For some reason, he wanted to wallow a bit longer before Daemyn did his humble routine. "You have a right to be angry with me. You don't have to forgive and forget and all that right this moment. I turned on you. Had you thrown in a dungeon, which led to you getting beaten. That's too big for a couple of words to make this all right."

Out of the corner of his eye, Alex could see Daemyn rest his elbows on his knees. He was staring off into the fields stretching into the distance behind the manor house. "Forgiveness doesn't mean much if it can't take the hard things as well as the easy. So, yes. I'm going to forgive you right this moment. Because the anger will only get worse if I let it linger."

Alex should've felt better, but he didn't miss Daemyn's admission that he was angry. Of course he was.

"The worst part is that I could've stopped it. I knew what was happening, and I let it. Was I really so desperate that I thought being in a fake relationship caused by a curse was better than being alone?" Alex scrubbed his hands over his face. He was so pathetic. "How did you manage to do it? Be content alone for a hundred years?"

"I didn't have a romantic relationship, but I wasn't alone. Friendships can be deep and fulfilling. Perhaps in a different way, but still real." Daemyn glanced over at Alex before staring back at the field filled with dry cornstalks and the bright dots of yellow squash and orange pumpkins. "Friendships can keep you from feeling alone."

Alex's shoulders sagged. Daemyn had been blessed with a large family and abundant friends because of it.

But Alex never had any siblings. And because of his arrogance and his place as high prince, he'd never managed to make any true friendships either. He'd thought himself close with Mirabelle, but they spent more time kissing than talking. Not the sort of romantic relationship that had depth.

The only friend he'd ever had a chance of having was Daemyn, and Alex made a royal mess out of that. Friends didn't throw their friends into dungeons or order them about like a manservant they expected to lick their boots or take them away from their families for ten years without ever giving them a chance to go home or pretty much anything Alex had ever done to Daemyn.

Yet Daemyn was here. Would he offer friendship once again?

Alex had no clue how to be a friend any more than last time he'd attempted it. If they were supposed to be friends or family or whatever, then Alex was more like an evil step-brother to Daemyn than anything else.

Daemyn rubbed at a scar cutting across his palm. "But it was hard. Those first few years, I watched my brothers and sisters grow up, get married, start families. It hurt, knowing I couldn't have that happiness when they could."

Alex nodded. He understood that ache. Some of it, anyway. His reasons for not wanting to be alone weren't nearly as noble as Daemyn's. Daemyn talked about a wife, a family, a home to call his own. Alex just wanted the romance and kissing and shallow stuff without wanting what truly made those things matter, like family and sharing a heart and life together.

Daemyn shrugged and stopped rubbing the scar. "I learned contentment doesn't always mean being free from a good desire for something, but it's a joy in your life as it currently is, knowing that what you've been given whether it's an abundance or a lack is good because the Highest King has declared it to be so. Because in the end, the only thing we truly need is the Highest King's favor."

The favor that granted access to that crystal throne room. Alex had knelt in the light of that throne, yet he'd acted as if it wasn't enough. What sort of fool did that make him?

"For most of the hundred years, the desire for marriage was taken away so that particular struggle for contentment wasn't one I had to fight all those decades." Daemyn shook his head, his gaze still focused on the fields in the distance. "And, looking back, I'm grateful for the life I lived. If I'd had a wife and children of my own, I never would have grown as close to my nieces and nephews. It was a gift to see so many faithful generations that I never should've taken for granted. But eventually, I let myself slip past contentment into a numbness without joy."

It shouldn't make Alex feel better to hear Daemyn admit to a weakness, but it did. Daemyn always seemed to know the right thing to do. But perhaps that's what came of having a hundred years to practice.

"That's the way of things. You can tip off either side of the canoe, but you end up in the river no matter what." Daemyn gave another shrug, his mouth quirking into something of a wry smile before the expression faded back to serious again. "My pa's motto in life was *Before honor is humility.* He always said that meant there was great honor in being humble, doing humble work, and being content with the humble place you've been given."

"Your pa was a good man." Alex had only met him once, briefly, a hundred years ago. He'd barely dared interact with the man with the first stirrings of shame eating away at him.

Before honor is humility. If Daemyn had to learn to find the joy in life once again, Alex had fallen off the opposite side with desiring too much in all the wrong ways.

At the end of the hundred years' sleep, Alex had knelt before the Highest Prince, too horrified by what he'd done to raise his head. That same horror gripped him now. It wasn't only Daemyn Alex had wronged. *Give place to your pride no more,* he'd been told. Yet he'd woken up and blithely went about trying to be better all on his own. As if he was somehow good enough and strong enough to make himself a better person by sheer power of will.

He wasn't that strong or good. The power to be better could only come from the Highest King.

When he closed his eyes, it was as if he was again kneeling on that crystal floor in the brightness that would overwhelm without the Highest Prince standing between him and the throne, even though he could feel the cold stone of the step beneath him and still hear the dry rustle of the cornstalks as the breeze whispered between them and curled around Alex.

What he said now would echo in those halls, heard and answered. He couldn't think of anything more eloquent to ask besides a simple *Make me better than what I am. Please.*

He had the feeling it was something he would have to ask today. And tomorrow. And the day after that. Perhaps for the rest of his life, he'd always be begging for the strength to be better than he was by nature. Because his nature was weak and proud and cursed.

Alex released a long sigh, the breeze strangely cool against his forehead, but warm as it wrapped around him. This wasn't going to be easy, trying to repair everything he had broken. But with the strength of the Highest Prince, he had to try. "I'm glad you have Rosanna. And she has you. I think I may have said some things that sounded like I was jealous."

"I know you didn't mean them." Daemyn's posture stiffened a fraction. As if he was saying what he was supposed to say instead of what he truly wanted to say.

"We've been over this. No holding back. You and I both know that isn't true. This curse only worked because the emotions were already there." Alex needed the brutal honesty. He'd deluded himself right into this mess. Only hard truth beaming sharp and hot onto his heart would expose everything that needed to be ripped out and tossed aside.

Jealousy. *Tug.*

Anger. *Yank.*

Pride. *Rip.*

He was wrung out and empty. Weary. But more clear-headed than he'd been in a long time. Perhaps even before falling into this curse.

Daemyn leaned back on his hands, though something in him was stiff and wary. But a smile touched his face, even if it was probably forced. "In that case, Your Highness, you said a great deal that you might want to apologize for. As much as you probably want to linger out here, it won't solve anything."

No, it wouldn't. If only he was home at Castle Eyota where things were familiar, and he'd have his mother to remind him he wasn't as all alone in the world as he sometimes felt. He needed time to sort out what kind of person and high king he ought to be.

But he was still in Pohatomie, surrounded by enemies with only a few allies to stand with him, if they would after the mess he'd just made. King Cassius was still a threat. He might not have succeeded in having Alex spark another war, but it had been a near thing. And Alex had certainly done plenty to lessen the respect the kingdoms would have for him.

He had been gifted with intelligence. A gift he tended to ignore the moment his emotions got involved.

With one last deep breath, Alex pushed himself to his feet, faced Daemyn, and held out a hand. "I could use the wisdom of my advisor, if you're still willing."

It wasn't what he wanted to ask. But it seemed like pushing too hard to say he could use a friend to stand beside him.

"Of course, Your Highness." Daemyn took his offered hand and levered himself to his feet.

They would have to start over on this friendship thing. Again. Alex wouldn't blame Daemyn if he hightailed it back to the hills of Buckhannock and settled down by the descendants of his family.

Alex straightened his shoulders and strode into the manor house. The wooden floor creaked under his feet, and under Daemyn's as he followed. Alex kept his head high as he stepped back into the parlor.

Most of the people hadn't moved, as if they didn't dare. Captain Taum still gripped Baroness Hackett's arm while her daughters clustered by her, though they now sat against the wall with their arms around their knees. Major Stefan Vinzen leaned against the far wall, arms crossed, while Rosanna had her back to the corner by the door to keep an eye on everyone. Isi stood next to her, also watching the others in the room warily.

The buffalo boy was pacing in the center of the room, hands behind his back. He glanced up as Alex strolled in, and his shoulders sagged.

It was time to be a high king and sort this mess out. Especially since he was the one who caused it in the first place. "Captain Taum, please release the baroness. She is no longer under arrest."

Captain Taum started untying her hands so fast it was as if he'd been waiting for the order. By the way the rope fell off after two tugs, he hadn't tied it tightly.

Her daughters jumped to their feet and hugged her. The younger of the two had tears streaking down her face.

Alex faced Baroness Hackett. "I apologize for this..." He nearly said misunderstanding but gave himself a good internal shake. He couldn't minimize what he'd done. "This wrongful arrest. By my own mistakes, I was under the influence of a curse, and it made me perceive things not as they were. I especially apologize for the terror I caused your daughters."

Baroness Hackett wrapped an arm around each of her daughters, holding them tightly. "Thank you for your apology, Your Majesty."

A throat cleared behind Alex. He turned and found himself face-to-face with the girl he'd asked to marry him. Several times, if he remembered right. He still didn't know her name.

The only reason he even knew it was her was something about the shape of her face and the look in her eyes. The rest of her looked nothing like what he'd seen when he was under the curse. Instead of blue-eyed and black-haired, she had light blonde, straight hair and deep, brown eyes. She was pretty enough in her own way, but not the delicate beauty he'd thought she'd had thanks to the curse.

She had been wearing a red ball gown a moment ago, but now she was dressed in a light blue, homespun dress with an apron over it. Her feet were wrapped in white bandages, no glass slippers in sight.

He waited for a jolt in his chest, a surge to his heartbeat. None came. It was awkward seeing her and knowing what a fool he'd made of himself. But he wasn't in love with her or even all that attracted to her anymore.

That came with a sense of loss. He didn't truly want to be in love with her, but the hope of having someone to love and be loved in return had been nearly worth it.

Nearly. Now it was just pathetic.

The buffalo boy took a step toward the girl, his mouth working as if he wanted to say something, but he cleared his throat and looked away.

The girl twisted her hands in front of her, her gaze flicking from Alex to the floor. "I'm sorry for this, Your Majesty. I never meant to pull you into a curse."

"You're not the only one at fault. I could have resisted the curse's pull, but I willingly gave in." Alex's throat ached at having to admit his failings publicly. Again.

He began to pace. How was he going to think his way out of this? The immediate threat of the curse was gone, but King Cassius still needed to be dealt with. Alex didn't have the resources to start a war with Pohatomie, nor did he want to spark a war that would spread across all of Tallahatchia.

He needed something clever. Almost manipulative to combat King Cassius's plotting.

A bluff. That's all he had. He glanced around at the

people in this room, an idea sparking. It would take all of them to pull this off.

"Daemyn." He spun on his heel. Daemyn was standing close to Rosanna, their shoulders brushing. For a moment, Alex's throat tightened, a burn in his chest. That's what he wanted. Closeness. Companionship.

Alex swallowed it down. He was going to be content as he was, no matter how hard it was. He forced a smile on his face. "I have an idea, and I think I'm going to need your advice to make sure it will work."

Daemyn met his gaze and nodded, his shoulders straightening as if he was mentally steeling himself to go to war if necessary.

Alex turned to Major Vinzen. "And I think we're going to need your help to pull this off."

Major Vinzen shifted, his gaze flicking past Alex to Daemyn. "I know I haven't helped as much as you would've liked. But Pohatomie is my home, and King Cassius my king."

"It isn't fair to demand your loyalty based on a promise my sister—your great-grandmother—made decades ago." Daemyn shook his head. "Besides, that promise was fulfilled the moment High King Alexander woke. I have no reason to demand loyalty any longer."

Major Vinzen glanced toward the doorway, as if he could see through the wall to where Zeke and Prince Josiah must be guarding the squad of Pohatomie soldiers. "That hasn't stopped the Buckhannock side of the family. But they remained closer to you than other branches, I think."

Alex cleared his throat. "Actually, I think my plan won't violate your loyalties, not if you wish to prevent your king from starting a war. If we do this right, he won't even know you helped us."

Major Vinzen slowly nodded. "I'll have to hear your plan, but if it's something that won't harm my king or my kingdom, I'm willing to listen."

Alex felt something in him settle. Perhaps this would work after all.

CHAPTER 35

ALEXANDER

"When will your mysterious girl arrive, Your Majesty?" King Cassius smiled, slick and smooth.

Alex forced his grin to remain too wide, his expression empty of everything besides a vague, drooling infatuation. It had taken some practice before Elara, as he'd learned her name was, Rosanna, and Isi assured him that he'd gotten it right.

The expression turned his stomach now. But he had to act like it only a few more minutes. "My beloved will be here." He waved his hand expressively, slopping the water in his glass. He kept waving and talking as if he didn't notice. "And then before this entire assembly, I will declare my undying love."

King Cassius's eyes were sharp as he sipped at his glass of water.

Was he even fooling King Cassius? Alex had managed to convince him to call yet another ball the moment he'd returned—via a canoe down the Pohatomie River since he had refused to get back in that elk cart.

But had King Cassius called the ball because the king thought his plan to humiliate Alex publicly was working? Or had he realized his plan partially failed and planned to use this ball to manipulate Alex one last time?

"What did you say happened to the squad of guards I sent with you?" King Cassius's tone was much too casual for the gleam to his eyes. Alex had told him this information once already, but King Cassius was testing him. Searching for any holes in his story.

Alex beamed as bright and empty-headed as he possibly could. "Didn't I tell you? It must have slipped my mind. I've been so enraptured with my darling that I haven't been able to think straight. I sent them throughout the countryside to proclaim the invite to this ball. I knew you wouldn't mind. You said you would cooperate with anything I needed, and I need this ball to declare my true love before everyone. There wasn't time to wait for you to give your official permission. I hope I didn't overstep? I am the high king, after all."

Alex tried to blink at King Cassius with an innocent expression. After all, most of what he said was true. The soldiers had been reluctant to go, and only Major Vinzen telling them that the whole getting attacked and tied up thing was a misunderstanding had finally convinced them to leave. They'd had no reason to doubt the word of their seneschal, so they'd gone. Major Vinzen had gone with them to claim innocence in Alex's plan tonight.

Spreading the word would keep them away from Castle Fonthaven long enough that they couldn't report the attack to King Cassius. And it had been the only way to invite as many of the nearby citizens—noble and common—to the castle on short notice.

Alex scanned the crowd of dancers again, though it was hard to concentrate on what he was seeing while keeping the vapid expression.

Princess Rosanna danced with Prince Josiah. King Cassius didn't have a way to prove they had helped Daemyn escape the dungeon, nor could he be sure they'd been the ones who had left the castle thanks to Asa and Captain Degotaga covering for them. They looked tense enough that King Cassius might assume Princess Rosanna was angry with being slighted by Alex, and Prince Josiah was miffed on behalf of his ally.

Zeke, Isi, and Daemyn were around somewhere, but Alex probably wouldn't spot them. All of their guards lurked nearby in case they had to flee Castle Fonthaven in a hurry if Alex's plan failed.

Hopefully that wouldn't be necessary.

Monica, Baroness Hackett's oldest daughter, had claimed a dance with Prince Tyrell. The Monongadotte prince towered over her, an effect made even more noticeable by the huge elk antlers he wore perched on a crown on his head. Compared to the fur-covered Tyrell, Monica was a delicate daisy of yellow hair and slim build.

She had confessed her part in King Cassius's plan, small as it was, and Alex almost wished he had fallen for a girl like her. She was kind, sweet, and gentle. All things he should desire in the woman he married.

Maybe someday. As the past few days had shown, he wasn't ready for marriage or desiring the right things in a lady just yet.

The stir at the far end of the room was expected. After

all, Baroness Hackett and her younger daughter Beatrice had been stationed near the doorway to make sure there was enough commotion, gasps of shock, and whispers when Elara made one, last grand entrance.

This time, she came as herself, her blonde hair styled by Isi and wearing a dress borrowed from Monica. Without the extra *something* the cursed glass slippers had given her, she wasn't all that breath-taking or someone who should be capable of rendering an entire ball room speechless.

But thanks to Alex's allies causing a stir, she'd stopped the entire ballroom. She shifted, hands clasped in front of her.

Alex couldn't let the moment linger too long. If he did, King Cassius may suspect something even more than he already did. Instead, Alex forced his inane grin to grow even wider. He strode straight down the length of the ball-room, making several people jump out of his way as if he was too enamored to notice the people standing between him and Elara.

When he reached her side, he held out an arm and asked through his fake grin, "Are you ready for this?"

"Not really." Her tone was tight, as if her teeth were clenched behind her smile as she set her hand on his arm.

"It will be over in a few minutes." Alex patted her hand. It should have felt comfortable, considering how many times they'd walked like this over the past few days. But her touch on his arm was as foreign to him as her real hair and eyes.

He strolled back through the crowd of halted dancers until he reached King Cassius. With one last hopelessly lovestruck grin, Alex faced the gathering with Elara at his side. "Good people of Pohatomie as well as distinguished guests from Neskahana, Monongadotte, and Buckhannock, I have an announcement to make."

To his left, King Cassius straightened, the hint of a smile flickering at the corners of his mouth. As if this was just the announcement he'd been waiting for. The moment, he thought, Alex was going to make an utter fool of himself.

Alex took a deep breath and let the annoying grin and vague expression drop. "It has come to my attention that it's rumored Princess Rosanna and I are courting. It's an understandable assumption, given that she woke me from my cursed sleep, but she's actually courting my chief advisor and friend, Daemyn Rand."

Princess Rosanna had halted across the ballroom near the doors to the garden. As Alex watched, Daemyn appeared from the darkness outside and joined her.

When the crowd turned to look in their direction, Rosanna slipped a hand into Daemyn's.

King Cassius stiffened, his eyes narrowing.

"Many of you heard me give the order to have Daemyn Rand arrested the other night. I hereby revoke that order." Alex met Daemyn's gaze, and Daemyn gave him a small nod. Another reassurance of forgiveness. "For the past few days, I have been under the influence of a curse that stole my critical thinking and made me fall madly in love with a girl I didn't even know."

Elara dropped Alex's arm, took a step back, and curtsied. Alex gave her a nod in return, and she joined Baroness Hackett, Monica, and Beatrice, who had worked their way through the crowd to stand nearby.

King Cassius's smile had tightened into something more like a grimace. His hand closed on his long knife, but he didn't draw it.

"Under this curse, I made a fool of myself. I went harrying off to force many of your daughters to try on a glass slipper to find the girl I thought I loved." Alex swept his glance around the room. He had their attention. Both noble families in their mix of silks and linens to the common folk who had come wearing their finest buckskins and homespun. "In doing so, I had the opportunity to see your kingdom. I met many of you. I learned more about your struggles. I know Pohatomie is a sharp contrast between the wealth here in Castle Fonthaven and the existence you grow from the earth."

King Cassius made a sound, as if he meant to protest, but stopped. He too would be able the feel the way the gathered people were listening. With Prince Tyrell from Monongadotte, Princess Rosanna, and Prince Josiah in attendance, King Cassius wouldn't dare openly oppose Alex.

"Hear me now, Pohatomie. I see you. My mother is from Pohatomie. My name, Alexander, is a Pohatomie name. In me, you have one of your own on the high king's throne." Alex held his head high. It was a bold claim but calculated to take the river of public sentiment from under King Cassius's canoe.

King Cassius made the people of Pohatomie feel overlooked. By his actions and his arguments, he pushed to get rid of the high king and let each kingdom rule alone. Alex needed the people of Pohatomie to see him as *their* high king, not just a random person sitting on the throne in Castle Eyota.

"You are an important part of Tallahatchia. Your fields feed all seven kingdoms. You may have a humble job, but there is great honor in the dirt under your fingernails and the sweat on your skin." Alex once again found himself looking across the ballroom toward Daemyn. "A wise man once told me that before honor is humility. That is something I needed to learn through this curse."

Across the way, Daemyn's mouth quirked with a smile.

It was time to set aside honor, crush pride, and kneel. Only twice had Alex truly bowed before another, and that had been in the throne room Beyond before the Highest King and before the Highest Prince in his dream before waking from the cursed sleep.

In that dream, the Highest Prince too had knelt. If the Prince of All could kneel, then surely Alex of all people should be willing to kneel before his fellow men and women.

Alex faced the crowd. "For that reason, I bow before you, good people of Pohatomie. Know that from this day forward you will always be held in great honor in all of Tallahatchia."

With a deep breath, Alex went down on one knee, rested a hand on the floor, and bowed his head as a subject would to his king. He held the position for several moments, feeling the stillness in the room, as if no one dared move while their high king knelt on the floor before them.

Alex straightened and spun to face King Cassius. The king's face was tinged red while his mouth flattened in a taut line. Alex stared right back. "And you, King Cassius. I know how you plotted against me. You wanted to nudge me into making a fool of myself before the royalty of Monongadotte, Buckhannock, and Neskahana. In that, you succeeded. But in manipulating them and me into sparking another war, you failed. The only kingdom you have isolated is your own."

King Cassius flexed his fingers on his long knife. "You cannot isolate Pohatomie. The other six kingdoms need us more than we need them. We can live without your gold or beadwork or silks, but you need our corn."

"Yes, we do. But look around you. Look at your fields that need Buckhannock's iron to turn the soil, Monongadotte's skill with leather for the harnesses your buffalo wear, and Neskahana's pottery to store your produce. Look at the gold plating on your ceilings and the silks of your shirt. You are not as self-sufficient as you would like. This is what the high kings have always stood for. Unity between the seven kingdoms." Alex half-turned to face King Cassius as well as Prince Tyrell. "A hundred years ago, perhaps the voices of the individual kingdoms weren't being heard and the high king lorded his position over the other kings."

Alex swallowed. It was even harder to speak of his late father failing than it was to acknowledge his own mistakes.

But he needed to continue this speech. He had Prince Tyrell nodding, the elk antlers tipping precariously with the movement.

Alex gestured to encompass the whole room in what he was about to say. "For this reason, I hereby establish a counsel and invite a representative from each of the kingdoms to come to Castle Eyota that they may be the voices of their people. From now on, you will be heard. And for this, I bow to you."

Alex bowed from the waist in Prince Tyrell's direction. The prince from Monongadotte swept the antler crown from his head and bowed in return.

Finding Prince Josiah a few paces from Daemyn and Rosanna, Alex bowed to him. Prince Josiah's mouth twitched, like he was fighting a grin, as he returned the gesture.

Alex turned back to King Cassius and bent at the waist. It may have been stiffer than the others, but he still bowed.

King Cassius's acknowledging bow was stilted and his words sharp-edged. "I bow to your wisdom, Your Majesty."

After straightening, Alex strode toward Rosanna and Daemyn, the crowd parting before him. Once he was in front of them, he bowed to Princess Rosanna. She curtsied, and the gesture seemed somehow right with the mix of buckskin and silk she wore.

Alex faced Daemyn and squared his shoulders. He'd publicly tossed Daemyn in a dungeon. He needed to just as publicly honor him now.

Alex raised his voice so that the entire room would be able to hear him. "And, for my most loyal advisor, I bow that everyone may know the honor that I hold for him."

He went down onto both knees and knelt lower than he had to everyone else in the room, staying there, head bent, face to the floor. This was the person he needed to be. The kind of man who was willing to bow. Willing to humble himself.

"Your Highness. What are you doing?" Daemyn's voice was pitched low enough few besides Alex would hear.

"Doing what I should have done a long time ago." Alex glanced up, and nearly laughed at the wide-eyed look of what could only be sheer horror on Daemyn's face. "Enjoy it. You know your brother Luke is cheering in his grave about now."

"I think Zeke is doing the cheering for him." Daemyn shook his head and held out a hand. Alex took it and let Daemyn pull him to his feet. As if they were friends. Or brothers. Or at least a high king and an advisor that mostly tolerated each other.

Alex turned to King Cassius once again. "Thank you for your hospitality, but I believe my companions and I will be leaving immediately."

King Cassius stepped forward. Behind him, his guards moved as if to draw their long knives and attack.

A bow creaked next to Alex. He didn't have to look to know it was Zeke, stepping from the shadows with an arrow aimed directly at King Cassius now that Alex had conveniently cleared the path of bystanders when he'd walked over to Rosanna and Daemyn.

Instead, Alex kept his gaze focused on King Cassius. "I might be alone and without an heir at the moment, but so are you. It would be a pity if the line of the Pohatomie kings ended with you. Perhaps, instead of manipulating the affairs of others, you should see to your own house first."

"I will keep your suggestion in mind, Your Majesty." King Cassius's mouth curled at the corner, but he dropped his hand from his long knife. There was something in his eyes. A pain even he couldn't fully hide.

How close had Alex's words come to the truth? King Cassius was in his mid-thirties. Not ancient by any means, but older than would be expected for a king to remain unmarried. Did he too have a woman he lost in the past? A woman he loved but couldn't be with for political reasons? Perhaps, for a manipulator like King Cassius, it wasn't easy finding love when all he could see were devious plots and suspect motives.

Then the look was gone, and King Cassius's expression smoothed. "If that is all, I bid you farewell. I do hope your journey home is uneventful. It would be a pity if the line of the high kings ended due to an unfortunate accident."

Alex's smile was sharp. King Cassius would like for his journey to Castle Eyota to be anything but safe, but between Daemyn and Zeke, it would be fine.

But King Cassius's jab still hit too close to the aching place in his chest. Even if he was content alone, Alex needed to marry, sooner rather than later. Would it even matter if he wanted love and happiness? Or would he have to be content arranging a political match for himself?

The princess of Neskahana was taken, but perhaps one of the twelve princesses of Tuckawassee would be a good option to solidify peace in Tallahatchia. Maybe even one of Baroness Hackett's daughters for an alliance with Pohatomie.

All worries for another day. Tonight, all he had to do was leave Pohatomie safely while protecting those who had fought for him this night.

Alex met and held King Cassius's gaze a final time. "One more thing. Baroness Hackett, her daughters, and her maidservant were under my orders tonight. Please do not fault them for obeying me after you gave the orders that I be given full cooperation in hearing of many at the ball that night. I expect they will be allowed to carry on their lives without interference."

"Of course, Your Majesty." King Cassius's voice was even more tight.

Hopefully it would be enough. If King Cassius tried to punish them now, they had a whole ballroom full of witnesses who heard him say he wouldn't hold them responsible for this.

With one last glance at Castle Fonthaven's glittering ballroom, Alex stepped into the night. As Daemyn and Rosanna joined him on one side, Zeke and Isi on the other, he drew in a deep breath of the night breeze, and something inside him relaxed in a way it never had before.

His chest still ached with dreams left unfulfilled. But he wasn't alone. For now, he'd be content. There was something satisfying in the laughter and grins and jokes of a friendship.

A true smile eased onto his face as he stared at the stars high above. "Let's go home."

CHAPTER 36

ELARA

Elara slipped from the ballroom while High King Alexander was giving a stirring speech. She didn't belong there, even though many of the common folk had been invited. She'd thought she wanted the glittering ballrooms and fancy dresses. But the gilt had tarnished and the silk frayed.

The guards paid her little mind as she walked with her head down from the castle courtyard, out the gate, and down the causeway. Her bandaged feet ached inside her moccasins, but this pain healed.

At the end of the causeway, she paused and glanced toward the river. A breeze curled toward her, heavy with the scents of wet earth and muddy river. Elara closed her eyes and breathed deeply. Last time she'd slipped away from a ball like this, she'd run in that direction.

This time, she hiked down the mountain toward the barn and Terrence's shack behind it. It was the direction she should've gone back then. Not because Terrence was the answer to all her problems. But because, if she had, it would've meant she had been seeking the right things in life —friendship, wise words, contentment—instead of superficial silk dresses and a handsome prince. There wasn't anything necessarily wrong with nice dresses. But they shouldn't become the focus they had for her.

Yet without this curse, she might never had seen the truth so clearly. Perhaps she would've gone on longing for silks and princes even if she'd sought Terrence's advice that night. And Terrence might never have admitted his true feelings for her. In this, the curse had turned into a gift.

In the silver light of the moon, its circle only a sliver less than full, Terrence's silhouette leaned against the tall fence of the paddock with the white buffalo Toho by the rails. Beyond him, the two elk grazed, their antlers curving points of silver in the moonlight.

Elara reached between the rails and buried her fingers in Toho's thick ruff. Her heart was beating harder in her ears than she thought it would, her stomach more knotted than Toho's fur.

Next to her, Terrence stiffened as he continued to scratch Toho's broad forehead. Elara didn't blame him. They hadn't had a chance to talk since he'd confessed he loved her. From the moment she'd walked back into the parlor in Hackettsville, she'd been swept into a whirlwind of planning for tonight, then whisked off by Monica to pick out a ball gown, and finally bundled off in the canoe while Terrence followed behind in the elk cart with the high king's guards.

Terrence heaved a sigh and rested his head against the top rail. "I'm sorry. I shouldn't have said...I mean, you probably don't...what I'm trying to say is, things can go back to what they were. Just pretend I never said..."

"I'm glad you said it." Her heart in her throat, Elara

threaded her fingers through the buffalo's fur, letting the animal's solid warmth keep her steady as everything in her was off-kilter. "And I think I might be falling in love with you too."

Terrence stilled before he turned to her. "You do? You are?"

Elara nodded, but she couldn't meet his gaze. "I'm obviously not a good judge of what love is. But I do know that what I have with you is better than silk dresses and fancy castles and all the princes in Tallahatchia."

"Are you sure? I'm never going to be able to give you fancy dresses or a magnificent home." Terrence gestured at her, and she remembered she still wore the soft pink ball gown Monica had lent her for tonight.

Elara smoothed her fingers over the silk, and a part of her still ached with longing. She still loved pretty things. Still wanted them.

But she needed to want deeper things more. Like the love she could have with Terrence. Maybe they would be living in a tiny log cabin with a dirt floor, and she'd have nothing but homespun dresses and one nice hair ribbon.

But if she had love, laughter, Terrence's smile, and, most of all, the comfort of the Highest Prince, then she could be content. Happy.

"I know." Elara stepped closer and took Terrence's hand. There was a flutter in her stomach, her breath catching in her throat. She swayed as if they were dancing in the gilt ballroom of the castle towering into the night sky behind them. "But I've learned those things are empty by themselves. A life spent serving the Highest King and shared with those also serving him is what truly matters."

Terrence took her other hand, and they danced to the music of the tree frogs and crickets. Their movements were stilted and wobbly compared to the gliding dances Elara had experienced with High King Alexander. While those dances had sent flutters to her stomach and heat to her head, this one made her smile and laugh, filling her with a warmth that radiated from deep inside her chest.

It wasn't nearly as awkward as she would've thought, going from just friends to something a bit more than friends. She was all too aware of the feel of his hand around hers, kind of awkward and sweet all at once. When he bent down and gently kissed her forehead, it sent tingles down her spine, even if something like relief also surged through her. She wasn't ready for a kiss on the lips yet, and it would probably be the most awkward, fumbling, don't-know-what-they-were-doing kiss in the history of Tallahatchia.

But that was all right. This was only the start, after all. Romances didn't have to be crammed into a few short days. They could be little moments that added into something more eventually.

Terrence stepped back, letting go of her hands. "I think they're gathering at the river to leave."

Elara swallowed and glanced over her shoulder. Sure enough, dark silhouettes of people bustled by the canoes they'd left tied to the docks. "I need to go."

When she turned back to him, Terrence was giving Toho a pat on the neck. There was something final in the gesture. Almost as if he was saying goodbye. He bent and picked up a sack Elara hadn't noticed lying on the ground in the shadows beside the fence. "I'm going with you."

"What do you mean?" Elara stared at the bulging sack he slung over his shoulder. He couldn't possibly mean that. He loved the white buffalo Toho and the elk pair Kal and Kio.

"I told Major Vinzen I resigned before he left to spread

the word about the ball tonight. King Cassius is going to have to find another buffalo boy. I won't work for him any longer, and I want to be closer to you in case he decides to punish you." Terrence brushed his hand against her lower back, steering her toward the river with the lightest touch. "I plan to ask Baroness Hackett for a job. Perhaps she'll have a plot of land I can farm, and I can help the neighboring farmers with training their buffalo. Or if she has a place big enough, I can catch and tame elk and buffalo to sell."

Terrence had a way with animals. If anyone could make a living at taming the wild buffalo into beasts of burden, he could.

He halted and drew in a deep breath. "You were partially right, I think. There are times when we should stay and be content where we are, but there are other times when we need to go, and I didn't let myself see that it was time for me to move on. I'm allowed to dream, committing those dreams to the Highest King."

"I like your dreams." Elara peeked up at him. They were the kind of dreams to aspire to. Perhaps, in time, she too would figure out the balance of contentment and dreams.

She and Terrence arrived at the river as the high king's guards loaded his canoes with his luggage. Based on the number of canoes and guards, it looked like Princess Rosanna and Prince Josiah were also leaving tonight.

High King Alexander gave a half-bow to Baroness Hackett. "I can't guarantee there won't be reprisals against you for standing with us. You would be welcome in Kanawhee, if you would like to go with us."

"Or Neskahana." Princess Rosanna glanced over her

shoulder before she went back to tying down a pack in the center of a canoe.

"And Buckhannock." Prince Josiah had his arms full with a pile of sacks and luggage while his guards sorted through it before hauling the packs to their proper places.

Baroness Hackett drew her shoulders straighter. "Thank you for your offers, Your Majesty and Your Highnesses. But Pohatomie is my home, and I can't abandon my people."

"In that case, I'm sure it can be arranged for someone from Buckhannock to check in once a month or so for the next while." High King Alexander turned toward his advisor, Daemyn.

Daemyn gave a nod before he joined Princess Rosanna in strapping down another pack.

"That would be appreciated. I'll send word if there's trouble." Baroness Hackett curtsied before she headed for the long, dugout canoe that dwarfed the smaller birchbark canoes used by the others.

High King Alexander faced Elara. "The offer stands for you as well."

A month ago, she would have been tempted. As a guest of the high king, she would probably be treated like visiting nobility.

But she'd learned where her heart lay, and it wasn't in a far-off castle.

"Thank you, Your Majesty. But I have friends here who will keep me safe." Elara glanced up at Terrence and reached for his hand. Their fingers met, and there was an awkward moment of adjusting as they tried to figure out how to fit their hands together comfortably. But she still found herself smiling. Terrence's smile answering her filled her with a rush of warmth and tingles and every bit of romance she'd ever dreamed of. "I've found my home right here."

CHAPTER 37

DAEMYN

As they set up camp on a flat, sheltered spot along a gorge in early afternoon, Daemyn let his muscles relax for the first time since leaving Pohatomie a week ago. Perhaps they weren't much safer here in the northern edge of Kanawhee than they'd been in Pohatomie, but the distance was reassuring.

Not to mention the excess of guards since Josiah still traveled with them. He'd decided to head straight to Castle Eyota to represent Buckhannock, probably to make sure he secured the position and adventure before his grandfather assigned it to one of his brothers.

Down below, a river meandered through the cliffs of the gorge, a steady rumble providing background music to the chatter of three sets of guards organizing the camp.

Daemyn eyed the wall of the gorge that guarded one side of camp, the screen of cedars and hemlocks and the river on the other. Between Asa, Captain Taum, and Captain Degotaga, there wasn't anything left for him to do.

No nephews to wrangle. No curse to break. No high king to serve at that particular moment.

Just his princess leaning precariously over the edge of a rocky ledge, her face turned to catch the mist-laden breeze swirling down the gorge from one of the waterfalls farther upstream.

After joining her, he held out a hand. "Would you like to go exploring?"

"Do you need to ask?" She took his hand, her dark brown eyes shining. "Where are we going?"

Josiah jumped to his feet. "Are you going to the swimming hole?"

"I reckon that's a good idea." Zeke sniffed at his sleeve and grimaced. "We're all a mite ripe. Might as well wash, clothes and all."

Nephews. He'd hoped for a few moments alone with Rosanna, sharing the waterfalls and the view along this gorge. No matter. This could still work.

Captain Degotaga nodded and barked out orders, dividing the guards in half. Over the past week, he'd ended up more or less in charge, even though the guards were from Neskahana, Buckhannock, and Kanawhee.

With the guard detail arranged, Daemyn finally headed up the gorge. Rosanna's stride matched his at a comfortable pace while Josiah, Zeke, Isi, and Alex trailed behind them with Captain Taum and Asa heading the guards sent with them.

The thin, dirt track followed the boulder-strewn river. Daemyn took his time, trying to ignore the passel of guards and nephews trailing along and giving Rosanna a chance to enjoy the hike. He was in no hurry, after all. He had nowhere else he needed to be except beside her in this moment.

Ahead, the river widened into a calm pool with a five-foot tall waterfall at the far end along with a dry stretch of brown-orange rock. The late afternoon sunlight shimmered over the water, especially at the far end of the calm pool where the water shone a lighter green over a sandbar. Above the sandbar, the far side of the river rose in a steep cliff with dense trees. Even if an enemy approached from that direction, they would have a hard time attacking.

On their side, large rocks jutted into the deep part of the river while the mountain rose steeply at their backs. The guards with them spread out, finding positions among the trees.

"This is it. Glimmer Falls." Daemyn unbuckled the knife from his belt and set it on a nearby rock.

"Best swimming hole in this part of Kanawhee." Zeke removed his quiver from his back and leaned it against a tree.

Josiah let out a holler, took a running start, and jumped off the rock jutting into the river. He splashed into the deep section, and when his head popped up, he was several feet downriver thanks to the current.

On the large, flat rock, Isi stared down into the water. "It looks cold. And wet."

Zeke rested his hands on her shoulders. "It ain't that bad. And worth it. Trust me."

With a grin and a glance at Daemyn, Rosanna let out a whooping yell, dashed past Zeke and Isi, and jumped. When her head broke the surface, she swam across the current until she reached the sandbar that took up most of the river on the far side. When she stood up, the water only reached her knees.

She kicked at the water. "You've got to see this, Isi. The

water is sparkling. There's flakes of something shiny that gets stirred up when I move."

"Fine." Isi patted Zeke's arm. "But you're going first."

Zeke grinned and launched himself from the rock. Isi followed a moment later, and they both swam to the shallows formed by the sandbar.

Rosanna trailed her fingers through the water as if mesmerized. Even from across the river, the water had an extra shimmer caused by the mineral flakes in the sand. For a moment, Daemyn couldn't tear his eyes from the soft tilt of her grin and the wonder shining in her eyes.

He'd discovered this spot decades ago, back when he'd been going by the name Jubal. It was one of his favorite places in all Kanawhee. And now he could share it with her.

Alex crept onto the rock, as if he feared falling in, and peered down into the water. He crossed his arms, his shoulders hunched, and watched the others as they laughed and splashed on the sandbar on the far side.

Daemyn eyed him, studying the way he shifted from foot to foot. Alex didn't know how to interact with others. Not as a friend. He'd been raised to be a high king. Never to be just Alex in a friendship. Had he ever laughed? Daemyn had been his manservant since age ten, and he didn't think he'd ever seen it.

If he wanted things to change, then it was up to him to teach Alex how to be a friend by being Alex's friend first. He needed to act more like Alex's advisor than manservant. After all, how could Alex see Daemyn as an advisor and a friend if he didn't see himself that way?

He strode across the rock until he was next to Alex. "Am I your friend or manservant at the moment, Your Highness?"

Alex started, his expression smoothing from something that had almost been longing to a carefully composed smile. "Friend. If you're still offering."

"Good. I just wanted to be clear on that." Daemyn grinned and positioned his feet. "You might want to hold your breath."

"Wait. Why would—"

Daemyn took Alex across the chest with an arm and propelled both of them off the rock. Alex had time for one startled shout before they hit the water.

Cold water closed over Daemyn's head, seeping through his buckskins to shiver along his skin. His bruises and ribs ached, but he brushed the pain aside. He kicked his way to the surface, dragging Alex with him by a firm grip on his shirt.

Alex came up sputtering. He swiped a hand over his face, then blinked at Daemyn. "What is it with you and dunking me underwater?"

"If I do it enough, maybe it'll shock some sense into you." Daemyn kept his tone light, his smile in place. Small steps.

"I don't think it's working." Alex grimaced and swiped his dripping hair from his face with one hand while treading water with the other.

"It's worth a try." Daemyn stroked through the water, the current a firm pressure against his right side. He matched his pace to Alex's since Alex wasn't nearly as strong at swimming. He didn't want to accidentally let the high king get swept downriver, though Alex should catch himself on one of the boulders bordering this sheltered area if it came to that.

Daemyn clambered to his feet on the sandbar, then

reached out a hand. Taking it, Alex staggered upright, panting.

Zeke splashed toward them. "If you get to dunk the high king, Uncle Daemyn, does that mean I can too?"

"Wait. No, don't you..." Alex backed up a step, his foot falling into the deeper section of river. He tumbled over backwards, hitting the water with a splash.

Daemyn sighed and fished Alex out of the river. "Zeke, he ain't too good at this relaxing and socializing thing yet. Take it easy on him."

Alex grimaced and attempted to wring out the end of his sleeve. "I think I agree with Isi. Being wet isn't pleasant."

"See? I'm not the only one." Isi dipped her hands in the water and came up with a handful of the river sand. "But in this case, being wet is worth it."

Leaving Alex to fend for himself for a few minutes, Daemyn splashed to Rosanna. "Would you like to go behind the waterfall?"

Water streamed from the fringes of her shirt and leggings while droplets shimmered on her black braids. She glanced from him to the waterfall. "We can go behind it? How?"

"You'll see." Daemyn clasped her hand. The movement was confident, their fingers fitting together without fumbling or hesitation.

They tromped over the sandbar, climbed onto the flat rock, and strode next to the short cliff near the waterfall, its roar growing louder. At the waterfall, Daemyn lowered to his hands and knees. "There's a ledge here. The water will push on you for a moment, then you'll be through. I'll be there to help if you need it."

Rosanna nodded, her grin wide, her eyes sparkling as much as the river behind them.

Daemyn took a deep breath and crawled forward. The waterfall's spray washed over his face, then he crawled into the downpour. It pummeled his head, then his shoulders, strong as a pair of hands shoving him backwards. He dug his toes into the rock behind him and pushed forward.

The pressure of the water eased. Daemyn blinked and crawled into a space a couple of feet wide. A smooth wall of rock curved into a foot-wide ledge. The waterfall was a white, frothing wall next to him, its thunder echoing in the small space and reverberating inside his bones.

He crawled farther inside and maneuvered around, wincing at the ache in his ribs, to help Rosanna if she needed it.

She came sputtering through the wall of water, rivulets cascading from her face and braid. He gripped her hand, and she hauled herself forward the rest of the way inside.

Swiping water from her face, she sat cross-legged on the ledge, leaned forward, and trailed her fingers through the back of the waterfall before them. She let loose a laugh. "This is amazing!"

Daemyn sat on the ledge next to her, so close their shoulders were touching, his gaze focused on her face as she peered around them.

This was the Rosanna he'd fallen in love with. Not the princess in the fancy ball gown. But the adventurer dressed in buckskins who saw the wonder in each tree and mountain the way he did. Appreciating the Highest King's handiwork.

Yet perhaps he needed the princess part of her just as much as the adventurer. If he was to truly claim a place as Alex's advisor, then he would have to learn how to navigate life in Castle Eyota's court. He couldn't be the invisible manservant or the elusive mountain man he'd been for the past hundred years.

Rosanna managed to be a princess without losing the mountain girl inside her. He, too, could be both mountain and castle, moving between those worlds with her at his side, a princess in ball gowns or buckskins.

She turned, as if finally noticing that he was staring at her instead of the waterfall. Her grin quirked at the corners. "Can they hear what we're saying?"

"They'll hear that we are shouting to each other but can't make out the words." Daemyn took her hand in his. He probably hadn't planned this well. Words like the ones he needed to say were supposed to be whispered beneath the stars, not shouted at the top of his lungs while they sat in sopping wet buckskins beneath a waterfall.

But it was time he stopped dancing away from this like a shy whitetail deer and be active in this relationship. He had to give her himself—every last complicated piece of his past and every uncertain dream for the future.

And he needed to be himself. Not Jadon, the invisible manservant who died decades ago. Not Jubal or Arlen or all the other names he'd worn and killed off over the years.

But Daemyn. The man who had lived all of those things and been changed by them. He wasn't who he'd been a hundred years ago as Jadon. Back then, he wouldn't have fallen in love with Rosanna. He'd been quieter. Less adventurous. All he'd wanted was to marry a mountain girl and settle down in a small cabin.

He didn't want that now. Not that he would mind spending some of their time sharing a cabin near the Buckhannock family homestead. But all of Tallahatchia was his home now, and he longed to show her every mountain, every waterfall, every mist-filled gorge just to see the way her eyes lit up and her face softened as if she could hear the ancient song it was said the mountains sang before the world was cursed.

He swallowed and tried to piece his thoughts together. At least the waterfall's thunder pounded louder than the beating of his heart. Since he felt daring, he touched her cheek, then tipped her chin up. In the end, it all came down to three words. "I love you."

"I love you too." Rosanna shifted closer to him. She was warm against him while all around was cold water and colder stone. "I'm going to ask my father to make me Neskahana's representative so I can stay at Castle Eyota with you."

He pulled back just enough to see her face. "But you love Neskahana. And your family and the Onohio River."

He didn't want to take her away from her family or the mountains she loved so much. Of all people, he understood what it was like to leave home and miss a family left behind.

She rested a hand on his chest, her hand warm even through his buckskin shirt. "I wasn't ready to leave a few months ago, but I am now. Just ask my family how restless I was. It's time I started a new home and adventure in Kanawhee with you."

Those months had been too much like the ten years he'd spent as Alex's manservant. Stuck at Castle Eyota while his heart was elsewhere.

"We'll visit them as often as we can." If there was one thing he knew, it was how to love a far-flung family. He brushed his fingers over her cheek. They were both dripping wet, the spray from the waterfall shining on their skin and clothes. He was leaning closer, his thoughts growing muddier. Still, he hesitated to close the last few inches. "I reckon I'd like to marry you someday."

"I reckon I do too." Rosanna swayed closer, their faces only inches apart. "Is this later?"

His promise from the moonlit river in Pohatomie. He leaned down and softly kissed her, his pulse drumming loud and very much alive in his ears.

Tonight, when Asa pulled out his fiddle, Daemyn would let the music carry him away into a mountain jig the likes of which he hadn't had the heart to dance in years, all toes a-tapping and knees a-wobbling and legs a-high-kicking in a prance that was more footwork and innocent fun than anything else.

And he'd let himself be so full up with joy that he'd laugh a deep-down, heart-and-soul laugh and remember what it was like to truly *live*.

Don't Miss the Next Adventure!

Poison's Dance

If he falls to the lure of the curse, the dance might trap him forever.

Alex has survived his first year as high king. The new counsel has improved cooperation between the kingdoms, and peace seems achievable. When the Tuckawassee queen sends him an invitation he can't refuse, Alex must once again face his greatest threat for the sake of peace.

Princess Tamya of Tuckawassee, along with her eleven sisters, has danced from sunset until sunrise every night of her life. It is her gift and her curse. When Queen Valinda wishes to use the power their cursed dance gives them to rule all of Tallahatchia, Tamya must decide if she will do what is right even if it betrays her own sister.

Daemyn Rand has survived a hundred years' worth of battles. All he wants to do now is safely marry his princess. Will he be forced to choose between the love of his life and the high king he has loyally served for years?

They have faced certain death before. This time, they might not make it out alive.

Don't miss this re-envisioning of the Twelve Dancing Princesses fairy tale.

Buy Now!

Acknowledgments

Thank you so much for picking up *Midnight's Curse*. I hope it touched your heart and brought a smile to your face. I appreciate each and every one of you. If you would care to take the time, reviews on Goodreads and Amazon are greatly appreciated and help spread the word to help others find the book.

Thanks once again to my parents. To my mom, whose favorite fairy tale is Cinderella and who introduced me to Rogers and Hammerstein's 1953 version of Cinderella. To my dad for once again reading an early copy and loving the book.

To my twin-in-law Alyssa who gets a special mention for reading this book so quickly in order to give me last minute feedback before it went to my editor. Her insight is always so helpful and appreciated!

To my sister-in-law Abby who read most of an early draft out loud to my brother on a road trip so they both could read it. Thanks to both of you for picking *Midnight's Curse* over your stack of audiobooks.

To my brothers Ethan, Josh, and Andy who keep my guy characters real. Though I am glad pun wars are not our family's thing, lol.

To Bri for helping to brainstorm this book into such an

easy outline to write and for the Romeo and Juliet reference.

Thank to Paula and Jill for asking how the writing was going and always being supportive, even when I don't always remember to be social when the stories are calling me.

Sierra, I don't know how this book would have been written if not for our mini writing retreat. The inspiration and word counts helped me push through to the end.

Thanks to the Mitchtam crew for the ideas for bad romance clichés for me to add. It is probably the only time I will ever ask for clichés to purposefully include them in a book.

A special thanks to Jaye, Morgan, Nadine, Katie, Ashley, and all my Realmie Roomies and other writer friends too numerous to name. I never would've guessed the author community I would find when I started this journey, and I don't know what I'd do without your support and encouragement.

Thanks to the PR writer group. It has been fun meeting with you guys and finding a critique group!

Thank you to Tom and Mindy Bergman for pushing through all the technology headaches to get this book proofed in time. You make a stellar proofreading duo! Thank you, Bethany, for an additional proofread before the release of *Goose Princess*.

But most of all, all glory belongs to my Heavenly Father. He has abundantly blessed me with His love and grace.